BITE OF VENGEANCE

BLOOD OATH
BOOK THREE

R.L. CAULDER

WHITE RABBIT PUBLISHING

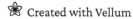 Created with Vellum

CHAPTER 1

ALINA

I knew you were just a slut who would bend over for me after I found you fingering yourself in that window.

My chest burned with a fire that stole my breath and threatened to consume me whole. I felt ashamed and angry, burning with humiliation despite knowing Andrei didn't mean his callous words.

With each breath I took, the fire scorched me from the inside out. How was I supposed to douse it when the biting sting of rejection fueled my fury and hurt?

No—that wasn't the Andrei I'd bound myself to. That was the Andrei that Jeoffrey had pinned beneath his foot. *Stop doubting it, Alina, fuck.*

It was so damn hard to just let it go, though. My natural instinct was to protect myself and my heart first, fuck everything else. Letting go of that internal conflict would never be as simple as snapping my fingers to poof it away.

Andrei's lifeless eyes plagued me. What did Jeoffrey manage to do to him in such a short time to break his spirit so completely?

I let out a groan as my fingers twitched at my sides, aching to touch the blood drop on the back of my neck that reminded me that we were *supposed* to be together. We were entwined, forever. Fated mates.

But there lay the second, arguably bigger, issue. Could I place my faith in the fact that we were supposed to be together, or was Fate playing her cruelest joke on me yet?

Was I worthy enough of such a gift?

"Alina!" Lo called out, her voice cutting through the thoughts plaguing me.

Her warm smile brought one to my face as well as she approached with a tall, slender man at her side. An intricate black tattoo crept up from beneath the white dress shirt he wore and up his throat. Messy, white hair that was an adorable juxtaposition to the crisp, tailored lines of his suit, fell into his warm brown eyes.

"This is Rin," she introduced as he held out his hand, showcasing a similar tattoo to the one on his neck crawling up his hand and onto his fingers. "He's a Pawn on the board and our most recent induction before you joined us."

"Hello," I mumbled as I offered my hand in return.

I knew I should probably show more interest in meeting these members, but my mind wasn't here at all, completely consumed by the situation with Andrei.

"Pleasure you to meet the new queen," his deep voice rumbled as his large hand swallowed my smaller one in a quick, polite shake. "Please don't hesitate to let me know if you need anything."

A deep rumble came from Drake at those words, but Lo was quick to slap him on the chest and reprimand, "He didn't mean it like that, you caveman," before turning to Rin and tucking her hand into the crook of his elbow. "Let's go, Rin."

As they walked away, my eyes darted to Andrei's back as he chatted with a raven-haired beauty at his side. Her tight, floor-length dress shimmered with the black sequins that covered every inch of the fabric. She had a killer body, and a flare of jealousy rose within me at the sight of Andrei with her. Drake led us in their direction, but it was as if Andrei sensed me the second I got within a hundred feet, excusing himself.

"Pleasure talking to you, Silvyn."

Was this how it would be between us now? Unable to even be in the same vicinity?

My chest burned, and my throat constricted with the unpleasant thoughts rolling through me.

As soon as I opened my heart to the realization of my feelings for Andrei, I opened the door to a heap of unwelcome, emotional demons as well. Anxiety over being wrong, fear of another rejection if I tried to pursue him after this, desperation to prove the truth of what I knew about his father.

I hadn't realized I felt so strongly already about Andrei until the precious words fell through my lips. Panic had set in when I felt like I was losing him for good, but it was too late to stuff them back down my throat now. I'd told him I loved him—it was the first time I'd uttered them to a man who wasn't a part of my family—and of course it ended with him walking away from me. *That* was par for the course.

The woman turned on our approach, her striking purple eyes catching me off guard. Her eyes were wide and gentle, full lips splitting into a smile as Drake introduced her.

"Alina, this is Silvyn. She's a Rook on the board."

She offered me a nod, lifting her glass of champagne. "Welcome to the board, Alina. Cheers to finally finding the most powerful piece to stand next to our King."

"Thank you," I responded with a curt nod. "I look forward to getting to know you all more as we work together."

I watched her go as she disappeared quickly, excusing herself to fill her glass. I wasn't sure how I felt about her after that short interaction. She seemed like a quiet and reserved woman from what I gathered. Not openly extroverted, but still kind.

Drake's large hand stayed on my lower back the rest of the night, cradling me as he guided me through the party. His strong fingers pressed into my skin, leaving a faint warmth behind like a comforting kiss that traveled straight through to my soul.

I thought that in front of these people, he would never show any sign of affection—as if doing so would make him vulnerable or an easy target for manipulation. I was pleasantly surprised, and thankful, that I was wrong. The gentle caresses and heated embrace were a tether keeping me centered and grounded in the midst of chaotic energy and unfamiliar faces.

He mentioned that fated mates could sense each other's emotions, so I was betting he could sense my distress. He knew something was wrong, but we couldn't disappear now that we were in the lion's den.

There's no hiding from this life, now.

He made the rest of the introductions, but the board members' names and faces all melted into one big blur the rest of the night. I couldn't shake Andrei's harsh words from my mind, leaving me unable to properly focus.

The anxiety rising in my chest was like a wild animal, desperate to be freed. It clawed at my stomach, trying to escape, and it hissed a million possible disasters in my mind. No matter how much I tried to break free of it, the beast was chained to me, refusing to leave. I knew I had to learn how to manage the feelings and accept them as part of my life, despite knowing they didn't reflect the truth of my soul.

Bile churned, and acid crept up my throat, searing it until I silently gagged as I nodded absent-mindedly at the Pawn Drake introduced me to. I had no idea what the man was saying to me as I wrestled with myself to not look over his shoulder at the clear view I had of Andrei and Jeoffrey.

It took everything within me to not go over to his father and call on Devorare before slicing her cleanly through his neck. Every laugh he gave sounded like nails on a chalkboard, grating and sharp. I swore I could feel my ears bleeding at the heinous sound.

Jeoffrey was seemingly the most jovial of the entire board, but the more I watched him, it became clear that he had his talons hooked in deep to everyone here. Silvyn laughed at his side next to the other Rook, whose name I thought was Tania.

Taking a deep breath, I pictured all of my churning anxiety and fear flowing from the dark well at the center of my stomach. Slowly, it pooled into a throbbing black ball, as if it was a live entity. Staring daggers into the back of Jeoffrey's head, I imagined the ball exiting my body and shooting at him.

He could have back all the shit he'd stirred within me. A small smirk curved my lips upward as I pictured the ball morphing into a large middle finger before it seeped into him.

I wouldn't let him sink his claws into me with

the mind games he was playing. That was the only way he could attempt to take me down, and I needed to hold strong in the belief that my gut was right. He was a piece of shit, and I just had to figure out how to prove that to the blinded board members who hung onto his every word.

As soon as my eyes met his, a sinister smirk spread across his face. I glared at him, unflinching and resolute, my jaw clenched, and my hands balled into fists. He seemed to sense the danger emanating from me, and his expression shifted. His Adam's apple bobbed as if he struggled to swallow, the smirk locking into a tight, forced smile that looked as though it could shatter any second.

My lips curled into a snarl as I let my fangs lengthen. His piercing eyes burned with a promise of violence, as if he was trying to make me cower and look away—but I was born to hunt monsters. I wouldn't let him see any fear.

I was unafraid to show him I knew what lurked beneath his mask. He thought he was the biggest, baddest creature here, but I knew otherwise, and I would make sure he learned that fact the hard way.

The night of my family's death, of my own trans-formation, I thought I was all alone in the world. But

I was wrong. As my strength grew, so did my determination to avenge those I'd lost. Jeoffrey and any other vampires on his side wouldn't take away what I'd found...A spark of friendship, of love, of hope.

No one would take anything else from me.

I could no longer hide from the truth or wallow in self-pity. Fate had brought me here, and now it was time to take control of my destiny.

I still had a bone to pick with Fate for the actions she took to get me to this point in my life, but I wouldn't use it as a crutch anymore.

Drake's strong arms pulled me close, making me let go of the violent thoughts of beheading his Knight I had been entertaining. His lips moved against my temple as he spoke, the warmth of his breath sending a shiver down my spine. "Darling, I can sense your distress, and I'm barely keeping myself in check from the urge to rip out the throats of anyone in this room who's making you feel this way. Let's get out of here now that you've met everyone, shall we?"

He looked down at me with a gaze that felt like it was boring into my soul. His presence loomed over me, and I was overcome with a mix of fear and exhilaration. I answered his question with a silent nod, and he took my hand in his, leading me away from the jostling crowd.

My brows furrowed together at his words finally filtering through to my mind, though. *Shit,* I'd met everyone on the board already? Time really had gotten away from me.

I'd done my best to not stare at Andrei all night, not wanting people to see my lingering gaze and possibly placing more unwanted attention on him, but I was growing weak. I wanted to catch his eye, desperately wanting to see a flicker of the man I'd come to love in his gaze. I wanted the reassurance that he would be okay once he left this party.

The only thing I *was* fearful of was the emotional and physical pain that he would be forced to endure by his father's hand the longer he was stuck with him. Could I help heal him, or would that be a journey he needed to take alone once I ensured Jeoffrey was gone for good? Could we fix this chasm between us after that? Was I capable of forgetting the vile words he'd spat at me, even if I forgave him?

I needed to make peace with the fact that I wasn't going to get any of those answers right now. It fucking hurt but wallowing in it wouldn't fix anything. Actions would.

"Whatever it is, Alina, you can trust in me to

help fix it," Drake whispered before pressing a lingering kiss to my forehead. My toes curled, and I could feel my core heating. This man was like catnip for my soul.

I'd have thought anyone completely mad if they had told me *Dracula* would be the one to lend me strength and kindness in a moment of need. Yet here he was, being everything I needed without me even uttering those needs to him.

My faith in him was new and precarious still, and I'd be a liar if I didn't say the change in Andrei wasn't rattling me enough to question all of my mates.

As Drake gently guided me back toward the entrance to the castle, I noticed the subtle nod he gave to Lo who stood with another woman I faintly remembered might be named Heather. Drake had introduced me to her last. What I knew for certain was that her grey-blue eyes had radiated a kindness toward me that felt genuine during our introduction.

The jester who announced us upon our entrance quickly reappeared with his small trumpet in hand. "Are you leaving, your majesties?"

For a short second, my eyes widened in confusion, and I looked over my shoulder for who he was speaking to until I recalled that he had announced me as the Queen of Sanguis tonight. Being addressed as that would take time, and I wasn't certain I'd ever feel like I was worthy of being anyone's queen, but for now, I'd play the game as necessary.

"Yes, Timothy," Drake answered with a polite nod before the jester ran up the steps toward the door and blew his horn, dragging everyone's attention from their conversations.

A hush descended upon the room as I sensed invisible eyes burning into my skin. My muscles tensed, but I steeled myself against the urge to squirm beneath the board's collective gaze. I held my head high and waited for Timothy to speak, my heart pounding like thunder in my chest.

"Greetings, all," he boomed. "While this night has been as magnificent as a fresh stream of blood from an artery, I must announce it is drawing to a close as your King and Queen depart for the night, therefore you must get the fuck out."

Fates, did he really just say that?

My hand flew to my mouth to stifle a laugh at his words. I wasn't expecting that in the least, but perhaps he was known for his callousness as everyone in the crowd seemed to chuckle good naturedly.

Drake spun us around and confidently waved at the sea of people, but my attempt to save face was shattered as my eyes paused on Andrei's. His vibrant green eyes held mine for what felt like an eternity, piercing through me with a fathomless void. Jeoffrey's sharp gaze snapped toward Andrei, his body tensed with indignation. The air seemed to sizzle with animosity as I tried to avert my gaze and regain my composure.

Motherfucker.

Before Jeoffrey could take in the sight of his son, Andrei's mask was back up and a venomous sneer had replaced the emptiness I'd seen on his face. Jeoffrey seemed satisfied, nodding curtly before plastering his fake, sickening smile back onto his face as he slowly turned back around to us.

Rage welled inside of me as I took in the wave of command that Jeoffrey held over Andrei. My blood burned like fire through my veins, and I felt the unmistakable prickle of heat all over my skin as a bloodhaze began to take over. My gums seared in agony as my fangs threatened to break free from their confinement.

I would destroy him, though giving him a swift

death would be too kind. I wanted to fuck with his mind and make him scream for mercy before laughing in his face and taunting him with the fact that I would keep him alive as long as it served my amusement.

He seemed to think that everyone else was alive to cater to his needs, and nothing would give me more pleasure than turning the tables on him. I wanted to see the moment the fight bled from his eyes as his body sagged in defeat with the realization that he wasn't the one in control anymore.

I was.

Dropping my hand, my fingers curled inward as my nails dug into my palms.

Shit, I needed to leave before I showed my whole ass with this bloodhaze.

Tugging on Drake's arm lightly, I indicated that we needed to leave right fucking now or else my first act as queen would be to show that I let my base emotions control me like a fledgling vampire.

With one last look over my shoulder at Andrei, who already had his back to me, we crossed the threshold into the castle.

Hang in there, Andrei. I won't let you fight this battle alone.

CHAPTER 2
ALINA

I knew he couldn't hear my words with the wall he had in place, but it made me feel better to speak to them through our bond anyway. Manifesting and all that shit, right?

The heavy doors thudded shut as Drake grabbed me, spinning me into his chambers in a flurry. He set me down, and my own legs felt weak beneath me, like I might collapse at any second. For a moment, I felt his hands, soft and warm on my face as the darkness that surrounded him dissipated to reveal his bright, piercing blue eyes. I felt a sudden rush of relief at the sight of them, the tension in my body melting away. Yet, his eyes were filled with an intense anger that seemed to radiate off him and draw me in. I could sense the ferocity of his rage while simultaneously feeling like he would do anything to protect me no matter the cost.

My breath caught in my throat as I gazed into his blazing eyes. I realized, with a jolt, that I felt safe with him. He made me feel protected, like I wasn't standing alone in my fight, and that was maybe the biggest gift anyone had given me since losing my family and friends.

"Alina, what the hell happened out there?" He hissed through gritted teeth, his fingers lightly tracing the contours of my face.

I had to wonder how he could be so gentle with me despite the distress I detected in him.

His eyes roamed my features, searching desperately for the answer I wasn't sure how to give him. I closed my eyes and took a deep breath, feeling my body slump against the wall behind me. "I know I didn't do what I should have tonight, but I—"

"Do not apologize to me, Alina," he commanded, and my eyes flew open at the sharp tone. "I felt a deep anguish within you as you spoke with Andrei. Yet you managed to compose yourself and greet an entire crowd of vampires with a smile and polite handshake, whom if I must remind you, were your sworn enemies not too long ago. You did more than anyone else I know could have in your position, darling."

Was that true?

While I was thinking of all the ways I'd fucked up, he focused on the strength he saw in me. My mouth dropped open, and I searched his face as I tried to put into words the way I appreciated him. He'd never given up on me and our bond despite my stubborn desperation to prove he was the villain in my story.

My knees felt weak as he brushed his thumb across my lower lip and whispered, "I'm proud of you."

Fuck. I was officially a goner.

I wasn't sure if it was his kind words or the way his eyes bled with adoration as he uttered them to me, but the wall I'd pulled up around my fragile emotions tonight crumbled in an instant. His hands fell away as I launched myself at him, throwing my arms around his neck tightly as I buried my face against his collarbone, breathing in his soothing scent of the woods and vanilla.

He finally felt like home, just like Lincoln and Andrei did.

I was his.

"Tell me this isn't a facade between us," I

breathed out in a soft plea as my eyes slammed shut. My hands balled into fists, nails digging into the fleshy part of my palms as I tried to ground myself through pain once more.

I ached to hear the raw truth and vulnerability I always sensed in Drake's words as Andrei's vile comments rolled through my mind.

It's pathetic, the way you crumbled at the first crumb of kindness I showed you. It was so damn easy. You are so damn easy.

Drake's arm wrapped around my waist, pressing me against him tightly as his hand came to cup the back of my head gently. "Darling, I can say with the utmost certainty that only two people in this world have seen the part of me that isn't a facade—and you are one of them. I've shown you the real me, in the hope that you could find something redeemable within me to be worthy enough of your affection, and hopefully one day, your love."

My heart fluttered as I bit my lip, my breath hitching in my chest.

"I may not be the easiest person to care for, but what you never need to worry about is if our bond is a facade or not. It is the single most pure thing in my life that I will guard and nurture like my most prized possession because it is. You are my *Comoară.*"

His admission was like soothing balm on my gaping emotional wounds. I felt myself relaxing within his hold as I pulled back enough to look up at him as I asked, "What does that mean?"

The way he rolled the r might have single-handedly made it sound like the most beautiful word I've ever heard, but I didn't recognize it at all.

His hand brushed away the wetness from my cheeks before he pressed a kiss to my forehead. His lips grazed my skin as he whispered, "It means *my treasure* in Romanian."

Oh, be still my fucking heart. My throat bobbed as I struggled to swallow around the thick emotion bubbling up.

"I spent much of my life there before I became... this," he admitted and looked away, the emotion in the air palpable. He had only shared a few sentences about his life before, so surely this was harder for him to open up about.

My eyes widened. The small tidbit made me hungry to ask him a million questions to understand exactly who he was. My mind whirled with all the possibilities.

Sometimes I forgot that not all vampires were born...that they had lives before this. But he was supposedly the first vampire. How was he turned?

Why did he have the ability to pull the darkness into his eyes? Was there anything else that was different about him compared to other vampires? What was his life like before this?

Did he...have a past love?

I couldn't help but ponder the possibility. A wave of uncertainty surged through me. Could I compete with someone else's memory if he had? He had no doubt shared his bed with others before me, but did he have a true connection to any? My mind raced with questions, and I tried to push away the feeling of jealousy that kept creeping in.

We were all just an accumulation of our past moments, whether good or bad, and I wanted to know every detail about each of my mates, no matter what. I stopped myself from the barrage of questions that were on the tip of my tongue, though, knowing that I needed to be ready to give him that side of myself as well. I wasn't there yet, despite wanting to be. Somehow, telling Andrei I loved him was a hell of a lot less scary than baring my soul, jagged edges and all.

One day I'd get there. One day I'd stop fearing that the people I loved would leave me if they knew the real me.

As he pulled back, comfortable silence stretched

between us, and I found my fingers playing with the hair at the nape of his neck as we stared at each other. This was uncharted territory for us, and I was terrified of fucking it up, as if I was one misstep away from popping an illusion, despite his reassurances.

In an effort to show him the real me, I forced my mouth open to speak a question I asked myself constantly. My tongue felt like sludge, but I forced the words out, "Why do I feel like every step forward I make sends me ten steps back a moment later? I feel like I'm lost in the dark on what to do at any given moment. I'm terrified that I'll ruin everything."

His thumb came up to stroke my cheek as he smiled softly, offering a flash of his dimples that made my core heat. "Even the stars need darkness to shine, *Comoară*. Sometimes we need the lights off and to feel lost in order to find our own path out. That path can never be wrong when it's the path your soul leads you down."

I shook my head, in complete awe of his words.

This man...vampire...manpire? How was he mine?

Thank the Fates I couldn't actually kill him back when I tried. What a shame that would have been.

A strangled laugh bubbled out of me as I stared up at him with an incredulous, wide-eyed look. "How do you always manage to say the right thing? Do you have a handbook on how to navigate Alina Van Helsing, because if so, I would really like to borrow it from you."

The way Drake seemed to navigate every hurdle with me—*and there were plenty*—truly left me in awe. I had been hellbent on thinking the way he treated me was an act this entire time, because truly, how could someone be *that* great?

I swear I could hear Fate whispering to me, *"That's why we made you soulmates, you dumb bitch. Do you believe us now?"*

Truly, I was becoming a believer.

I moved on instinct, raising onto my tiptoes to seal my lips to his, craving the feeling of his touch as much as I craved his emotional intensity. I melted into him and greedily deepened the kiss when his arms enveloped me before he tipped me back with a firm hand resting above my ass. While we had kissed before, something about this moment felt so much more special to me.

As I thought deeper on it, I came to the realization that this was the first moment I gave Drake all of me without reservations. He was deserving of my trust, and I was damn proud of myself for not allowing the hiccup with Andrei to detract from what I was building with Drake because it was pretty damn special.

Without a doubt, we had obstacles to work through, but I knew by everything we'd gone through so far that Drake would stand by my side as we figured it out.

That damn dimple made an appearance as he pulled back to answer my question. "I don't have a handbook as much as I'd kill for one, but that's why the Fates put us together as mates, *Comoară*. We complement each other's souls and give the other what they need as naturally as we breathe air."

Without giving me a moment to do anything more than smile, his face descended toward mine once more. Peppering small kisses along my cheeks, he made me giggle from the way his trimmed beard tickled my skin. As he straightened us to stand once more, my smile deepened into a full grin as he trailed his hands down to squeeze my arms lightly. His bright blue eyes seemed to be staring into what felt like the deepest part of myself that even I struggled to connect with.

I didn't flinch away from it, though.

No part of me wanted to run at the invasive look.

I simply stared back, hoping that he could see me for me, without me having to announce all of my fears, traumas, and insecurities.

I wanted him to see me.

I wanted him to understand me.

I wanted him to know exactly what he was tying himself to before we decided to complete our bond.

I wanted to know that he'd see it all and accept me...flaws and all.

Somehow, I'd convinced myself that if he did see and understand all of me, he would run. I felt the same about each of my mates, which is why I struggled to let my walls down and utter the truth from my own mouth.

It boiled down to me spending my entire life feeling I was inadequate to the slayers and my House. I'd never wanted to stick to their traditions and just accept my fate. I pushed back where I could, but ultimately, I would have had to fall in line and accept the role that I was born into. I would have never been trusted to run our faction if I'd shown the real me, and I would have disgraced my entire family—the slayers would have chosen a new House to rule, with me being the only heir to the Van Helsing.

Somewhere along the line, I'd convinced myself

that I truly wasn't good enough as I was, and what had occurred with my family the last night I was in our territory...It had cemented that feeling as a fact, and now I couldn't break free of it.

Drake's hand came up to cradle my cheek, and I found myself instantly leaning into it, craving the support I felt from every little touch he gave me.

"You're so strong, Alina," he murmured, brushing his thumb against my skin lightly. "I see the pain that lingers in your eyes and the weight of the world you seem to carry on your shoulders. I admire the way you fight every day and refuse to bend when the average person would have caved."

My breath caught in my throat, and my eyes pricked with tears. I wanted to brush them away, hating how emotional I looked, but he blocked my hand as I moved. Grabbing my hand tightly in his, he brought it back down to my side as his lips moved to kiss a stray tear that had rolled down my cheek.

"Do not ever hide your tears from me," he commanded between kisses, alternating to my other cheek. "Your tears are my tears. Your fears are my fears. We are a team now. We lose together and win together. Every little thing in between is ours to carry the weight of together."

I sniffled as I nodded my head, lifting my chin to stare up at him as he pulled back. More tears fell down my cheeks, but I didn't feel ashamed this time. I felt the conviction and truth in every word that fell from his plush lips. My heart slammed in my chest, loud and erratic as his words washed over me.

He was saying everything I wanted—no, needed —him to say.

Moving his hand from my cheek to grip my chin lightly, his eyes danced around my face before he whispered, "You've never looked more beautiful, *Comoară*. Thank you for letting me see you."

My body was on fire, a need roaring through me that I ached to satiate immediately. Every one of my nerve-endings felt like it was tingling as my tears subsided, and I let my desire bleed into my gaze.

I wanted him—now.

CHAPTER 3
ALINA

A grumble of appreciation came from his throat as his eyes dropped to my heaving chest. He let go of my chin to run his hand through his dark hair roughly, pulling on the roots as he shook his head. "Darling, I know exactly what you want, but I cannot continue a single moment longer without knowing what happened out there. It is eating me up alive inside."

Dammit.

Lincoln always let me push the issues to the side when I wanted his touch. We were the most similar in the way we reacted impulsively, seemingly coping in similar manners. I should have known that Drake wouldn't do the same. Every move he made seemed so controlled, as if he had an actual grip on not letting his emotions fuel his actions completely.

Logic? I didn't know her.

The thought of Lincoln dropped my heart into my stomach. I missed him deeply.

I found myself craving his presence during my turmoil with Andrei, knowing he'd let me bury the pain while we devoured each other. Maybe it was for the best that Drake wasn't letting me get away with that shit, though. I wasn't sure how I would tell him what happened with Andrei, knowing how volatile their own relationship was. As bad as that might be, I knew the bigger bomb would be telling Lincoln that I was going to explore this with Drake openly now.

There was no way I could continue to live these separate lives. I had to find a way to bring them together.

Dropping my eyes to Drake's wide chest, I absentmindedly pulled my hands down to undo his tie.

His fingers came back to my chin, forcing my gaze back up to his, which had morphed from the tender look to concern as his dark brows slammed together. "Please, trust me."

I was a fool to think he would let the extreme

tension and anxiety he'd felt from me go with my silence. Unfortunately, I was pretty sure this conversation would kill the mood entirely...At least we had forever to get to the good stuff? What a jarring thought. The concept of fated mates was something I was still trying to wrap my mind around.

I inhaled deeply before blowing it out and nodding once in acceptance. I needed to trust in him once and for all. If I was going to pursue this bond, I needed to be all in. "You have to promise me to listen to everything I have to say and not act rashly, okay?" I ended my question with a single brow raised, knowing that Lincoln or Andrei would have reacted instantly if the roles were reversed.

But this was Drake—my even-tempered and controlled mate. That would take some getting used to.

His eyes narrowed suspiciously as he nodded hesitantly, voice dropping an octave as he conceded, "Okay."

Taking a deep breath as I struggled to figure out what to share and what to keep inside, I recalled how I didn't share with Lincoln or Andrei that Lo and Drake had this softer side to them. They didn't allow anyone else to see that softness, so I'd held onto information in respect of their privacy.

The abuse I suspected Andrei was facing from his father felt even more intrusive to share. It didn't help that I had no proof to back up such a serious allegation against someone who had been on Drake's board for who knows how long. The allegation could backfire on me so damn badly.

Even if Drake believed me, I had a bone-deep fear that if Jeoffrey felt like Drake was going after him, all the repercussions would fall onto Andrei before we could help him. I needed to believe in my gut, though, and it was telling me to confide in Drake with some of the information.

"Andrei told me that completing the bond with me was a mistake and that he didn't want me," I started, licking my lips after as I formulated my next sentence.

But before I could continue, his eyes burned a bright crimson as his fist blew through the wall behind me, startling at the sudden aggression. I flinched at the small pieces of stone that bounced off my cheek and shoulder as I stared up at the very pissed off manpire.

"He fucking said that to you?" Drake roared, chest heaving as his nostrils flared with deep breaths, eyes completely trained on me in an eerily piercing manner. "I will end him, Alina. No one disrespects you."

Whelp, I was wrong. I really thought he would be the calmest mate of mine, but I was quickly realizing that he wasn't like that in relation to anything that had to do with me. Lovely.

I shook my head and let out a huff as I resisted the urge to face palm. I thought he wouldn't be as reactive after seeing his steady, calm, and calculating nature recently.

"You just promised to listen to everything I had to say and not act rashly!" I reminded him in a stern tone that reminded me of my mother scolding my father.

For once, the thought of them didn't make my heart want to split and swallow me whole. Instead, the memory of them brought a warmth in the center of my chest and reminded me of everything that we had on the line between Sanguis and the slayers as a whole. I'd never let the fate that befell my family happen to any families on either side of this convoluted war.

Despite how all-consuming this issue with Andrei and Jeoffrey felt, I needed to remember that I took on this role to find out who had orchestrated the murder of my family and to hopefully fix some of the miscommunication and misconceptions between our two peoples. This feud needed to end.

Drake seemed contemplative for a moment before he inclined his head and growled out in a mumble, "Yes, I did say that, and I listened to everything I needed to hear." As I opened my mouth to disagree, he beat me to it, tacking on, "I also punched the wall instead of instantly going back out there to kill him, so truly I did rein in my instinctual reaction, *Comoară*."

My mouth snapped shut as I mulled his words over.

I couldn't really argue that, seeing as he truly could have gone back out there and killed Andrei with absolutely no repercussions for his actions, other than facing my wrath as a result. It was also really hard to be upset when he called me *Comoară*. Something about the endearment turned me instantly to putty in his hands every time he said it.

All I could do was sigh heavily before continuing in hopes that he would actually listen, despite his rage.

"He said a lot of hurtful things to me when I tried to talk to him in private, but I know he didn't mean any of them." I kept eye contact with Drake, and my tongue darted out to wet my lips as I prepared to launch into the tricky part of this conversation. "I think there is something going on with his father that controls his actions and words toward me."

At my words, Drake's previously confident posture seemed to shrink. His eyes widened and his eyebrows raised as he asked in a curious voice, "You mean Jeoffrey, my Knight?"

My heartrate quickened, and it felt like cement had suddenly been poured into my mouth, coating my tongue and making me unable to speak. Was this a mistake? What if he went and straight-up told Jeoffrey of my accusations? It could put Andrei in even further danger.

Trust him to believe you, Alina. You've given him every reason to run and forget about you already, and yet he's stood fast at your side.

Squaring my shoulders, I lifted my chin and nodded in affirmation. "Yes. There's something not right about him, Drake. Have you never felt that way about him?"

The man made my fucking skin crawl in his presence. He was a shady bastard, and I wasn't sure how he'd lasted this long without having a mile-long list of enemies that wanted to kill him.

Drake's dark brows rose as he tilted his head to

the side in a contemplative manner. Clicking his tongue in his mouth, he tapped his foot at the same time, following the same beat for both. Suddenly, he stopped, letting his gaze fall back to rest on me.

"Well, honestly, darling, I'm suspicious of everyone on my board besides you and Lo right now." My heart soared but took a nose dive as he continued, "However, Jeoffrey has been one of the longest standing members of my board and has never once shirked his duties or gone against my orders."

My stomach sank like a bag of bricks. *Shit.*

As his eyes settled on my face once more, he added, "But that doesn't mean that he isn't a manipulative fuck that has managed to create a solid persona."

Instantly, the weight lifted from me. *Holy emotional rollercoaster.*

With a heavy sigh, he backed away from me to pace as he rubbed his chin. I watched him prowl like a caged predator in front of his massive four-post black bed, waiting to hear what else he had to say before I mentioned anything further. It was a lot to digest, and I didn't want to rush him.

He came to an abrupt stop after a few minutes, turning to face me. "He has only ever spoken with a fond and proud tone in reference to Andrei. I know he aspires to get him on the board as well and has pushed for me to take him into consideration for an empty spot. While I've wondered why he's pushed so hard for that, I remind myself that shouldn't every father want the best for their child? Being on the board is a prestigious accomplishment that comes with titles, money, and a set future."

I was relieved to hear the wheels turning in his mind and the pieces coming together, but it also sparked the memory of what Andrei had mentioned to me earlier.

You acted like you hated Maya for cheating her way to the top, but how the fuck can you say that and turn around and do it the exact same way? You slept your way to the top of the leaderboard and knocked me off after just one week of being here. I've been here for years adding points to my score.

Holding my hands up in a stopping motion, I instantly blurted out, "Sorry to change the subject like this." He raised a brow in question. "Do you happen to know how the hell I would be at the top of the leaderboard back at the Academy? I haven't been there long enough to knock Andrei from his spot, yet he told me I was first tonight during our little chat. That shouldn't be possible."

While it probably seemed like an abrupt change of conversation to him, there was no way it couldn't be a coincidence that Andrei was suddenly having issues with his dad on the same night he mentioned it to me. Drake said it himself; Jeoffrey wanted his son on the board, and Andrei made it clear to me that he needed to achieve that in order to keep his father sated.

The fucker had the decency to at least have a sheepish look on his face, making it clear he had a hand in me being at the top of the leaderboard.

Fates give me the strength to not try to kill Drake again.

He'd unknowingly set off Jeoffrey into whatever sick fucking plan he'd enacted, and he'd damn well help me fix this now.

Nodding in confirmation, he admitted, "I might have told Lincoln during our fight at the Academy when we met that you showed the most promise and deserved additional points for managing to catch me off guard and knock me into a vulnerable position." He paused to widen his stance and cross his arms across his chest, offering me a nonchalant shrug. "But I stand by that being the truth of the situation."

A small growl bubbled in my throat as I crossed

my arms against my chest in defiance. Staring him down, I took deep breaths and pushed down the Alina that would have blown up on him for trying to get me what I wanted without even working for it. I wanted to deserve every damn thing I got in life, and this was a prime example of him using his power to get me what I *wanted* to work hard for.

I'd be having a stern talk with Lincoln as well for going along with this bullshit. Fucking...manpires.

"I'm going to ignore that blatant issue for now, as we have bigger fish to fry," I finally relented with a heavy sigh, tossing my hands into the air. "Let's focus on one thing at a time. Jeoffrey needs Andrei to be in first on our leaderboard to have a chance at getting a spot with you, right?"

Letting one arm drop to the side while the other worked at loosening the tie around his neck, his head tilted side to side before he dropped onto the edge of his bed. He leaned back onto his hands, and I chastised myself as I thought of how great his current position would be for me to ride him. *Fuck, focus, you horn dog—you're no better than a man right now.*

"Not necessarily. I've never looked at the students at the Academy purely because I have never felt like they had enough life experience to get on the board and handle everything that comes along with it. It doesn't matter if anyone's number one academically."

My lips thinned as I considered his words. That actually made a hell of a lot of sense.

While I knew Drake was suspicious of everyone on his board, I think there was still a part of him that didn't want to believe that he was wrong about any of them...That any of them would betray him.

It felt worth reiterating to him, and if he truly meant that I was going to rule at his side as the Queen, I needed him to listen to my input and truly keep it in mind while making decisions for Sanguis.

Crossing the distance to stand between his legs, I grabbed the ends of his undone tie, lightly pulling him forward. "I think that you don't know the true intentions of all those on your board, and we both know that it was likely someone who holds that kind of power that would have been able to orchestrate the slaughter of my family. You need to look into Jeoffrey further, please."

His large hands splayed over my hips as he pressed a kiss to my stomach over my dress. Despite the heels adding inches to my height and him sitting, he still somehow managed to make me feel tiny compared to his size. I couldn't deny that I absolutely loved how all three of my mates made me feel like that. Being a tall girl, I was used to being the intimidating one, never the small one who let others protect her.

Tilting his head up and resting his chin against me, his eyes bore into mine with a sincerity that stole my breath. "I will, I promise."

He batted his eyes at me in the perfect "puppy dog" manner, and I instantly chuckled. "What do you want, you little devil?"

The innocent look was gone in a flash, replaced by a promising smirk and a narrowed gaze.

"What do I want?" he echoed before humming. "Hmm, let's see."

His fingers drummed against my hips as he pulled his head back. Cocking his head to the side, his dimple indented in his trimmed beard as his lips split into a wicked smile.

Dropping his hands back down to rest behind him, his eyes wandered down my body lazily. Drawing his bottom lip into his mouth and biting it briefly, he let it fall free before growling, "That's a dangerous question, *Comoară*. There are many things I want from you, but I don't quite know your boundaries yet."

Clearly, I was so fucking wrong earlier that

having that hard conversation would kill the mood. It was back in an instant and somehow even stronger than before. It felt...healthy to have made it through the conversation, both parties listening to what the other had to say. No fighting. No toxicity. No jumping to conclusions.

Vic would be so proud of my progress.

It solidified my faith in this growing relationship between us, and I couldn't help but love that I seemed to become a better version of myself the more I was around Drake. Isn't that what we all should strive for? Finding someone who pushes you to be the best version of you.

He deserved a reward.

Offering him a smirk of my own, I sassed, "Name it."

CHAPTER 4

DRAKE

"Name it," she sassed, placing her hand on her slender waist and cocking her hip to the side.

I wanted to fuck her perfect, pouty lips so damn bad. I needed her choking on my cock until she was unable to sass me anymore. While I always wanted my *Comoară* to cum before me, multiple times even, she made her needs so fucking blatant in these moments. She was testing my willpower, and I wouldn't let her get to me so easily. She wasn't the one in charge between us, despite my desire to cater to her every whim and cherish her.

If I wanted to feast on her wet cunt right now, the very one that was teasing my nose with the scent of her arousal, then I would.

If I wanted to fling the castle doors open and fuck her in the entryway so that her cries of pleasure echoed through Sanguis from the mountain we were on, I would.

Earlier, when I'd lapped at her pussy like a starved animal, my needs had been sated by watching her fucking explode on my tongue. I'd denied her when she tried to gain access to my cock because there was no way I'd fuck her in that emotional state, uncertain of how she actually felt for me.

But now...Now she was my *Comoară,* and I wasn't sure I possessed even an ounce of self-control anymore.

"Or are you too scared?" she taunted as I stared at her with my nostrils flaring and chest heaving. Need roared through me like a drug I needed my next hit of.

Trailing her hand slowly up from her wrist, she dragged the tiny strap of the dress off her shoulder before repeating the motion with the other side. Her nipples poked through the thin dress, begging for my tongue to lavish them before I used clamps on them.

I forced down the growl burbling in my throat at her goading question.

The monster inside of me wanted to bend her to my will until she broke and knew nothing past the haze of pleasure we could bring her. It wanted to see her bleed for us. Ever since seeing Lincoln marked with her blood as she protected him from us, we wanted to drown in her life force. Her blood was mine.

My arms shook as my fingers dug into the comforter, struggling to keep those urges at bay. No one knew that the side of me that was able to create vampires felt like a different entity at times. I could call upon its strength, rage, and features like the black eyes, long fangs, and obsidian claws.

But I hadn't felt at peace in my own body since it merged within me. It was so long ago that I barely remembered the life I led before we became one.

Alina's blue-grey eyes were wicked as she kept my gaze the entire time, smirking enough to show her little baby fangs pushing into her bottom lip.

Concern filled me in an instant. Did she need to feed? With the extreme control she seemed to have in such a short time, I kept forgetting that she was still technically a fledgling. I needed to do better at making sure her health needs were met.

It continued to shock me, the way my concern for her was able to push down those dark desires so swiftly. It had been so damn long since I'd taken a woman, unable to control my urges when they surged back then.

I'd given up on the possibility that I even had a mate as the years passed. The women I'd taken didn't mean shit to me—they were merely a way to pass the seemingly endless time I'd been alive. I'd seriously injured a few of them in the height of my monstrous side taking over in the middle of fucking. I'd barely managed to pull back long enough for them to escape, and the only microscopic saving grace was that I knew they would heal after feeding. But it wasn't worth it, even when every single one of them told me it was okay and that they wanted a taste of the *beast* again, as many of them had called it.

There was so much blood on my hands from when I was first turned into this...I'd concluded that my celibacy was karma for the lives I'd taken and those I'd forcibly turned into vampires.

There was nothing I could do in my life to make up for the way I lost myself to the monster during those early years. It's why I cared so deeply for Sanguis and everyone in it now, fighting with everything within me to create a community that protected each other and built prosperous lives. It was the least of what I owed to every single one of them.

"Do you want me to grab you some blood bags?" I asked, voice filled with concern, despite my thick arousal trying to break through my dress pants and the somber memories filling my mind.

Alina...My life had instantly changed when she entered it. Despite wanting to feel her blood coating my skin, I didn't want to actually harm her. If anything, I felt my monster almost purr like a house cat around her. She's the first thing we've ever agreed on.

I knew I would never lose my control around her and that she could take me. She was meant for me, even all of the fucked up, jagged pieces of me that I tried to act like didn't exist.

A tinkling laugh fell from her lips as she shook her head at me. "No, that's not why my fangs are out."

My gaze ran the length of her until it sunk into my thick skull that her eyes weren't tinted red in the slightest. This wasn't an episode of bloodlust. *She was fine.* The knee jerk reactions that she pulled from me were so out of character after forcing myself to have such finite control with the beast within me spurring me on. But I couldn't help the way I easily agreed with his temper and bloodlust when it came to her being hurt, emotionally or physically.

Intrigue bled into all the pieces of my brain that had been previously concerned.

Raising a brow at her, the tension bled from my body, and I forced myself to relax again, asking, "Then why are those cute little fangs out, darling?"

I remember thinking that it was adorable the first time she flashed them at me in her rage while she attempted to murder me. Now felt like the proper time to be able to talk about the baby fangs without it furthering her hatred of me. Although, she did seem like she'd get into a dick measuring contest with any man and claim her metaphorical dick was bigger than theirs, so maybe it would offend her, calling them small.

Her brows slammed together immediately as a look of hurt crossed her face.

Damn it. I shouldn't have said that.

As I opened my mouth to apologize and tell her that her fangs were big and scary, she snapped at me, "Don't call me that anymore," and glanced to the side as her weight shifted from foot to foot, betraying her discomfort.

It was on the tip of my tongue to ask what she meant, but then it clicked. She didn't care about the fangs. She cared that I called her darling. What an interesting turn of events.

It was damn hard to keep the knowing smirk off my face. "What am I supposed to call you now?" I teased, loving that she'd latched onto her new nickname so quickly and fiercely.

My little Comoară.

A dramatic sniffle came from her as she turned her nose up and flipped her long hair over one shoulder before crossing her arms. I couldn't fight off the smirk any further with that small act of sass.

This woman was the most dramatic little creature I'd ever met, and somehow it never made me any less intrigued by her. It turned my cock as hard as a diamond. Even if she frustrated me with her sass at times, it was sexy as hell the way she stood her ground, firm in her beliefs, even if they were slightly misguided at times. She'd already shown exceptional growth in expanding her preconceived notions as a born and raised slayer, but thankfully she hadn't lost her spunk in the process.

"Comoară," she mumbled finally as she lowered her eyes to my face, stumbling a little over the pronunciation, but it was cute. "I feel like darling is what you only called before we became..." She

trailed off before uncrossing her arms and gesturing between us with wide eyes, "This."

I let out a huff of laughter at that.

I'd already felt the shift between us, but to hear that she recognized the change and wasn't running away from it...It was ecstasy.

Pushing off my hands, I grabbed her hips in a flash, dragging her to straddle me and pushing the hem of her red satin dress up before she could inhale her next breath. Digging my fingers in, I pushed her down onto my erection as I rolled my hips up just a fraction, showing her exactly what her little attempt at being in control did to me.

I needed her, but there was something else I needed from her first.

Her lips parted, and the air around us became heavy with the tension of our need. Her eyes glowed with a smoldering heat, and my heart raced with anticipation. As I leaned closer, her breath hitched, and a soft sigh escaped her lips. It was like a symphony being played on the air, and I found myself craving to hear it again, louder this time. I wanted to hear the beautiful moans she'd cried out for me earlier in her room even more, though. Already, I was addicted to the sound.

Would it be too far if I recorded her without her

knowing and set it as my alarm clock in the morning? The beast in me rumbled his appreciation. I'd circle back to that at a later time.

As her head tilted back to meet my eyes, I descended toward her lips slowly. Just before I could kiss her, I stopped. Looking into her eyes I growled out, "What is *this*, *Comoară*? I want to hear you say it."

How I'd fucking ached for her to accept me as her mate since the first time my eyes had fallen on her. I wasn't letting her have even an inch of my cock in her pussy until she admitted it to me.

When I took her for the first time, I wanted her to openly admit to herself that she'd be coming on my cock for the rest of her fucking life. I wasn't a fling or an itch she could just scratch and get out of her system. She was going to look into my eyes when she came and know that this was just the fucking beginning.

My cock pulsed beneath her as she stared at me and without missing a beat, admitted, "I'm your mate, and you are mine."

Those sweet, sweet, words made the shackles on my restraint explode. I wanted to exchange blood with her to make it official and for her to wear my mark, but I'd settle for her confession...for now.

I felt like a teenager who had never gotten his dick wet before as she reached down to pull her dress up slowly, revealing more and more of her beautiful, tanned skin until the tiny scrap of black fabric that separated her pussy from me was revealed.

I had her pinned beneath me in an instant with her hips high in the air and her chest on the bed. "Fuck, warn a girl," she breathed out heavily, words thick with desire as her cheek was pushed into the bed with the swift change.

A deep wave of pleasure rolled through my body as I beheld the sight of her before me. Her tanned, smooth skin begged to be touched, always glowing, as if caressed by the sun even at night. Those endless legs of hers captivated me with every movement, the heels only adding to the allure. As she lay outstretched, her back curved in perfect symmetry, her full chest pressing against the bed. Her supple body was incredibly flexible, igniting my imagination with all that I could do with it in the future.

Fucking beautiful.

It didn't escape me the way she didn't try to move from the stance I'd put her in, despite all of her sass and bravado to be in charge. It only further cemented what I thought she was looking for, and I was more than ready to play.

"There's only one warning I'll ever give you, *Comoară*," I murmured as I trailed my hands down her spine and over the swell of her hips. She quivered at my touch, and my cock swelled with desire for her. I caressed her softly, feeling the heat radiating from her body. She leaned into me, yearning to feel more of me.

She wanted me as much as I wanted her —finally.

Bringing my hand down in a firm swat to her ass, I watched her gasp at the delicious friction. The sound reverberated powerfully through the open space, and even with clothing shielding her skin, I knew it would leave a delightful sting.

The scent of her arousal grew stronger, driving me closer to the edge of ecstasy as I inhaled it deeply, my eyes rolling back as I did.

"W...what's that?" she asked, words slightly muffled by the comforter pushing into her mouth.

A deep chuckle escaped my throat as I carefully and slowly tore away the fabric of her dress that shielded her from my adoration. It cascaded away from her like a waterfall, embracing her curves in a way that I couldn't.

My fingertips brushed against her long hair, gathering strands to twine around my hand. Gently, I tugged, bringing her back to meet mine until she was arching for me. Her pulse raced beneath my touch, and her breaths came out in short, ragged pants, inviting me to explore her further.

I leaned into her, pressing my body against hers as I whispered into her ear. "I'm warning you that I'm going to make you cum whenever the fuck I want. No matter where we are or who is around."

CHAPTER 5
ALINA

I shivered beneath him, a quiet cry spilling from my lips.

He let go of my hair, letting my chest fall back onto the bed. I bounced slightly from the spring in the mattress. Deep, ragged breaths pushed through my slightly parted lips as my brain short-circuited.

I hadn't thought it possible for my panties to get any wetter than they already were, but when he whispered his warning that felt more like a promise, a new heat rushed between my legs.

I stifled a smirk at him saying he'd make me come no matter who was around. It seemed like Lincoln and him had a bit more in common than they thought.

An image of them sharing me appeared in my mind as I heard Drake drop to his knees behind me. The heat of his breath fanned across my center before he ran his nose along my soaked panties, letting out a groan that sounded like a mix of pain and pleasure.

Would they ever be able to share me like that? My cheeks burned at the idea.

Who would be around to watch if they did? Andrei's devastatingly handsome face suddenly appeared in my dream scenario.

A moan escaped me, spurred on by my thoughts and the way Drake ran his tongue against my heat, torturing me with the fabric that remained between us. Dragging my bottom lip between my teeth, I bit down. I needed more, now. I pulled my hand down with the intent of sliding it beneath me to pull the thong to the side, but my eyes widened at Drake's loud growl, and I stopped in my tracks.

"No."

No?

"Did you not hear me say I'd make you come whenever *I* want, *Comoară?*"

My mind raced, and I heard a low chuckle come from him as the sound of metal clinked from nearby. *What the hell was that?*

The cold bite of metal against my ankle made me jolt slightly as I tried to push up.

"Lay back down, *Comoară*," he demanded, and I...I fucking listened—without any act of defiance.

Who was I around this man?

The cold material was replaced with a softer one that wrapped around my ankle as the metal I'd felt before jingled lightly. He gently pulled my foot out and closer to the corner of the bed. Soft kisses were peppered across the back of my thigh, light enough to tease the skin in a sensual way I'd never experienced before.

"You don't get to control when you reach your orgasm, *Comoară*," he finally explained. "If I want you hanging on the edge for hours, begging for me to give you that final piece that you need to finally come for me, that's what's going to happen. You didn't listen to my words, so now I'm going to take that choice away from you."

Fuck. I'd never expected Drake to snatch control away from me in a way that made me want to purr for him. When Lincoln tried, the fun came from our fight for it...from the way I made him take it from me. I'd never rolled over for him and handed him the reins. But with Drake, there was an unwavering desire in me to see where he could take us when I gave in. I had a feeling it would be to heights I never imagined possible.

My pussy clenched as he moved to my other leg, dragging my foot toward the opposite corner before repeating the process there, spreading me for him.

How the fuck had I never noticed restraints attached to his bed? Those must have been hidden perfectly.

Fingers trailed up both of my thighs and over my ass, making me shiver at the feather-light touch.

Wait, did he use these often?

I blinked rapidly as the jealous thoughts raced through my mind. I knew it wasn't fair to be jealous or care who he'd fucked before me. I'd fucked other guys and had two other mates he knew he had to share me with.

"You're uncomfortable, *Comoară?*" He voiced, phrasing it as a question, but also implying he already knew without my answer. "I can release you if you don't like this."

Fuck, it was so easy to forget that he could sense my moods even without our bond being fully in place yet.

I pushed my face into the bedding, allowing my hair to fall over the sides and obscuring my embarrassment from his line of sight. "It's not about the restraints," I mumbled into the comforter, unsure of if he could even understand me like this.

Once more, he draped himself over my back as his fingers gathered my hair. But instead of pulling me back toward him, he guided my head to lay on my cheek once more. I stared at him out of the corner of my eye as he ran a finger against my cheek and let my hair cascade toward the other side of the bed.

"Then what?" he questioned, arching a single eyebrow.

Own up to it, Alina.

With a heavy sigh and shame spearing through my heart, I admitted, "I was wondering if you used these with other partners before and got jealous."

I waited for the mood to be ruined by my issues, but to my shock, he didn't even respond to it.

"Spread your arms out toward each corner of the bed, *Comoară,*" he instructed, peeling himself off my back as he moved to the left side, waiting for me to do as he said.

Was he not going to even acknowledge what I'd said? *Fuck it.* I wanted to continue to explore this moment with him, so if that's what he wanted to do, I'd roll with it.

As I extended my wrists toward the corners, my

hamstrings protested at the way my chest sank even further into the bed without my forearms helping hold my weight up.

With both of my wrists secured, I finally heard the rustling of clothes behind me. Pulling my head back as much as I could in this position, I got a glance of his large, bronze chest before my neck burned at the strain and I let it fall back to the bed in a frustrated huff.

Damn it, I really wanted to see his body beneath the dress clothes. While I found his impeccable clothing choices sexy as hell, I knew he'd look like a god beneath them.

The sound of his deep voice startled me from my thoughts as I tried to picture his naked body in full. "I promise to always ensure you are safe and enjoying what we do together, *Comoară,* but if at any time you want to stop, I need you to choose a safe word—make sure it's something you remember. I will stop immediately if you say it."

I almost blurted out that there was no way in hell I'd ever want him to stop anything, but the new, logical part of my brain that was forming knew I needed to take this seriously.

After mulling it over for a moment, I whispered, "Devour."

For some reason, my soul sword's English name came to mind quickly. She had always been my built-in safety net, and I knew that I would never be without a way to defend myself in any situation because of her. It brought me peace to choose her name, and she wouldn't accidentally come to me unless I spilled my blood and said it in Latin, so Drake was safe from her flames in this case.

A chuff came from behind me. "The name of your sword you called to try to behead me."

Damn, he'd understood me back then *and* remembered it.

My head jerked as I glanced at him out of my peripheral vision. "You speak Latin?"

A deep hum of confirmation came from him before he moved on, "Okay. If you say devour, I will stop. But, Alina, there's one more thing I need to make clear."

It was becoming near impossible to stop myself from trying to pull against the restraints to seek out his body as my desire burned, untouched and growing within me.

"Okay, what?" I questioned sharply, unable to contain the sexual frustration from bleeding into my tone.

He chuckled at my impatience before making me

gasp as my thong was finally ripped away from my body. I was completely spread out for him and on display, agonizing over the torturously slow pace he was setting for our night.

"Fuck!" I moaned as he shoved two fingers inside of my pussy, easily sliding in with the wetness pooling there.

As he curled them, hitting that perfect spot inside of me, my hips tried to move at their own pace. I wanted to fuck his hand and come already, but the restraints made it impossible.

Tsking at my attempts, he pulled his fingers out completely, making me cry out in a pitiful, needy way. Seconds later, he slapped my pussy, the contact making my clit feel like it was on fire for a brief moment. The tingles following it made my eyes roll back as euphoria flooded my brain.

"I've never used anything that is in this room with anyone," he admitted, his voice deep and rough as if he was struggling to hold back. "I got everything the day I met you, knowing that one day I'd have you. I have never had any partner in this castle, and I haven't fucked anyone in over a millennium."

My heart practically exploded as relief poured through me. A millennium? Hell, I knew he was old and considered immortal, but damn...I was more intrigued than ever to know more about his life before me. It hit me then, that he'd been waiting for a mate for that long...No wonder he'd been so hurt when he found me, and I'd tried to instantly kill him. Having that context explained so much.

Unable to keep the quip back this time, I sassed with a smile tugging at my lips, "A little presumptuous of you, don't you think? Getting all of this on the day you met me when that was also the day I tried to kill you."

"Mmm," he hummed before smacking my pussy, making me cry out and tug at my restraints before he continued, "but you're here now, restrained to my bed and on the cusp of begging me to fuck you, aren't you? Turns out my presumptions were correct."

I couldn't argue that logic, especially with the way all of my limbs were nearly shaking with need. At this point, I was so wound up that if he slapped my pussy one more time, I might actually come from it.

"I'm going to fuck you tonight, *Comoară,*" he growled as I felt the thick head of his cock rubbing up and down my wet slit.

My hips tried to push back despite knowing it

wouldn't get me anywhere, but I couldn't help myself. I wanted him inside of me—now.

"And I'm not going to use a condom," he tacked on, prodding at my entrance with the faintest push of his hips, driving me crazy. "I don't want anything between my cock and your pussy squeezing the cum out of it. I want to fill you up and watch it leak from you as you're cuffed to my bed, unable to stop it."

Fucking hell, did this man have a breeding kink, or did he just want to mark his territory? Either way, I loved it. I still had time on my last birth control shot, so I wasn't going to use my safe word to stop him. My center instantly pooled with heat at the thought of him doing exactly what he said.

"Mmm," I moaned, closing my eyes and dying to feel him. "Fuck me, Drake."

His hips pulled back, removing any touch from me. "Say please."

I'd get on my knees and beg if I could right now. I didn't care in the slightest. "Plea—"

He didn't even wait for me to say the entirety of the word, shoving his cock into me all the way to the base with one swift push. "Shit!" I hissed at his size. I was stretched so fully I wasn't sure how he'd even gotten all the way in with one go despite the help of my wetness.

His hips began to languidly pulse, making my toes curl. He easily had my body tightening and spiraling toward release within moments.

As I relaxed and adjusted to his size, he seemed to sense it and pulled out almost completely before slamming into me with precise thrusts to time up with his words. "Tell. Me. You're. Mine."

My orgasm crashed through me as I blurted, "I'm yours! I'm your mate."

He practically purred behind me as he slowed to a languid pace once more and spread his hands on my ass, digging his fingertips in slightly. "That's my good little *Comoară,* coming on my cock so quickly."

I was too busy floating in the euphoric clouds of my mind to say anything back. This was bliss. Every nerve ending in my body was vibrating at finally having found release after such torturous build up.

As his hands on my ass trailed toward my lower back, the light touch turned almost reverent as he brushed the skin lightly. His pace turned to a slow and steady one as he murmured, "I've spent my whole life looking to find a way to repent for the sins of my past, but it never felt like I had anyone listening. But I swear your pussy is the closest I've ever felt to heaven in my life, and if there's a god or goddess in Divinus listening right now, thank you for giving me such a perfect mate despite not deserving it."

His crass, yet sweet words had me slamming back into my body. I had one problem with them.

"You do deserve me," I argued, feeling an ember of fire sparking in my chest.

My brow scrunched at the way he seemed to have such little thought for his self-worth. What I saw in him was a man who cared about his people. A man who persevered through my crazy because he believed in what we could be one day. A man who was willing to anger some of his citizens in order to find justice for the senseless slaughter of my family —people who had killed many, many of his kind.

"Don't ever say that again," I demanded, feeling my eyes prick with angry tears.

What if he continued to think he didn't deserve me and left me one day?

"Shhh," he crooned, rubbing my back as he increased his pace, easily making my brain let go of the tiny bubble of anger around it in favor of pleasure. "Just because I don't deserve you doesn't mean I'd ever let you go, *Comoară*. I'm not that good of a man. I'm selfish when it comes to you."

His admission sated my fears instantly.

The way he so easily read between the lines of

my mood without even hearing my thoughts was borderline scary. It was like he was in tune with my body and soul—more so than even I was.

When he dropped a hand from my back, I wondered what he was doing, but was immediately rewarded with an answer as he reached down between my legs and brushed his fingers across my clit. I moaned at the contact.

I was already becoming the biggest fucking fan of this position.

"Tell me why you had your fangs out earlier," he demanded gruffly as he increased the pace of the dance of his fingers on my swollen bud.

Maybe I shouldn't have been thinking this far ahead in our relationship already. Maybe it was reckless and rushed—but if there was anything I'd learned in my life recently, it was that no day was guaranteed. Drake had proven he was worthy of our bond, and I wanted to enjoy everything it had to offer us.

My answer came out breathy and choppy as I struggled to speak with the pleasure coursing through me. "I...fuck, I...wanted to exchange... b...blood."

Everything came to a screeching halt as he stilled. My heart hammered in my chest, wondering if I'd fucked up by wanting that too soon. *Dammit.*

A blink of the eye later, my left wrist and ankle were uncuffed, and a moment later my right side. My shoulders ached a little bit when I pulled my arms in to push up off the bed. My back protested for a second as I straightened.

I'd totally fucked this up, but it didn't change how I felt. I wanted the bond, and I'd own that.

I whirled around, desperately seeking Drake. My breath escaped me as I spotted him, a vision before me on his knees. Unashamed as he gazed up at me from the floor.

My fingers grasped my chest as I stuttered, "Wh...What are you doing?"

My eyes feasted upon his body, firm and defined, each muscle begging to be touched. Yet I couldn't bring myself to look away from his piercing blue eyes, full of such raw desire that it almost scorched me.

He reached for the hand at my side and grabbed it, bringing it up to his mouth to kiss softly. Holding onto it, he squeezed, "I promise to honor our bond and put it first before everything else in my life. Nothing and no one supersedes you. I will protect not only your body, but your heart as well."

The hand on my chest lifted to cover my mouth as it popped open, completely stunned by this incredible man on his knees for me, vowing to cherish me and be the best mate he could be.

A cheeky grin popped his dimple back into existence as he tacked on, "Also, I know it's too soon, but I want you to wear a ring on this finger soon to mark you to everyone who can't see the mark on your neck when it's hidden by your hair," before lowering his lips to kiss my ring finger.

And here I thought *I* might have scared *him* by moving too fast.

I shook my head and laughed softly at his request. "We'll see about that," I mused, not completely opposed to the idea, but knowing it was something I needed to think on and discuss with my other mates. I didn't want to make choices with one when it impacted the others.

With a raised eyebrow that practically screamed *I'm going to put that ring on your fucking finger whether you want it or not,* he dropped my hand to lift his wrist to his mouth. Massive fangs descended and gleamed in the light as he opened wide before biting into his skin. His blood ran black as it poured from the wound and coated his lips as he retracted his fangs.

A flash of fear flickered in his eyes as he glanced from the dark liquid and back to me. "I know that the color looks grotesque, but it won't hurt you. It's just like any other vampire's blood."

The moment of insecurity had me kicking my heels off and dropping to my knees in front of him.

I wasn't scared of him, nor ashamed of anything that made him different.

Without hesitation, I gripped his wrist and brought it to my mouth, latching onto the wound and sucking on it long and hard. My tongue lapped at the blood, loving the rich flavor that exploded on my tongue.

A groan came from him, making my eyes pop open despite not realizing they'd closed. I saw his free hand stroking his cock and his lips parting as he watched me drink his blood.

"Fuck, *Comoară*," he hissed as I pulled away begrudgingly and let my own fangs descend before biting into my wrist and offering it to him.

His eyes darted back and forth between the offering and my face, his tongue darting out to lick his upper lip. "Are you sure? We can't go back."

Searching deep within my soul, I asked myself the same question. *Are you sure?*

The sting of the situation with Andrei was still

present, but more than ever, I felt determined to ensure I claimed what was mine and protect it.

With a slight nod of my head, I reaffirmed my choice. "I'm sure."

Then he was on me, quickly putting me on my back and settling between my legs before shoving into me as his fangs pierced my wrist all in one smooth move. As he pounded into me and drank from me, I had to agree with his earlier sentiment, this felt like the closest I'd ever get to heaven.

Once again, it was as if I hovered outside of my body as I felt our connection snap into place. My neck burned, and I smiled at the thought of finally being marked by all three of my men.

He growled like a wild animal, and I gasped as his eyes turned black, staring deep into my own. Little black veins appeared beneath his eyes, spreading out over his cheeks.

While it did catch me off guard, I wasn't afraid. I wanted all of him, and I wanted to know all of him. He was giving that to me and letting me see him— the real him.

He let go of my wrist and I reached up with both hands, brushing my fingers across his cheeks before digging my hands into his soft hair and tugging. "Fuck me like you mean it, Drake," I commanded, wanting to reassure him that I wasn't scared or going anywhere, and to toss in a healthy dose of bratty sass for good measure.

"Then scream my name like you mean it, *Comoară,*" he rebutted, smirking as his black eyes faded to reveal his beautiful blue ones once more before gripping my wrists in one of his hands and yanking them above my head.

And then he did exactly what I requested and fucked me like it was the last time he'd ever be able to do so. With a masterful touch on my clit, I saw stars as he fucked me at a pace that tapped into his vampire speed and took my breath away.

"Drake!" I screamed, making him rumble and smirk.

"That's right, *Comoară,*" he praised. "Be a good girl and come for me. Squeeze my cock and make me spill inside of your tight little pussy."

I wanted to do exactly that. I wanted to give him everything he wanted, and it scared the hell out of me. He'd somehow gotten me wrapped around his finger and cock so quickly after I accepted he wasn't responsible for my family's deaths.

I was placing a quantifiable fuck-ton of faith into this man by accepting our bond because he could very easily rip my heart to shreds.

His grip on my wrists was loosened, and moments later, I felt his hands sliding under my hip to my lower back. He lifted my hips with ease, giving him a new position that allowed him to hit even deeper inside of me.

"I'm going to come," I cried out, letting my eyes close as it threatened to slam into me.

"Look at me," he demanded.

I snapped my eyes back to his just as the crest of the wave rose and crashed into me. Crying out as my orgasm seeped into every inch of my body, he came right after me with a roar, his hips pulsing a few more times as I felt him spilling into me.

I closed my eyes as he dropped his head and pressed a kiss to my forehead.

His voice spoke into my mind for the first time.

This is just the beginning, Comoară.

CHAPTER 6
ALINA

A torrent of water cascaded down my arched back, my hair a murky curtain blanketing my face. I exhaled heavily as I leaned forward, the sounds of my pleasure echoing off the walls of the shower.

The warmth and safety I'd felt cuddled against Drake last night was unparalleled. We'd shared a night of intense emotions, passionate embraces, and unbridled pleasure. This morning, however, he seemed determined to etch our time together into my memory forever, to make sure I still felt the electric current that sizzled between us when I returned to the academy.

I gasped as his thumb tenderly grazed the inked lines of our mating bond on the back of my neck. All of our morning had been spent in positions that would allow him to look at and touch our mate bond mark. He was captivated by it, and I couldn't help but stare at it on his neck too, feeling an immense sense of pride now that it was a part of us both.

He was mine. All mine.

A pinch on my clit sent sparks of pleasure through me as he demanded, "Come for me, *Comoară.*"

"Fuck, Drake!" I moaned, pleasure cascading through my limbs as my body quivered with delight. His strong hands guided me through my climax as he joined me in his own.

I felt like I was floating as he lovingly bathed me with warm water, then enveloped me in a cozy towel. The intensity of the moment was palpable. He stood behind me, his gaze upon my reflection in the mirror as he leaned down to stake his claim with a gentle kiss. The bond between us was undeniable, and his appreciation for it was written across his face.

You're pretty adorable, I whispered to his mind.

A little nip to my skin made me jump slightly and chuckle as he stood back up and squeezed his arms around me.

Don't call me adorable, Comoară, unless you need another reminder of how adorable it is when I make you beg for my cock.

While I was almost certain that I'd always want that reminder, I couldn't deny I was a bit sore from our nonstop sessions. My stomach rumbled as I thought of food and healing. It had been too long since I'd had blood. The small amount from Drake last night hadn't even touched the hunger pooling in my stomach.

I knew he would have gotten me some blood from the kitchen last night if I'd asked, but sleep had dragged me under the second we fell into bed. I was paying for that this morning.

"Come," he said, ushering me into his room with a hand on my lower back. "Let's get you dressed and fed. We have a big day ahead of us."

As I pulled on the leggings and hoodie he'd grabbed from the side of my closet he'd prepared in this room, I chuckled at his persistence. "You know I have to go back to the Academy for classes today, Drake. I told you last night."

We'd had a tiny tiff over whether or not it was safe enough for me to go back right now, and after a lot of back and forth and a few orgasms scattered between, we'd finally come to an agreement.

Knowing that our mate bond wouldn't connect us across that distance, he was going to get me a phone to talk to me, and I was going to text him multiple times a day to check in.

When he suggested I drop out of the academy now that I had a duty to the board here, I'd truly considered it. I didn't need the academy to find a path to Dracula anymore. I consider myself a checkmate on that now, but there was something the academy provided me that I still needed, and that was my own space and room to figure things out. With Andrei. I'd have to find a way to juggle my duty to the board and my duty to my own life.

A heavy sigh fell from him as he buttoned the cuff of his white dress shirt. "But this castle has so much more room and protection for you, *Comoară*."

He wasn't wrong, but he'd never understand where I was coming from in this situation. That was okay, though, as long as he didn't think he could stop me from making my own decision on the matter.

That little dorm room had become my refuge away from everything and everyone. It was the one place I could call my own. Not only that, but there were the issues with the breach of security at the academy. I wasn't going to run away and leave my friends and classmates that remained to face whatever evil was lurking around the campus without me.

I wouldn't run away from my problems ever again. This was my era of facing them head on, even when it was the harder path to take.

Standing up straight and pulling the band of my leggings up, I doubled down. "No, I'm still sticking to my choice. But you can come visit me, remember?"

Our previous scheduled time together sounded awful now that I actually wanted to spend time with him. Only seeing him on the weekends wasn't going to cut it, but I was aching to spend more time with Lincoln and to have the opportunity to talk to Andrei without his father around, so Drake would have to come to me and be around them during the week.

He grumbled his begrudging understanding before ushering me out of the room once he was fully dressed in his dark navy suit. Damn, he was so beautiful. "We need to stop by the library in my office before grabbing you some blood in the kitchen."

My curiosity was piqued as I glanced up at him out of the corner of my eye. "Oh?"

His face was guarded, and as I tried to focus on how he was feeling, I got a sense of confusion from him. Channeling into his head, I got small pieces. Naturally, he'd always erected a solid wall around his mind as a defense mechanism, so he was working on letting me in slowly.

Bond.

Unusual.

Think he'd seen it before, though.

All night, I'd felt such contentness and warmth from him as I could feel him thinking about the bond, but this was the first time I'd picked up on something unusual.

As if he sensed me prodding his brain, he tossed me a lop-sided smirk as he turned the corner and guided me toward two large, dark double doors. "I promise I'll let you know when I find what I'm looking for. I don't want to misspeak on the matter before I can read up on it. It's not something I remember the details of well."

Uncertainty bled through me as anxiety knotted my insides.

A beautiful, curved wall of books on black, worn bookcases stared back at me as he pushed the doors open and strode inside. A heavy desk sat in the middle of the room atop a large, silver area rug. Two oversized chairs sat on either side of a small side table to the left of the room near the only window providing natural light.

Striding to the middle of the sun rays, I soaked in the warmth seeping in through the window as they hit my back. I watched Drake with rapt attention as he scratched at his beard, walking from one end of the room to the other, scouring the shelves for a book. He pulled an occasional few out, glancing at the front cover before mumbling to himself, "No, no. It's here somewhere," before placing them back.

As he reached for the top shelf on the bookcase closest to me, I mentally oohed and ahhed over the beautiful, dark purple leather-bound book that he pulled down. It had intricate gold fonts and symbols etched into the spine and cover, reflecting in the sun as he pulled it open.

A thrill ran through me, and I rushed over to sit in the empty chair across from him as he did the same. His eyes tracked the words on the page with single-minded focus as he furiously flipped through the pages. Finally, he must have found what he was looking for as he exclaimed, "Aha! I knew I'd seen it before. Have a look, *Comoară*."

Turning the book around, he extended it to my greedily waiting hands. Snatching it from him, I quickly scanned the top left of a passage next to a drawing of three dots with a line through it after settling it on top of my thighs.

My pointer finger brushed across the rough parchment as I read the dark, sprawling script out loud. "Although this has only occurred once in our recorded history, there remains the near impossible chance of what they called the *Coniuncta*, a soul bond involving the alignment of multiple souls."

My breath caught in my throat. Was he saying this was us?

Flicking my gaze up, I found his eyes trained on me, raptly listening as he rested his elbows on his knees and his chin in his hands. "Go on," he encouraged.

Wetting my lips as I glanced back down at the page, I took a deep breath before diving back in. "While there is only one recorded *Coniuncta* to go by, it was said that despite going years with three of her mates, the line between her mates never appeared until they happened upon her fourth. This leads us to believe that the *Coniuncta* isn't possible to achieve until all possible individual mate bonds have been established.

"This would explain why this type of bond is the rarest known. The chance of all of the souls finding each other and being alive at the same time would be nothing short of a miracle. The merging of these souls allowed the telepathy between mates to extend to all within the *Coniuncta,* making them a complete unit with a bond between each."

Confusion rocked through me. *This couldn't be us.*

Furrowing my brow, I sighed heavily before sitting back in the chair. "This is really interesting, Drake, but why are you showing this to me? I felt the small spot burning where your dot would go, but nothing running through them all."

He just stared at me for a moment before an arrogant smirk tugged the corner of his lip up. Arching a single eyebrow at me, he questioned, "Are you so sure about that, *Comoară?* Have you actually looked at your mark in the mirror since we bonded?"

My eyes furiously glanced around as I thought back over our time since then. Holy shit. My eyes widened as I breathed out, "Well, I...no, I haven't, but I knew what the previous two looked like, so I figured it would be the same."

Humming floated through the air from the direction of the kitchen, and I quickly raced to put the book down on his desk before darting toward the sound. It had to be Lo, and I needed to borrow her eyes right now.

"Lo!" I called out as I slid into the room, all but falling against the kitchen island as she spun around at the fridge door, her curls flying around in a movie star way that made me jealous.

Damn, she was so effortlessly beautiful.

"What's up, boo?" she chirped energetically before turning back to pull the fridge open. "You hungry?"

She tossed bags of animal blood in front of me before I could even answer, and I blinked at her. How was she so relaxed when I just raced into the kitchen like a demon, yelling her name?

Taking a moment to observe her, I noticed a seemingly permanent smile on her mouth and a faint blush to her cheeks. *Wait a second.*

My mouth popped open as I recognized the glow of sex. "Lo! Did you hook up with someone last night?"

Her blush deepened, and she actually looked bashful for a second. "Maybe," she cooed before turning to start the coffee maker.

Oh, she wasn't getting off that easily. "Girl, spill!" I demanded as she scooped the grounds in.

"Yeah, Lo," Drake taunted in a weird tone as I felt his presence at my back suddenly. "Spill."

His arms wrapped around my waist, and I

leaned back into his chest on instinct just as she spun back around to face us, this time with narrowed eyes and a warning in those irises.

She held a long spoon out like a knife, jabbing in the air as she responded. "Drake, do not get any ideas. I swear you are the worst cock block of my life, and if I have to live here and occasionally hear the two of you having the time of your life fucking, I'm going to have a fuck buddy of my own, okay?"

A growl spread through his chest before he dropped his chin to rest on top of my head. "I wouldn't have to cock block if you'd stop choosing the worst possible men to invite into your life," he rumbled.

I smirked at their familial banter. It was so adorable.

What did I say about calling me adorable, Comoară?

My smirk deepened as his voice in my mind.

Lo's fingers flew to pinch the bridge of her nose as she closed her eyes and whispered, "Fates, give me the strength." Her eyes popped back open as she cocked her head to the side and placed a hand on her hip and motioned with her hand in a sassy manner. "You don't think any man is good enough!"

Drake scoffed, "Well, that really sounds like a

personal problem now doesn't it, Lo? Choose better men, and we couldn't be in this predicament!"

They both exchanged low growls, but the coffee maker beeped, signaling it had finished its brewing cycle. It popped the tension between them, and Lo turned to pour three cups, adding the proper cream and sugar to each of ours as she mumbled, "Why can't a girl get laid around here in peace?"

Don't be so hard on her.

She deserves better.

His voice was matter of fact, like this conversation was not up for discussion. I lightly smacked his hand that hung around my waist.

That isn't up for you to decide. She might choose wrong at first, but she'll learn from each one. It's her life to live, Drake. You saved her once, but you can't save her from everything.

I felt the guilt pouring through him.

She's my responsibility.

She's her own woman. All we can do is support her and love her through any decision she makes.

"What did you need when you came in, Alina?" she questioned, pulling us from our chat after placing the cups in front of us.

I let out a sigh as I shook my head, stunned by

how quickly I'd forgotten. My attention span was severely lacking today.

Breaking out of Drake's grip, I rushed to her, turning around and pulling my hair to the side. "Tell me what my mate mark looks like."

"Uh, it has three black dots and a line through it. Why?"

Holy shit. We had a *Coniuncta* bond.

My mouth dropped open as I stared at Drake's shit eating *I told you so* grin.

Can you hear Lincoln or Andrei?

His head shook. **No, but we are probably too far from Lincoln, and you told me Andrei has his wall in place around his mind already. There's no way to test it right now.**

"Wait, what the fuck is happening right now?" Lo questioned, coming around to my side and staring a hole into my cheek. "Just because you have your bond in place doesn't mean you can leave me out of conversations!"

Drake reached for his cup and took a sip as I turned my head to face hers. Reaching out, I grabbed her hand and squeezed. "Sorry, Lo. It isn't on purpose; it just feels natural."

She sniffed dramatically. "Mhm. It's fine. So what were you talking about?"

I let out a laugh at her dramatics and dropped her hand to walk back to the counter and grab my cup. "Supposedly we have a unique bond that's only been recorded once in the history of vampires, but we don't have a way to test it until we're back at the academy."

She shrieked, "Say what now! Why aren't you back there yet?" Her fingers shooed us. "Go on, get!"

Drake let out an exasperated sigh as he shook his head at Lo's antics. "We should get going, *Comoară*. Drink your blood first, and then we'll head back."

After drinking down half the cup of coffee, I put it down and switched over to my blood bags.

Lo reached into her back pocket before sliding a sleek black phone onto the counter in front of me. "Drake asked me to pick you one up. It already has his number and mine programmed in."

I hummed in delight around the straw in my mouth as I grabbed the phone and slid it into the side pocket of the leggings.

"Thanks for doing that, Lo," Drake said, washing his cup in the sink before placing it back in front of the coffee maker. "Don't forget we have to have that chat about your schedule changing slightly when I get back."

She saluted him as she mumbled over her coffee, "Yes, Dracula, my liege."

The blood in my throat choked me as I somehow tried to laugh and swallow at the same time.

Gathering my empty bags, I cleared my throat as he cheekily asked, "Why do I keep you around, again?"

With a wink, she quipped back, "Because your ass would feel empty without my foot up it 24/7?"

Tossing my trash away, I soaked in the warmth and love that was always present with them when we were alone in the castle. I'd never had a sibling— the closest being Skye and Jade—and I found myself slowly coming to regard Lo as a sister of sorts, considering her relationship with Drake.

"For some reason, I just don't think that's the answer," he joked before offering me his hand. "Shall we take you back now, *Comoară?*"

Was I ready to face everything waiting for me back there? *I had to be.*

Taking a deep breath, I placed my hand in his. "Let's do it."

CHAPTER 7
ALINA

Like a dog shaking off water, I shook my body as if I could get off the weird, lingering sensation of traveling through the portal. "Ugh," I said, upper lip curling in slight disgust. "There's just something about using that thing that never quite feels natural."

Voices surrounded me then as I focused on the pavilion. There was a variety of students from each of the sectors standing around. Some in circles with only their own species, but much to my delight, there were a few mixed groups as well.

What were they all doing here?

My enhanced hearing picked up on a few conversations. Focusing in on a fae nearby I listened.

"Yeah, my mom freaked and didn't even give me the

choice of staying. I don't know if she's even going to let me come back next year."

The tall man who had an arm draped around her shoulders squeezed her gently. His scent wafted through the light breeze, and I picked up on his shifter blood.

"We'll figure it out, babe. For now, this is what's safest for you, and that's all I want."

My heart lurched at the sight of their relationship. They were two people from sectors in Praeditus that would probably never have crossed paths without DIA bringing them together. For some reason, it sparked hope in my chest that maybe one day I could bring the slayers and vampires together in a semblance of peace.

Another conversation further away jerked my attention toward them.

"Did you hear? All the dragon heirs went home last night. They took Bex right after the meeting and left."

Bex was gone. The thought made me a little sad at first, having enjoyed the few moments I'd had with the sweet dragon. But if she was gone, that meant she was safe, which was for the best. Hopefully one day our paths would cross again.

That left only Alexandra for me to check on.

"They must all be gathered here and waiting on Estrid to help get them home," Drake mused, pulling me against his side and dropping a kiss on my head. "I should help her if there are any vampires. This is a lot for her to handle alone."

Once again, he was proving to me how selfless and wonderful of a man he truly was.

Spitfire? Are you back?

Lincoln's deep timbre flowed through my mind, the feeling bringing a flood of euphoria to me. Fuck, I missed that prick.

I'm here, Sir. Come and get me.

Only if you promise to be a good girl.

Never.

My heart was practically beating out of my chest at the thought of seeing him. Despite it not having been that long since I'd seen him, everything that happened since made it feel like a lifetime.

Wrapping my arms around Drake, I looked up at him. "Hey, I have two requests for the King of Sanguis really quick before you go help."

"Go on," he responded as he kept his eyes on the crowd, seemingly always on surveillance in case of an attack.

This issue had been weighing on my heart in a really fucking annoying way ever since it happened.

And though I wasn't sure she deserved me sticking up for her, it still felt like the right thing to do.

"I know you had Maya kicked out of the academy for fucking with me, but I want you to get her back in and tell her family to send her back if that's what she wants. Even with the threat over the academy, it should be her choice."

Silence followed for a few moments until he eventually nodded. "Okay. The second request?"

"Don't wait too long to investigate Jeoffrey."

The sooner we had more information on him, the better. He was a fucking snake in the grass, and sooner or later, he would be exposed. I wouldn't rest until he was.

"Done on both accounts," he easily agreed before dropping his gaze to me. He lifted his hand to cup my face. "Now, may I make a request from the Queen of Sanguis?"

I let out a huff and shrugged. "Not sure I'll ever get used to that title, but sure. What is it?"

To my utter shock, he jerked me against his chest, knocking the breath from me as he dipped me back with a hand supporting me. His warm lips devoured me, and I opened for him, loving the public attention he was giving me. I was accustomed to him making a clear difference in his personality when we were in private versus outside the castle, and I was so pleased to see him not falling back into that pattern.

A throat cleared, and I was startled out of the moment with Drake.

"Welcome back, Princess."

Oh, fuck. Lincoln got here faster than I anticipated.

Disentangling myself from Drake, I straightened up and turned on my heel to face the vampire who drove me equally crazy and made me equally happy.

He looked like shit. Well, I still wanted to run my tongue along every inch of his body, but he was a disheveled mess. His dress shirt and pants were wrinkled, and his sleeves were rolled up to his elbow. His hair was normally perfectly slicked back in public, but right now it looked like he hadn't showered, slept, or done anything to his appearance since before I saw him last.

I could see the fatigue in his eyes, but there was a fire burning deep in them, and I sensed his frustration over finding Drake and I kissing. That fire was a lot more subdued than I would have expected. Whether that was from how tired he was or him starting to accept that I had other mates was yet to be seen, though.

Strutting right up to him, I grabbed his tie and pulled his lips down to mine. When they touched, it was like sparks danced in my heart. His hands quickly found the small of my back and dragged me in closer to him. Despite not looking like he'd taken care of himself, his scent was still his signature clean, minty aroma that made me melt into his embrace.

I needed to bottle up what each of my men smelled like to spray on my clothes when I missed them.

Well played, Comoară. He needed that.

It was only fair that I treat them as equals, even when I was in front of each of them. It was the only way I could think to make them realize I needed all of them, equally, and that I wasn't going to settle for one.

Drake's words made me pause, though, for multiple reasons. He seemed genuinely encouraging of this, and it sounded like he could sense Lincoln now too.

Can you pick up on his thoughts or feelings through the bond?

I can sense his moods like I could you before we completed our bond. I can't hear his thoughts, though. I think he has a wall up for anyone other

than you, but this confirms what we know about the Coniuncta bond. There is definitely a connection between us now that wasn't present before.

As Lincoln and I parted, he pressed a quick kiss to my forehead before tucking me against his side. He clicked his tongue a few times before asking, "So, who wants to explain why the fuck I feel this shit-head's emotions and him prodding at my mind?"

I nearly choked on my spit at the blunt manner in which he asked, and I looked at Drake immediately. He chuckled and shrugged back.

I think this is a conversation best had between you two in private, Comoară. If you want me to stay, I will, though.

No, you're right. I need to pull my big girl pants on and just lay it out there for him.

I think Lincoln and I actually would agree for once on the fact that we want you to pull your pants off.

His words made me roll my eyes and laugh.

Maybe it wouldn't be like talking to two equally obstinate brick walls about the idea of having to truly share me. Drake was really, really impressing me with his attitude about it today. It gave me hope that Lincoln would come around that quickly too.

With that cheeky statement and a wink, Drake

flashed over toward the portal and began talking to the few vampire students I recognized. We probably had the least number of students present in the pavilion, but I wasn't surprised by that. Our sector was used to danger and a cutthroat environment. It would have shocked me if a bunch of them left due to the threat hanging over the Academy.

Placing my hand on Lincoln's chest, I peered up at him as he stared a hole in Drake's back. "I'll explain it to you, but let's go to one of our rooms. It's a bit too hectic here for my liking."

As we spoke, I picked up on the conversation of a few nearby witches.

"Did you hear they're saying it's one of the freshman witches who killed the students?"

Holy hell. There was so much for Lincoln and me to talk about.

It was getting harder and harder to drown out the dozens of conversations going on, and I really wanted some peace and quiet for us to have this talk. Especially if it didn't go well. We didn't need an audience for that, considering he was still a member of the faculty, and I was now a representative of the board.

With a nod, we sped together toward our sector, not stopping until he opened his door and ushered me in. As soon as the door clicked shut behind us, he was on me. His hand wrapped around my throat, and he slowly backed me up step by step until my back smacked into the far wall.

"Tell me, Princess," he purred in a low rumble as his eyes swept over me from head to toe. "If I flip you around right now, am I going to see a third mate mark?"

What should have been a straight-forward question sounded instead like a veiled threat, and the rumble in his voice as he asked had my legs rubbing together.

That was the thing I'd never get enough of between Lincoln and me...the push and pull for control. I knew he didn't want me to have the mark. Fuck me, he *really* didn't want that to be the truth.

I also knew with his territorial ways that it would make him want to mark in a whole other way once I admitted it. Was it wrong that I wasn't mad about that fact? While I wanted them each to accept that they were all going to be a part of my life romantically moving forward, there was just something about a possessive, over the top jealous man that made my core tighten with lust.

Some may think that's trash, but hey, what's the saying? One woman's trash is another's treasure?

My tongue darted out to wet my lip, dragging his focus to my mouth. His nostrils flared as he slapped his palm onto the wall beside my head before he leaned down to be nose to nose with me. "Tell me, Princess," he demanded.

The veins on his exposed forearm bulged, matching the pulsing vein running through the middle of his forehead. Reaching up, I brushed some of his fallen hair out of his eyes, smirking at him the entire time and refusing to break eye contact.

"Why don't you just flip me around to get your answer?" I goaded, a smirk tugging at my lips. "I know you like me from behind, Sir."

Images flashed through my mind of the way he fucked me against the window in my room. You'd think I hadn't just been thoroughly fucked by Drake this morning with the way my body was coming alive for Lincoln, which just goes to show that I truly needed them all.

He sucked his bottom lip between his teeth, biting down hard as his chest rumbled. Hazel eyes bore into mine, promising to rip the answer from my mouth if I didn't give it willingly.

"Never the easy way, Spitfire," he mumbled, tightening his grip on my neck.

My mouth popped open as a small moan

escaped with the pressure. My eyes fluttered, and I gave in as he spun me around, pressing my cheek into the wall as his fingers deftly moved my hair to the side, exposing the mark.

I didn't breathe as I waited for him to make a comment.

"What does the line mean?" He finally asked, voice tight as he clearly held back a lot of what he wanted to say.

"It's a rare bond mark called a *Coniuncta,*" I breathed out, trying my best to get a glance at his face out of my peripheral vision but failing. "It means that you three are the only mates I have out there, and now that I've completed the bond with you each, a new one has snapped into place that connects each of you as well."

A growl tore from his throat as he let me go. Turning around, I found him pacing in front of bed as he shook his head. A scowl marred his handsome face. "I don't want a bond to either of them," he spat before stopping at looking into my eyes. "What are we supposed to be, some kind of fucked up love square?"

I couldn't fault him for not taking the news in stride. Not only did he have to accept that I officially had two other mates, but he also had to come to terms with the fact that the Fates gave them a connection to each other too. There was nothing he could do to change that, and a part of me did feel guilty that they had to live with the *Coniuncta bond* without consenting to it first, but I had no idea this would happen.

Trying to lighten the mood, I walked toward him and laid my hands on his biceps. Tilting my head to the side, I smirked and responded, "I'd like to think we're a little more like a rhombus—unusual and much more unique than a typical square. More personality if you will."

After the words escaped, I couldn't contain my own laughter at the horrible joke. Thankfully it was bad enough to pull a small smirk from him too.

"You're really fucking weird, Spitfire," he said, lifting a hand to cup my face. "Never change."

Turning my head to press my lips against his palm, I whispered softly, "I'm so sorry that you've been dragged into this. I didn't have the slightest idea that this was even a possibility until Drake and I stumbled across a book about it in his library this morning."

My gaze trailed to the ground as I pulled my cheek away from his hand. A fierce sense of guilt stirred in my gut. Would they despise me for this?

His hand moved to seize my chin, and he demanded, "Look at me, Alina." Fear and anxiety kept me from complying until he yanked a bit tighter and bellowed, "Now, Princess."

My entire body tensed as I met his gaze, our eyes locked in a battle of wills.

"Am I happy about this? No. But as long as I still get equal time with you, I'll deal with whatever weird shit comes along with our fucked-up rhombus."

My body trembled as I barely suppressed a grin. His confession sent my heart racing, and I felt a wave of relief wash over me. Lincoln and I had made such incredible progress, and it was tangible proof of our ability to communicate effectively without lashing out.

Launching myself forward, I threw my arms around his neck and pressed a fervent kiss against his cheek, whispering a heartfelt, "Thank you."

"Mhm," he murmured. "But I swear to the Fates if one of them tries to fuck with me and get us friendship bracelets, I'm going to string them all together and choke them out with it." His eyes narrowed, and the vein on his forehead pulsed once more. "Why can I so easily picture Andrei doing it to piss me off?"

Andrei...

"There's something that happened last night with Andrei and I that I have to tell you about," I admitted hesitantly, unsure of where to start.

Lincoln's body coiled around me, his energy tapping against my mental shields as if trying to break through. I clung to a thread of composure, knowing I had to handle this situation with delicacy or risk unleashing the fury of a raging vampire. His presence seeped into my bones, and I felt the clammy grip of fear wind its way through me.

"He swore to me that he wouldn't let you get hurt, Alina," he said dryly, pulling back from me to look into my eyes once more. "What the fuck did that kid do?"

Here we go.

CHAPTER 8
LINCOLN

The last time I could recall allowing such blinding rage to consume my thoughts and emotions was when Dracula, his guards, and everyone on the board turned their back on me when I came back to get help for my parents.

It was soul shattering the way I felt disposed of, like yesterday's steaming garbage.

But this? This rage had nothing to do with me and everything to do with the most precious thing in the world to me being tarnished by the vile words of a little boy with daddy issues.

"Lincoln," Alina's fingers moved like lightning, snapping quickly in front of my eyes. Yet I refused to blink or speak. "Hello? Are you going to say something?"

When she'd finished with her summary of the night, I was a man with a single-minded focus. She continued to ask me to speak, to tell her how I felt, or what I thought we should do moving forward, but I was an immovable statue right now.

My gaze remained transfixed on her blue eyes as I contemplated the malicious possibilities of what I could do with just one swift motion—obliterating every bone in that insolent twerp's face.

Oh, the pleasure it would bring me.

Rage boiled within me, my veins and muscles like hot wires beneath my skin, tautly coiling my body with a seething energy. My teeth clenched so hard they threatened to break, and my jaw locked tight with the effort it took to not unleash my fury on Alina. She was saved from the brunt of my wrath, which was meant for Andrei alone. Even in my haze, I wouldn't let her feel an ounce of it.

My lip curled as I tore my mask of indifference away, exposing a sinister and triumphant smirk. I could almost taste my sweet revenge as I thought of the smug face that had provoked me so many times before, throwing the protection of his father and the board in my face.

No longer could he use that excuse. Not when

the King of the board was damn well going to be on my side in this.

The horror in her eyes had my smile faltering as her fingers dug deep into my forearm.

Did she seriously want to protect him just because he was too chicken to go against his father? He had plenty of people who would help him if he'd grown the balls to make a stand against Jeoffrey. Just because I wasn't a fan of his before didn't mean I wouldn't have helped him. I knew more than anyone the way living under the dog and pony show of the board as a child warped you. He would have had nothing short of my respect for trying to expose the depravity of his father, but instead, he tucked tail and lashed out at the one person in this realm who would have had his back against anything.

That was perhaps the most beautiful thing about Alina's soul. She didn't let many people in, and she made you work to get there; but once you were in, she'd go to the ends of the earth for you.

Yet he spat in her face. The thought made my lip curl in disgust.

My attempt to turn away again only seemed to anger her more. She yanked me back roughly.

"Oh no you don't!" she growled out, breathing

heavily in her attempt to stop me as she dug her heels into the floor. "He probably already feels awful enough, Lincoln. I told you all of this because I wanted to game plan how to handle Jeoffrey, not how to hurt Andrei!"

A dark laugh fell from my lips, and I could feel my brows shooting toward my hairline with my shock. "How are you defending him, Alina? There's no excuse for his actions. You would have helped him, and so would Drake and I, yet he chose the coward's way out."

Fury sparked in her eyes in defiance as she stared me down and gritted out, "He chose the survivor's way. You told me how horrible life is as a child attached to the board, Lincoln. He doesn't have parents that want out. He has a father who is willing to do anything to claim more power and control."

We stood toe-to-toe, our heated breath the only sound in the silence stretching between us. I felt the anger radiating from her body in waves, blazing like an autumn bonfire. We stood there for a beat, neither of us backing down from our stance.

She finally broke the silence when I made it clear I had nothing to say, seething as she faced me like an avenging angel. "Don't you dare sit on your high horse and act like you can judge him for his actions. Or are you so quick to forget that you even made mistakes and walked away from me after saying hurtful things?"

I gritted my teeth and shook my head. That blow stung.

I had made mistakes, but unlike Andrei, I hadn't purposely tried to hurt her. I'd been overwhelmed, confused, and shocked.

I'd realized so fucking quickly how badly I messed up and took immediate steps to try to fix it.

How could she expect me to not want to rip his head from his body?

Everyone from Sanguis and throughout Praeditus knew how precious our mates were to us with the rarity of the bond. If you were going to attack or insult someone's mate, you had the retribution coming, and you'd better say a prayer to the gods and goddesses in Divinus to protect you from that wrath.

Deciding to take a different approach, I tossed my hands in the air, causing her to take a step back. "Fine, I won't hurt him, but I'm going to get some fucking answers from him."

At the very least, I wanted to hear him own up to his mistakes. He broke his promise to me the one time I gave him a chance to prove himself. He could earn back an ounce of respect if he did own up to it, because right now all he'd proved was that his word meant nothing.

It was time for the little boy to become a man.

My pulse raced as I rushed out the door and thundered down the stairs, the bottom of my dress shoes echoing on the cold stone. The open layout seemed to amplify my name as Alina shouted it after me. I was already on the second floor, racing toward his room.

"Show your face, Andrei!" My voice erupted like thunder, reverberating around the hall as I headed toward his room in the corner.

Doors flew open with a bang as people cautiously peered out, only to be met with my withering glare. "If your name isn't Andrei, get back in your rooms this instant!"

The doors slammed shut as quickly as they opened, but not before I heard Alina's voice behind me. "Lincoln," she hissed, her fingers biting into the fabric of my shirt. "This isn't the way I want to handle this. Does that mean nothing to you?"

Fates, how did she not understand? She meant everything to me, and that was exactly why I wouldn't stand to see her treated this way by someone she'd chosen to share her heart with.

Whirling on her, I gripped her upper arms as I

lowered my nose to hers. My nostrils flared as I tried to contain myself enough to speak calmly with her, failing instantly as my voice boomed, "I refuse to stand back and watch the woman I'm falling in love with treated like a plaything to use and discard when he decides you're not worth it anymore!"

She sucked in a breath, and the fight seemed to bleed out of her at my words.

Lowering my voice, I whispered, "I know I've fucked up before, Alina, but that's exactly why I refuse to stand back and watch you get hurt again. I'll never let anyone disrespect you and get away with it." Turning on my heel, I whispered, "You're worth any consequence that comes from my actions."

"How fucking cute," Andrei's voice was laced with contempt as it echoed through the hallway.

His words made my fingers curl into a tight ball, and I quickly released Alina from my embrace and spun around. I found him leaning against the doorway of his room, shoulder against the frame with his arms crossed over his chest.

His expression was cold and unyielding. There was no apology or remorse in his gaze, only disdain as he stared at us like he wanted to get this over with and go kick puppies or whatever the hell he did to pass his time.

"Shut the fuck up, little boy," I snapped, taking a menacing step toward him before I remembered I promised not to hurt him.

A smug smirk tugged his lips up as he lazily said, "There's nothing little about me. Your girl can attest to that."

My eyes fluttered closed as I clung to the single percent of self-control I had left in this moment.

If I was being brutally honest with myself, I felt hurt by his actions toward Alina on a deeper level than simply how it impacted her. I had begun to realize that Alina wasn't going to choose only one of us and was beginning to come around to the idea of not being as hard on him or Drake—for the sake of making her happy.

When I'd entrusted him with her safety and he'd made that promise to me, it was an olive branch from me to prove that we were on the same team at the end of the day. A team that worked toward ensuring her happiness and safety in the fucking insanity that was the breach of the academy's security and the dangers of the board. I was a big enough man to know I couldn't protect her from all of that by myself, especially when I had to stay at the academy when she went to Sanguis.

I was fucking disappointed in him. I was mad that he ruined the first opportunity for us all to come together for this incredible woman who brought us together and made us better men.

Alina's soft voice piped up as my eyes popped open in time to see her walking in front of me toward him, "Andrei, there's no need to act like this now. Your dad isn't here. Can we please talk about what happened?"

He might think he's a good actor, but there was no hiding the distinct look of pain in his eyes as he moved his gaze from me to her. His throat bobbed as he shook his head and pushed off the door and moved to close it, "We have nothing else to talk about, Alina."

Before he could shut it though, she slammed her palm into the door. It cracked back against the wall with a splintering sound. That door was definitely broken.

Her voice rang out, strong and unwavering. "No. You don't get to shut me out like this. You gave up that option when you exchanged blood with me and completed our bond."

That was my Spitfire. Fuck, I loved her. I was

absolutely in love with everything about her and couldn't imagine anything that would make me give her up like Andrei had.

I decided to stay back and let her take the lead now that she seemed to be calling him on his shit.

A lifeless chuckle came from him as he shook his head. "I already made it clear to you that I got what I wanted from you—a quick fuck. I'm going to get a tattoo to cover up the bond mark like the mistake it was."

This time her voice shook as she laughed right back in his face. "You're so lucky that you're a horrible actor, otherwise my fist would have been through your teeth by now, Andrei. But I hope you know that you're digging yourself further and further into a hole that even a lifetime worth of groveling might never get you out of once you realize there are people here to help you out of the situation with your dad."

Silence ensued, and I knew her words had actually infiltrated his pea brain. There was no false bravado or arrogance on his face now...just emptiness.

Dammit, even this small look into how he truly felt inside tampered my rage. Alina was right when she said I knew better than anyone the way board members and their families were trapped in these situations. Could I check my own emotions in regard to Alina and still offer him a way out?

Despite having my mental wall up, I knew she could sense my emotions by the way she glanced over her slender shoulder at me with those big, pleading eyes.

Letting out a sigh, I put on a burst of speed to stand at her back. Placing a reassuring hand on the small of her back, I forced myself to try one more time for my Spitfire. If nothing else, I could do this for her.

"While I don't have the same reservations about punching your teeth in for breaking your promise to me and hurting Alina," I started, and a shadow of amusement bloomed on his face as one of his eyebrows quirked up. Taking a steadying breath, I continued, ready to share something personal that might help him realize that I truly understood where he was coming from and that there was another path forward, if he would just choose to take it.

"I know how hard it is to get out. My parents died when we fled to the human realm to escape the deadly atmosphere. Hunters found us and killed them. When I came back, the board sent me to live as a ward of Sanguis."

Alina leaned back into me, silently lending me her support as I tried to figure out how to best phrase my thoughts.

Andrei's eyes snapped to meet mine as I breathed out, "I know the board won't help you or listen, but *we will* if you cut your shit out and let us."

So much anguish and hope curled through Alina, projecting so loudly onto me that it made my chest tighten.

This was his chance. We'd find a way to forgive him and move on if he took it.

I wanted him to take it so damn badly, purely for the pain it was putting her through. But all you could do was lead a horse to water, you couldn't force it to drink.

CHAPTER 9
ANDREI

Alina's blue eyes were wide and glassy, her lips trembling as she leaned back against Lincoln's chest. His hands rose to rest gently on her shoulders, his expression sympathetic. I tried to keep my composure, clenching my teeth so hard that I felt my jaw lock, but it was no use. My fists clenched and unclenched, my nails digging into the skin of my palms as I tried to keep from fucking screaming into the void.

I wanted to be the man who could provide that security and be a safe place for her, yet I might have ruined that with a few wrong decisions and my inability to believe anyone could help me.

Fucking hell.

I couldn't do this anymore. I couldn't keep

acting like I was the cold, cocky little shit who only cared about himself. Not when the truth was that life felt fucking worthless without Alina in my arms.

Agony threatened to overtake me as I stood before the woman I was so in love with, trying desperately to maintain the mask of arrogant confidence that I had worn as armor for so long. It felt like a million tiny daggers were piercing my skin, and the longer I tried to maintain the facade, the deeper they cut.

With each passing moment since she'd pulled me into the tent and confessed that she loved me, I felt more and more of my integrity being stolen away. It felt as if all that remained was the shell of a man who foolishly thought he had to handle this fucked up situation alone.

I fought so hard for the bond that I knew we had, even after she was marked by Lincoln, and yet I'd lost faith that we would be able to tackle my shit-hole of a situation together.

I didn't deserve to call myself her mate, and I wasn't sure how she'd be able to forgive me for everything I'd said. But the fact of the matter was that I wasn't capable of doing this for a second longer. The longer I tried to keep this up, the more I lost not only her, but the version of myself that I had slowly begun to like with Alina in my life.

Letting the mask crumble away, angry tears threatened to spill over as I thought of the damage I'd done in such a short amount of time. My jaw clenched as I tried to keep the tears at bay, still fighting the stigma that I couldn't show emotion, but I quickly failed. The first drop of salty water slid down my face and lingered on my chin before it dropped to the floor.

"I never wanted to hurt you, Alina," I croaked out, the emotion pouring from my heart and up into my throat, choking me. "I'm sorry. I know that sounds like a bullshit thing to say after what I've done, but I made the decision that I thought was the only option in the heat of the moment."

The words sounded empty, even to my own ears. But what could I say to justify my actions? Nothing would ever sound good enough.

Lincoln stood with his arms crossed, his expression stony. His lips were pressed together in a firm line, and wrinkles of trepidation had settled into the corners of his mouth. His eyes were unreadable, and I knew that he wouldn't show any real emotion or sympathy, no matter what I said. It was exactly what I expected of him after our years together.

What absolutely fucking destroyed me as my gaze slid to Alina was the way her lips pressed together in a tight, emotionless line as her body became rigid. Her eyes grew distant, and a shield dropped over her features in response to my apology.

It's what I deserved, though. I'd take it without argument.

I closed my eyes and took a deep breath, feeling the tightness of my throat constricting me like a coiled snake around its prey, and I found myself struggling to breathe.

I lost her.

She'd admitted her love for me, and I'd somehow thought that wasn't enough of a reason to let her in, to stop and think even for a second that I wasn't in this alone. *I was such a fool.* It was so painfully obvious now that her love was worth everything.

My face felt hot and stiff, and my jaw clenched so tightly that my teeth ached, but my eyes startled open as soft fingertips brushed against my jaw.

A hesitant smile graced her face as she cupped my face and whispered, "There you are. I knew you were still in there."

A few more tears of relief rolled down my cheeks

as I brought my hand up to cover hers, holding it to me in case she wanted to pull it away. I ached, needing to soak in her touch for as long as I could because I wasn't foolish enough to believe this meant that we'd ever be able to get back to where we were before. If this was the last crumb of affection she ever showed me, I was going to burn it into my memory.

The image of her was blurry behind the wetness pooling in my eyes, but I'd never be more in awe of such beauty in my life. Not just in her physical appearance, but in her ability to chase after me and want to try to help me despite the way I'd lashed out at her.

Crumbling to my knees, she quickly followed me, dropping down and grabbing both sides of my face to force me to look at her when all I wanted was to look at the ground. "Look at me, Andrei," she demanded softly. I dragged my eyes up.

Her chest rose as she took in a deep breath. Blowing it out, she leveled with me. "I'm not going to lie and say that your actions and words didn't threaten to break me, but I knew in my heart that they weren't your truth. I knew that they were sourced from fear and desperation."

Apparently, I wasn't as good at playing my role

as I thought. Or maybe it was because the second Alina Van Helsing bumped into me, my entire life changed. She was the first person to make me question if I really did have to sit there and take whatever my father doled out. She was the first person who allowed me to share the man I was on the inside without feeling like I was weak for it or fear that she would exploit the softer side I hid from everyone. She was the first person to see *me*.

Lincoln approached, the bottom of his dress shoes smacking against the floor and making me look up just as he reached down to put a hand on my shoulder.

I know they won't help you or listen, but we will.

The silence stretched between the three of us as the memory of Lincoln's words echoed through my mind. He was right, there was no one on the board I trusted to be on my side—to even listen to me if I told them the truth about the man that Jeoffrey truly was. What I should have trusted in, though, was my mate.

"We all make mistakes," his deep voice rumbled out as his hazel eyes gazed down at me, softer than they ever had been when directed at me. "What matters from here is how you rectify your decisions and learn from them. That will show the kind of man you truly are."

Alina's small, surprised gasp matched exactly how I felt.

His fingers on my shoulder tightened before he tacked on, "But if you break another promise to me again, I'm breaking something of yours in return. Are we clear?"

Ahh, there he was. For some reason, I breathed out a heavy sigh of relief, feeling a lot more comfortable with this version of Lincoln that I'd come to know over the past couple years.

He stood back to his full height before glancing around. "We need to take this somewhere more private before we go any further on details. Let's go to my room."

Fuck, it hadn't even crossed my mind that students could be listening in, even with the walls between us. Fear spiked in my heart at the thought. I had no idea how vast my father's reach was, but I knew it was immense.

"My mom!" I gasped, eyes wide as the implications of our situation settled in. "We have to get her. We have to take her somewhere safe. We—"

Alina's voice soothed me along with her hands

brushing up and down my arms, "Andrei, take a breath. Breathe. That's good."

She praised me as I did as she requested. The blood pounding in my ears subsided with each inhale and exhale.

"Come on," she murmured, pulling me up with her as Lincoln offered her a quick nod.

Making our way up to the top floor, we piled into his room quickly. Not even a second passed before I forced myself to try to rationally explain the situation as I began pacing. "We have to get her out of the manor in case my father gets wind of me talking to you, Alina. He threatened to either kill you or her if I fell out of line."

Their shocked expressions quickly morphed into ones of concern as Alina whipped a phone out of the side pocket of her leggings.

"Piece of shit," Lincoln seethed, rubbing his jaw harshly.

Her eyes flicked up to me as she halted in the middle of typing out a message. "Are you okay if I ask Drake to go get her? I don't want to do something you don't feel comfortable with, but he's our quickest option to have her extracted."

Could I trust him? My father had served on his board since before I was born, and the way he shipped me straight to him when we got to Sanguis for the party proved that he thought absolutely nothing amiss with him.

Alina's eyes searched my face for an answer, and it hit me then that if she trusted him, then it was good enough for me. I wouldn't doubt her ever again.

With a sharp nod, I agreed. "Do it."

It felt like all of the air was sucked out of the room as she typed out a quick text. A whoosh sound accompanied the message being sent, and my heart dropped into my stomach at the thought that we might be too late.

No. Mom had to be okay. We were quick.

It was so easy to assume the worst when I'd witnessed first-hand the way my father followed through with every other threat he'd made to me before. They weren't empty promises.

Alina crossed the room to stand next to me, sliding her hand into mine and squeezing tightly as her eyes were glued to the phone screen, seemingly waiting for a response.

It astounded me the way she was still willing to help me after all of this. I knew that we were far from moving on from what I'd done, but the way she selflessly tucked her own issues away in order to help my mom and I was why she owned my heart and soul.

"Thank you," I rasped, pulling her focus as I pressed a kiss to her hand. Turning to Lincoln, I said, "Thank you as well. I know that if the roles were reversed, I would hold the same animosity toward me for what I did to Alina."

Truly, I'd want to fucking kill him.

His throat bobbed as he swallowed. He took a deep breath before answering, "It's not up to me to forgive you for what you've done to her, and I know I've made my own mistakes with Alina that I will continue to try to make up to her for the rest of our lives." He paused, running his tongue along his teeth. "But don't forget that just because someone finds it in them to forgive doesn't mean that they're going to forget the pain you caused them."

At that, Alina's gaze dropped away from me and returned to her phone.

I knew we had so much to talk about still, one on one, and I hoped that we'd have that private moment soon. I knew I could start one with her if I let down the mental wall, but it felt really unfair of me to bombard her like that. It was so much to work through, even in my own mind, that I didn't want it to overwhelm her. This had to go at her pace. If she wasn't ready to talk yet, I'd respect that and give her the distance she needed until she was ready.

All I could do was nod in acceptance of Lincoln's words. Without a doubt, they were the truth.

A ping sounded, and I jumped, my heart in my throat as I waited for her to read off the text she'd received.

She let go of my hand, tucking a long strand of hair behind her ear in a move that I had observed in the past as her nervous tick. "He said he was in the middle of an interrogation but that he's going there now."

I didn't miss the way her brow subtly scrunched for a second as she said interrogation. I wanted to ask what that was about, but I had no fucking right to ask for private information with the precarious situation I was already in.

A heavy sigh came from Lincoln as he looked at his watch. "I have to run for another meeting with the fucking faculty. Hopefully we don't sit around pointing fucking fingers like children at this one like we did last night."

It hit me then that while I had been so preoccupied with my own situation, I'd completely forgotten about the breach of security and attacks on students in the other sectors.

Fates, do you think you have it in you to cut us a fucking break? Sincerely, one tired motherfucker.

"Classes are still canceled until further notice, but stay inside this building, both of you, unless we tell you otherwise," he instructed.

"Okay." Alina breathed out, walking over to press a quick kiss to his lips before sliding her phone into his hands and requesting, "Can you put your number in really quick before you go? I know we have our mental connection, but it didn't extend to Sanguis, so I always want a way to contact you."

His fingers deftly navigated the phone, doing as she asked before handing it back with a smirk on his face. "Are you sure that's the only reason why you want my number?"

Her cheeks burned with a tinge of pink as she batted her eyes at him coyly. "That's for me to know and you to find out when I want you to, Sir."

My stomach lurched at the easy banter and affection they shared. I wasn't jealous in the slightest, but I was instantly reminded of what I'd given up. For once, it actually made me thankful that she had Lincoln to lean on while I put her through hell.

It also didn't escape me how she spoke about Drake differently now. For one, she wasn't calling him Dracula at all anymore, and there was no malice or suspicion in her tone when she spoke of him. The trust she had in him to get my mother spoke volumes of where they were at, and I had to wonder where they stood. Officially, *and* unofficially.

As Lincoln brushed by me, he clapped me on the shoulder before his voice filled my mind, making me jolt.

Don't fuck this up, buttercup.

CHAPTER 10
ALINA

Nerves blossomed in my stomach as the door clicked shut gently with Lincoln's departure. While initially I was pissed at Lincoln for forcing the issue with Andrei, I couldn't deny that I was relieved with the way it unfolded.

But now...Now I wasn't sure where it left Andrei and me.

There was also the matter of Lincoln saying he was falling in love with me. Fates, each day felt like ten with the number of changes and revelations that seemed to be coming at me recently.

Opening my mind to Lincoln, I tried to feel for him through our bond.

Miss me already, Princess?

Maybe.

I swear I heard a faint echo of his laugh.

Glancing at Andrei as he sat down on the edge of Lincoln's bed and dropped his face into his hands and rubbed at his eyes gently, I found myself wanting to comfort him. He looked absolutely exhausted and stress-riddled, but the devil on my shoulder was telling me that I needed to make him grovel before I let him back. It wanted me to get even and make him feel how I felt. But I knew, in the end, that would only make me feel like shit.

Maybe the old Alina wouldn't have given in, but this wasn't about getting even. This was about healing.

I actually wanted to tell you thank you for giving Andrei a chance and offering him your support. I know you were really heated and only did that because of me. It means a lot.

Don't ever tell the kid I said this, but I do feel for him. When he mentioned his dad's threat against you and his mom, it made me realize that just because I also grew up around the board doesn't mean we have the same life. I was lucky enough to have two loving parents who cared

*about each other and me. I don't agree with the
way he handled this, but I can feel his thoughts
and moods now because of the bond. He knows he
fucked up and doesn't expect you to even forgive
him right now.*

I had to stifle a little gasp. Reaching out through
my bond to Andrei, I still got nothing. There was
complete radio silence and a concrete wall
around him.

*I still can't get through our bond to him. I can't
believe he let you in.*

**I don't think he even knew he let me in. As soon
as he made the decision to cut the bullshit and let
us help, the wall came down between us. I picked
up on him not wanting to overwhelm you with
everything going on at once. He wants to have that
conversation out loud.**

I'd never felt such awkward tension between
Andrei and I, but now it was almost overwhelming
without Lincoln here with us. I had already made
peace in my heart that I knew Andrei's words and
actions last night were driven from a place of abuse
and fear, yet now that we were here, I didn't know
what to say.

That spoke volumes—I *always* had a lot to say.

My shoulders heaved with the sigh that puffed

over my lips as I walked toward Andrei. Dropping down next to him, I tried to clear my mind a little, desperate to not overthink everything. Leaning my head onto his shoulder, I felt him tense up.

What's he thinking now?

Oh, I have no fucking clue. As soon as I was walking out the door, I spoke into his mind and told him not to fuck it up, and he slammed his mental wall in place.

Of course you did.

I'm starting to see some of the perks of this new bond.

You're the biggest shit talker, I swear.

I learn from the best, Princess.

I couldn't hold back the chuckle of amusement before musing aloud, "So, how do you feel about Lincoln speaking into your mind?"

Andrei's shoulders shook, jostling me slightly before he murmured, "He called me buttercup, so I'm pretty sure he loves me now."

I'd always been drawn to his humor, feeling like it was so similar to my own, and for a brief moment, it felt like it did before the board party. Easy and companionable. But then reality quickly set back in, and I lifted my head away from him, twiddling my hands in my lap as I did.

Silence ensued for a few agonizing seconds.

"So—"

"Alina, I—"

We spoke over each other before we both quickly stopped, glancing at each other and waiting for the other to continue. I dropped my eyes, hating the way I felt like I couldn't even look him in the eye without remembering how his face had morphed into a mask of cruelty as he spat his hateful, vitriolic words at me.

I forgave him, but I needed something...something to replace the memory so I could move on and remember the good, not the bad.

Fuck, this was so weird. I hated it. I wanted the guy back who brought butterflies to my stomach and bantered back and forth with me like it was his favorite hobby. Everything in me wished that last night with Andrei hadn't happened.

However, it had paved the way for Drake and me to have a very intimate and emotional moment afterwards. So, in some ways, I wouldn't want to change what happened, but it left me wondering where we went from here.

When he finally spoke again, his voice was soft. "My dad threatening to kill you is my fault."

Jerking my head back, I shifted my weight on the bed to turn and look at him fully. "How so?"

I didn't believe that for one fucking second. His father was a narcissistic, manipulative abuser, but it was clear there was something Andrei wanted to get off his chest, so I wouldn't interrupt. For now.

He threaded his fingers together as he stared intently at them. "He beat the shit out of my mom as punishment for losing my first spot. We had a deal that he wouldn't touch her if I kept it."

My eyelids fell shut for a brief moment, guilt rapidly churning through me at having a hand in this— even if it was unintentional and way out of my control.

"He told me I needed to do whatever it took to get you out of the way—even if it meant killing you. He said he would use his connections to clean it up, but that I was to take back that spot immediately."

Why was it so imperative that Andrei retain that spot? I didn't fucking understand. He wanted me dead because of it? I'd understand him wanting me dead due to me being a Van Helsing, but this? Jeoffrey's mind was something I was coming to realize I'd never be able to rationalize. Maybe that was a good thing. If one day I found myself understanding the man, I'd be concerned about my own mental state.

Opening my eyes, I reached for his forearm, resting my hand on him and squeezing in silent support as his voice cracked with raw emotion, recalling the events. I had to resist reaching up to brush back the longer strands of hair that fell into his face as he let his head hang down.

"I told him I'd never kill you—that I couldn't—because you were my mate," he whispered. "I thought admitting it to him would make him see that his demands were impossible, that maybe there was a small ounce of understanding in him."

Andrei shook his head and blew out a long breath before tilting his head toward me, his usual bright green eyes shadowed with guilt. "I should have known by now that he wasn't capable of mercy or compassion. Instead, I played right into his hand when he faked those things, asking if I cared about you. I was a fucking idiot. His soft tone and genuine curiosity had the little boy in me—the one who wanted his father's attention and love—eating out of his palm."

I'd already wanted to eviscerate Jeoffrey before, but this...It renewed and amped up my determination to do so.

"Andrei," I murmured, squeezing his arm. "You're not weak or wrong for wanting to find that within him. I think it shows the depth of your heart for being willing to try to find the good in someone who has clearly done nothing to deserve it."

A dry chuckle bubbled up from his chest. "All it did was give him a way to further manipulate and use me. He choked my mom in front of me and said *'Focus on your task at hand, get the seat on the board, and your mother is safe. Choose your mate, and your mother dies.'*"

I'd made the educated guess that his father was abusive, but the fact that he hung Andrei's mother's life over his head like that added a whole new layer of complicated, fucked-up emotional abuse that I hadn't suspected. My heart broke for her. I couldn't even begin to imagine the emotional and physical abuse she'd faced well before Andrei was born, nor what she'd faced in the years after.

He sucked his bottom lip between his teeth, nibbling on it as he let his face fall back toward his feet on the floor. He released his lip and began tapping his feet lightly. "I hit him for the first time last night. I'd never fought back before then. It felt fucking good until he reminded me why I'd never done that before."

I sensed there was more to the end of the sentence, but the grimace that took over his face made me wonder if I even wanted to know.

"I told him I'd fall in line and do as he said to protect her from him," he whispered before reaching for my hand on his forearm and placing his over mine before squeezing. "I knew Lincoln and Drake would protect you, but she has no one except me."

His admission took my breath away. How could I blame him for making that choice? *I couldn't.*

He continued, "I knew you'd fight for me. For us. I thought I had to make you resent me and our bond to keep you safe, baby girl. I didn't see a way to protect my mother and have you in my life at the same time, and my mind was too clouded in the moment to step back from my emotions and think of other options."

I nodded despite knowing he wasn't looking at me. Even before knowing the extent of this situation, I knew he made his decision rooted in fear and in survival mode.

"It's been drilled into my head since birth that what a man should do is never show his true emotions. I donned my asshole persona without even considering there was another route when shit hit the fan. I know that just sounds like a shitty excuse, but whenever I'm around my father, it's like all logic flies right out the window."

I cut him off, pushing his hand from my arm to give me the freedom of movement to grab his face and turn it toward me. Staring deep into his eyes, I infused my voice with as much strength as I could, despite the feeling of my heart breaking in my chest at learning all of these details. "It is not an excuse, Andrei. It's a coping mechanism that you've used to protect yourself."

He tried to pull his head away, whether it be shame or denial driving the action, I wasn't allowing it. "While I hate that you didn't think there was another route, at the end of the day, we really haven't known each other for that long. Trust comes with time. I hope one day you'll know that we are all in this together now—you, me, Lincoln, and Drake."

His mouth parted before closing, and he blinked rapidly before he finally found his words. "How are you sitting here forgiving me?"

I swallowed hard as I considered his question, but the answer came almost instantaneously.

I didn't want to be judged for the awful things I'd done without being in control of the situation.

"I killed one of my best friends right after I was turned into a vampire when the bloodlust consumed me. I lost everything that night. My family, my friends, my life." I had to take a breath as the memories washed through my mind, clogging my throat with emotion. I cleared my throat before continuing, "I've hurt people in ways I can't possibly atone for, but I've had to learn to accept that I didn't make that choice with the intent to hurt, and that's what matters."

While I'd never forget the feeling of Skye's blood coating me, or the way that the last time she looked at me was in fear, I hoped that in the afterlife she knew I would never have hurt her if I had been in control of myself. I hope she knew, without a single doubt, that I would find the person truly responsible and avenge her death.

Andrei and I had each done things we regret, but that didn't mean they defined who we were or what we stood for.

Didn't we all deserve a chance to prove that?

I wasn't sure if he made the first move or if I did. All I knew was that seconds later our hands were in each other's hair, and we consumed each other's very breath as our lips melded together. I swear angels sang, and my soul felt complete at long last.

I finally had each of my mates at my side.

His teeth nipped at my lower lip, dragging it into

his mouth to suck on as I flipped myself around to straddle him, grinding my hips down over the erection already pressing into me. All of the questions and anxiety I had been feeling fled through the window as I lost myself in his touch.

It would take time to develop true trust between us, but this was a start that I was more than happy to take. I wasn't ready to take this further than where we were now with kissing and remembering each other's touch, but I was open to us working toward that once more. It would take time and action on Andrei's part to prove that I could let him back in without fear of him turning his back on us the moment things got hard again.

For now, I was content to feel him and let my heart begin to heal in my own way.

My phone pinged then, breaking the spell his touch held me under. We broke apart, and my hand dove into my pocket to fish the phone out. I almost dropped it in my eagerness as I pulled it up and furiously swiped to the message.

All of the happiness within me bled away like the ocean going out with the tide.

"What did he say?" Andrei asked, eyes trying to peer around the back of the phone to see the screen.

I let out a deep sigh and the phone slipped

slowly from my hand, landing softly on my lap. Dragging my eyes up to his, I knew he could see the sadness in my gaze as his expression hardened, prepared for what I was about to say.

"They're gone, Andrei."

CHAPTER 11

ALINA

Neither of us dared speak, both of our bodies completely rigid in the wake of the news. Hell, I wasn't sure if we were even breathing until my phone pinged again, breaking us from our tense silence. Not even Lo's nickname for Drake in my phone could bring a smile to my face now.

Daddy Dracula: It's only Lo and I here, so no one else knows there is an issue. How do you want us to proceed? I can alert my Pawns, asking them to find them.

I read the message out to Andrei, knowing the decision needed to be his.

I'd want to hunt Jeoffrey down until the end of

time, but things were a hell of a lot more complicated now with his mom's life in jeopardy.

Andrei's tanned skin paled, like he'd suddenly passed into the afterlife, as he shook his head and murmured, "No. We can't trust anyone else on the board. In the middle of beating the shit out of me yesterday, he slipped up and mentioned that he already has some of the members on his side."

What the fuck?

Alarm bells blared in my head, and I rushed to ask, "Who? We need to know."

With a groan, his head fell back against the pillow, bouncing as he rubbed his face harshly. His voice was muffled behind his hands as he answered, "I don't know names. All he said was that he needed me to take an empty seat to have a majority of the board."

Holy shit. Majority of the board? I had a suspicion that Jeoffrey had people fooled about who he was, but this sounded like way fucking more than that.

Dropping his arms out to the side, he added, "When I made the decision yesterday to stay with him, I was going to try to play the dutiful son to get information and bring him down eventually, but with the way he seems to be spiraling, I feel like we don't have a lot of time until he makes a move."

"Is he trying to take over the board?" I asked pointedly, dread pooling in my stomach at the thought.

Another ping.

Daddy Dracula: ????

Andrei stared at me for a beat before answering, "Without a doubt. Because I never really understood why he pushed me so hard to take a spot on the board. At first, I thought it was just to make him look good, but after what I heard yesterday, the pieces are falling into place."

This was so much bigger than what I thought Jeoffrey was capable of. I mean, seriously, why the hell would anyone align themselves with him? Drake was a great ruler from what little I'd seen. What was there to gain from a shift of power?

I rubbed absentmindedly at my forehead, unsure of what to tell Drake before muttering, "Dammit."

Because life wasn't complicated enough already, right?

Dropping my hand back down, my fingers flew across the screen as I typed out my response.

Alina: No, don't alert anyone else to what is going on. But you and Lo need to come to DIA.

Tonight. Lincoln and I convinced Andrei to let us back in, and he has some information that you need to hear.

Daddy Dracula: Are you okay, *Comoară?*

Alina: I have to admit, I'm a bit overwhelmed right now, but I'm okay. Play nice tonight, please?

Pushing a swath of hair behind my ear, I sucked my bottom lip between my teeth and nibbled on it as several scenarios for how tonight could go wrong raced through my mind. It would be the first time I had all three of my mates together since accepting all of the bonds, and I wasn't sure my heart could take it if they were still at each other's throats. I was reaching my limit on the amount of patience I had for their bickering.

Daddy Dracula: For you? Anything, *Comoară.* Meet in the training room at 6:00. Too many ears in the dorms.

A soft smile tugged at my lips as relief washed over me. Lincoln had already demonstrated a new-found tolerance for Andrei, and now that I had Drake's word that he'd be good tonight, the only thing left for me to worry about was how Lincoln reacted to Drake. Baby steps...but I'd take all the wins I could get right now with them all but marking their territory with me.

"What's he saying?"

Tucking my phone back into my side pocket, I rolled onto my side, tucking myself against Andrei's warmth. He lifted his arm, running his fingers along the outside of my arm, and as doubt and fear crept up into my mind about whether it was smart to let him back in, I forced myself to breathe through it and let it go.

It wasn't fair to him to say I forgave him just to turn around and be distrusting and guarded. Saying one thing and then acting another way would only make this harder to work through.

Say what you mean, and mean what you say, Alina.

Lincoln's words to Andrei echoed back through my head. *Just because someone finds it in them to forgive, doesn't mean that they're going to forget the pain you caused them.*

Truer words had never been spoken.

Reaching up to rest my hand over Andrei's heart, I traced random paths over his shirt as I caught him up on the pertinent parts of the conversation.

He responded with a simple *'okay'* before growing quiet once more.

I reached out through our bond, expecting to find nothing there, but found I could sense the emotions running through him. It sparked a small kernel of hope in my chest, that he would let me in.

"You don't have to keep your walls up with me, unless that's something you need right now," I whispered.

His fingers paused on my arm for a moment before resuming their brushing. "The mental bond always felt like the most intimate part of our connection," he breathed out. "There's a bunch of shit going through my mind and heart right now, and it wouldn't be fair of me to overwhelm you with that so quickly after everything that's happened."

Scrunching my arm beneath me and using my hand on his chest as leverage, I pushed myself to balance on my hip. As I stared into his tortured eyes, a tiny burst of happiness fluttered through my chest at the realization that I didn't feel the need quickly to look away after a few seconds.

It spurred me on as I reached out to cup his cheek, loving the way he closed his eyes and leaned into my touch.

"Let me decide what's overwhelming for me," I answered softly. "Sometimes it's easier to use the bond to convey all the things that are too difficult to talk about or too complicated to put words to. I want to understand if you'll let me."

As I said that to Andrei, I realized that's exactly why I knew I was ready for the bond with Drake last night. I'd so desperately wanted to be understood by him but struggled to find the words. It was crazy how it was easier to let someone into your heart and mind than to try to find the words to convey all of the emotions out loud.

There's no room for interpretation with your tone or word choice—just pure, unfiltered you.

Without hesitation, the block was lifted between us, and all of his thoughts and emotions poured into me in a slow, steady stream. Closing my own eyes, I sifted through each thought slowly, not wanting to miss anything.

Rage and a deep pit of longing swirled together as thoughts about his father came through first. Hatred for the man Jeoffrey was, but beneath that was a desperate aching within Andrei that would forever want his father to become someone he could go to for guidance, acceptance, and love. To be a role model that he could use to become a better man himself. Resentment boiled up amidst that, for Jeoffrey's lessons and beatings morphing Andrei into someone he wasn't proud of, even despite trying to rebuke the grooming.

I felt myself wishing right alongside him that

Jeoffrey would suddenly show back up and repent for his sins, but my mind rejected the possibility. It wasn't in the realm of possibility of what was possible for an outcome of this fucked situation, but I knew Andrei would never stop wishing for it.

The hard part about diving into someone's psyche was that it was hard to separate their emotions from your own, so when his grief hit me next, it felt like I was physically hit in the chest alongside him. My eyes pinched shut tightly as all the breath was knocked from my lungs.

So much grief and...*guilt.* Guilt for choosing me over his mother.

"Andrei," I whispered, feeling my face heat and my eyes prick with emotion.

I had to make an impossible choice.

His mom's voice echoed through his mind as he pushed her words at me. *I'm sorry, baby boy. I'm so sorry. You should never have to give up the one that is fated for you.*

She said that to me last night when I told my father I'd fall in line to save her. I can't help but feel that if she's hurt, or...

Pain lanced through my heart, and I gasped. So much love poured through him as he thought of her and...me.

Or if she's killed, it will be my fault. But another part of me hopes and prays that she would understand me choosing you after what she said. That she would understand the love I have for you makes it impossible to do anything other than be by your side, despite trying not to.

When I opened my eyes, I found him staring up at me as a thought flitted through his mind subconsciously.

Please don't think poorly of me for not putting my mom first.

This poor man had been put in an impossible position, and, with this war waging within him, it was becoming clear to me that he still didn't grasp what our mate bond meant.

You aren't choosing between us, Andrei. You can love us both equally and want us both to be safe and protected. Having me in your life just means that we're both going to do everything within our power to protect the people we love. That means I'm going to fight to protect her too.

Relief shone brightly in his eyes, and through our bond, before his voice cracked and he whispered, "I love you so fucking much that sometimes it scares me, Alina."

My heart practically leapt into my throat at his

words. The words I'd ached to hear so fucking badly last night.

At first I didn't understand why it would scare him, but then I felt it. His fear of not being able to live up to the idea of the man he thought I deserved. The desire to consume every part of me until I was ingrained within him and there was no starting or ending between us. The way he thought he loved his mother and that she loved him before he felt the love between him and me.

You can feel that I mean it when I say loving you has changed everything in my life. You've taught me that love is patient, kind, and supportive. It's doing what is best for the other person, even when it hurts you. It's choosing that person day in and day out. It's accepting that, while that person may not be perfect, they are perfect for you.

As he spoke, the walls I'd continued to hold up with him began to crumble, and I openly welcomed him to see my own truth within. It was messy, confusing, and complicated, but it was me.

His lips parted, and a sharp inhale came from him. I slowly peeled back my layers, one by one, and sent each toward him.

All of my own fears and desires in regard to him and this new life as a whole.

The pain and suffering of my past.

The way my heart burned for three men equally.

How I ached to have my blood oath fulfilled in hopes that it would free my heart from the shackles of the guilt I carried around.

The unworthiness I felt for being a leader of Sanguis.

Everything was laid bare for him to see for the very first time.

He silently took in the moment, a smile growing on his handsome face as he stared deeply into my eyes. His hands reached for me, drawing me close and pressing me against his chest. The warmth of his lips on my forehead felt like coming home.

Thank you, baby girl, for letting me in. I know actions matter more than words, but I'm going to prove to you that I will never betray your trust or heart again.

Snuggling into his side further, I felt the sincerity echoing through every part of him.

Maybe, just maybe with all of my mates by my side finally, that we could face everything Fate had to give us now.

Give me everything you've got, Fate. I'm not backing down.

CHAPTER 12
ALINA

Alina.

I cracked an eye open as my name was called, rousing me from the lovely nap I'd been having. Andrei's warmth had me curling around him like a contented house cat as I stretched my limbs on top of him. A small moan slipped through my lips as my back hit a perfect angle, flooding me with euphoria. There was just something about a good stretch after a nap that hit right.

I hadn't realized how exhausted I was from the party, my long night with Drake, and then waking up early enough to get back here in time for classes that weren't even happening. Andrei and I had played twenty questions, going back to the basics to learn about each other, and somewhere after learning his zodiac sign was Gemini and before I heard his answer to what his favorite animal was, sleep claimed me.

*Princess, if you don't disentangle yourself from him and stop moaning while in **my** bed, I'm going to fuck you while you lay on him.*

Lincoln's words caused me to jolt up, my heart racing as I frantically looked around trying to recall where I was. Disoriented, I felt like I was still somewhere in that weird part of waking up where I could either be awake or still in a very vivid dream. Honestly, I was all for this being a dream where I sassed Lincoln back and he followed through on his threat, fucking me while I cuddled Andrei.

But when I felt the hair stuck to the edge of my mouth, cemented by drool that had pooled beneath my cheek and noticed the dark mark of my drool on Andrei's shirt beneath me, it hit me that this was reality, and there was no way I'd be getting what dream me wanted.

He's been staring at me and smirking the entire time I've been in the room.

Glancing between a fuming Lincoln, who had his legs spread in a wide stance with his arms crossed against his chest, to Andrei, who had his hands behind his head and propped up against the headboard with a pillow, all I could do was laugh. They were so opposite, and I was fairly certain there was no way they'd ever lose the goading tension between them. I wasn't mad about that fact.

Somehow, though, the vibe that I was getting between them had shifted. There was a palpable animosity between them before, but now what I felt was almost...brotherly in their rivalry?

"Rise and shine, baby girl," Andrei murmured, reaching out to pull the hair from my cheek before tucking it behind my ear. A smirk tugged a corner of his lip up as he added, "Sorry to wake you, but we have a guest."

Oh my. Did he seriously just refer to Lincoln as a guest? This was going to be interesting.

"A guest?" Lincoln bellowed right on cue, flinging his arms out and turning around in a circle dramatically. "Last time I checked, this was my fucking room!"

It's just too fucking easy to rile him, baby girl. Don't be mad at me.

Rolling my eyes and laughing at Andrei's words, I took a deep breath and pinned Lincoln with a look. "If you wouldn't have such big reactions, it wouldn't be so fun to rile you, ya know?"

This reminded me so much of the way Andrei and I actively tried to annoy Lincoln during class in the beginning, and the moment of levity was exactly what I needed in a moment where everything else we were facing felt so fucking overwhelming. It gave me hope that our little group could somehow find a way to amicably coexist.

Lincoln's hazel eyes bore into mine as his lips flattened into a thin line. The veins in his forearms bulged as his jaw tightened. A growl emanated from him before he took a deep breath and blew it out, tossing his hands out. "Youths. Fucking youths."

I couldn't contain my cackle of laughter at that. "What are you, a grandpa wanting to yell at kids to get off your lawn?"

Between all of us, Drake was without a doubt the oldest, but Lincoln just had this...dad energy to him that was honestly hilarious once you got to know him. At first, he just seemed like a douchebag who didn't like when anyone had fun or laughed, but now, his attitude just made me laugh.

"I caught him up on Drake's plan to meet in the training room at 6:00," Andrei said, smoothly changing the subject, making my brow tug up.

I hadn't heard them talking. I knew I was getting that good, good sleep just now, but I wasn't a heavy sleeper—if they were speaking, it would have woken me up.

"Wait," I said, glancing back and forth between them as I tried to figure out when and how that had happened. "Were you talking through your bond?"

Earlier, Lincoln mentioned Andrei put a wall up with him when he left us, but had that changed?

Lincoln let out an exaggerated groan as Andrei graced me with a toothy grin. "Yes, I've been able to confirm that he does actually love me—his buttercup. We're besties now."

Lincoln scoffed as he glared at his buttercup. "Dream on, kid." Turning his gaze back to me as I pushed from the bed and stretched out completely, he continued, "I told him about the new bond between all of us and how that came to be."

Andrei let out a huff as his eyebrows inched up his forehead, "That's seriously crazy, by the way. I've never heard of it before, but I can see how it can come in handy."

Lincoln made a choking noise as the two of them shared a look. Andrei looked like a child that had come up with a devious plan and was in the middle of trying to convince his sibling to help with it. No doubt they were talking about something, but for some reason I couldn't hear it.

Was I unable to hear a one-on-one conversation between them? I attempted to speak into their minds but was met with a wall.

What the hell?

As Andrei's smile turned into a wolfish, predatory thing, I watched Lincoln turn contemplative with a scrunched brow before it flattened out and he nodded, saying out loud, "I could see the perks of that, buttercup, but don't think that's happening anytime soon."

Well color me real fucking intrigued.

Exasperation at being left out filled me, and I huffed out, "Why can I not hear the conversation?"

"Oh, we talked about that as well," Andrei offered as he tucked his hands into his front pockets and shrugged. "He didn't hear any of the conversation we had earlier, and if you can't hear ours now, it confirms what we thought. It's like a built-in privacy wall it seems. The bond only allows one-on-one chats between each of us, not group talks."

Huh. I wasn't sure if that was a good or bad thing, but I suppose only time would tell.

"Thank the fates for that," Lincoln murmured before walking into the bathroom and turning on the faucet. "I wouldn't be able to handle the endless stream of chatter."

While I could sense the sarcasm and humor to his words, they also lacked their usual zing.

Tuning into our bond, I felt his desire to curl up with me in the bed like Andrei and I had been. I watched him splash water on his face, and it hit me again how tired he looked. Part of me felt guilty for napping while he handled everything going on at the school.

Glancing at the clock on his nightstand to see how much time we had before needing to meet Drake and Lo, I found we only had about twenty minutes.

Padding over to him, I stopped just behind him and ran my hands up and down his back. "Hey, is there anything we can do to help whatever is going on with the security of the school?"

Letting out a heavy breath, he grabbed the hand towel and patted his face dry. "It's such a shit show. The witches won't stop talking about a lunar witch being a possible culprit, but they haven't even canceled the classes in their sector, despite a student being hurt there. Meanwhile, the Queen of Hell threatened to pull all of the kids in the demon sector back to them. Oh, and the shifter royals fled yesterday, leaving the rest of the students in their sector scared about what that means for their safety."

I already knew that about Bex and the royals, but the rest was news to me.

We hadn't gotten to the section of Praeditus 101 that discussed the witches yet, so I wasn't quite sure what a lunar witch was. Nevertheless, I was shocked that they were conducting business as usual over there.

Part of me really wanted Queen Ama to pull Alexandra and her roommate Alora down to the safety of Hell. But I knew if they were anything like me, which I sensed they were, they wouldn't run from this, even if their queen demanded it.

I had to clear my throat, indecision plaguing me. I wasn't sure how I was supposed to help when everything sounded like a cluster fuck. "What does Estrid think needs to happen? I know she offered for students to leave if they didn't feel safe, but what about those who want to stay?"

Just the thought had my heart pounding and my stomach dropping. What if they shut the Academy down for now? Once again, I'd be without a home, with nowhere of my own to go. I knew Drake would tell me to move into his castle, but then how would I see Andrei and Lincoln?

Fates, please don't let that happen.

It hit me hard, the desire to have a house of my

own that no one could ever take away from me. I wanted to build a life that couldn't be altered at the drop of a hat like this. One where each of my men would feel welcomed and never like they were intruding on someone else's turf, so to speak.

But without a dime to my name now that I couldn't access my family's trust, I wasn't sure how exactly to make that happen. Where would I even build it if I could find the money? Sanguis? Nowhere felt safe right now.

Lincoln placed his hands on either side of the sink, leaning forward as he looked at me in the mirror. I continued to scratch his back gently as he answered, "We've done everything we can for security. We paid the highest-ranking witches to come and triple the wards around the school. It would quite literally take an act of a god or goddess to break through that—or at least, that's what the witches told us."

As if that meant shit.

I couldn't help but let out a huff of laughter before I said, "Yeah, I remember them telling my parents that as well, with the ward we paid for yearly maintenance on, and yet enough vampires were let in to slaughter my family. Also, I saw no sign of the ward being torn when I was forced to flee. Sound familiar?"

Chills crawled up my spine at the similarities.

Andrei's voice pulled our attention toward where he paced through the room, "So there's a corrupt witch. Whoever it is has to either be the one putting the wards up or someone powerful enough to create cracks in them to let enemies through while not unraveling, or destroying, the ward."

Taking in a deep breath, I blew it out and nodded in agreement. "Yup, my thoughts exactly."

Lincoln straightened and turned to grab my hips, pulling me to press against his front. I went easily, letting my hands flatten against his chest as I rested the side of my cheek on him. His heartbeat thrummed slowly and steadily against my ear, the sound grounding me and offering a sense of strength.

Lincoln's voice rumbled through me as he said, "The shifters will resume classes on Thursday, but it's up to me to decide what we're doing in this sector. I'm waiting to decide until after the meeting with Drake and Lo tonight since it seems we have more issues at hand than just what's going on within DIA."

Boy was that an understatement. If someone

had gotten word to Jeoffrey that quickly about Andrei speaking to Lincoln and me, then we definitely had more issues at hand.

"Speaking of," Andrei murmured as he glanced toward the clock. I felt a spike of anxiety from him, biting and strong through the bond. "We should head over there now."

While I loved seeing the light-hearted side of him that made me initially fall for him, I knew he wasn't back to normal yet. Not with his mom's life on the line and Jeoffrey's whereabouts unknown.

Pushing away from Lincoln, I crossed the space to Andrei and slipped my fingers through his, squeezing gently. "We'll get through this, okay? Together."

His chest rose as his nostrils widened. Sucking in a deep breath, he nodded as he slowly let it out. "Yes. Always together."

CHAPTER 13
ALINA

"In regard to your earlier thought," Lincoln murmured in my ear as we walked down the hallway to the training room, "I have more than enough saved away to build a house. If that's something you truly want, I'll make it happen."

A swarm of butterflies erupted in my stomach at his sweet offer. I hadn't been trying to project my thoughts during that moment, but I was attempting to not automatically put my mental walls back up. We seemed to be in the middle of a beautiful turning point for us—to truly understand each other and learn to rely on one another. I didn't want to ask them to share with me and then turn around and not be willing to do the same.

If that's something you also want, but let's get through all of the shit on our plate for now and then talk more about the possibility in the future.

Waking up to you every day and being able to fuck you in every room of the house without worrying about other students or faculty hearing us? Why wouldn't I want that?

Did you not hear the part where I wanted all three of you to feel like it's your home as well? It wouldn't just be you and I, Linc.

I felt his gaze burning into the side of my face as we continued to walk.

Knowing it wasn't just us now, was something I really needed him to understand if he truly wanted to create a home together. I refused to compromise on it, knowing in my heart that I wanted to work on making us all a team together, and hopefully one day a family.

I know, Princess, I know. I promise I've come to understand that just because they are also involved doesn't mean that I wouldn't be waking up to you every day and fucking you in every room like I want. It just means that I need to accept that they will be doing the same. It won't detract from us, right?

As Andrei opened the door to the room, I tugged

on Lincoln's hand to stop him for a second before we went in. Tossing my arms around his neck, I pressed onto the tips of my toes as he leaned down to capture my lips.

Never. I need you all equally.

I felt like a bubble of warmth wrapped around us in that moment, suspending us from reality. His tongue tangled gently with mine, coaxing a small moan from me as his hands worked their way down to grab my ass.

Then I'll be a happy man for the rest of our lives.

A cough echoed through the empty hall, startling me away from Lincoln and putting me on high alert. My shoulders instantly loosened as I saw who it was—Drake stood behind us at the door, leaning there with his hand in his pockets. He looked almost carefree, like he didn't have a possible mutiny on his hands and that he wasn't watching his mate tongue down her other mate.

For a second, I was too shocked at his appearance to say or do anything. I'd never seen him in sweatpants or a thin cotton long sleeve before, but damn. My mouth watered from the casual look.

"Please, don't let me interrupt," he drawled as a shit-eating grin split his lips before sarcastically adding, "it's not like we have anything important to discuss right now."

I sensed absolutely no jealousy through our bond—color me intrigued and shocked. It was amazing to see the strides he and Lincoln had made in learning to share, which was a massive fucking relief.

Hello, Comoară. Enjoying yourself?

His tone was cheeky, and I found myself smirking at him.

I was, before you startled me. You can't just sneak up on a girl when there's the small matter of all of our lives being in jeopardy at hand.

As if Lincoln, Lo, or I would ever let anything happen to you. Having us all together is the safest you've ever been.

It didn't escape me how he left Andrei off of that list. I couldn't say that I blamed him, really. The events of the previous night with Andrei probably left behind a really bitter taste, and without being around today as we worked through it all, I could understand why he still held reservations.

Everything in due time. Already, I saw massive leaps in Drake and Lincoln's respective tolerance for each other. For now, I'd take what I could get.

I wasn't sure what I expected Lincoln to do in return to Drake's words, but he caught me off guard.

He gripped my face as he backed me up against the wall, sealing our mouths together in a much more aggressive manner. Where our kiss had been gentle and loving before, *this* was all carnal desire.

Suddenly, he hoisted me and pinned against the wall, urging my legs to wrap around his waist. His erection pressed into my core, my body heating to his touch. What really set me on fire though, was when my eyes slid mid-kiss to look at Drake, and found him looking entirely turned on.

Holy shit, was he...into this?

I didn't think I'd care for this, Comoară, but the beast in me is intrigued and somehow accepting of Lincoln also being your mate now that we have a bond to him and understand his intentions.

Huh. What a turn of events. Not for the first time, I found myself feeling thankful as hell for the *Coniuncta* bond. At first, I'd felt guilt-ridden over forcing them all to have a bond to one another without having a say in it. Not that I'd done it on purpose, but still. Now it seemed like maybe it's exactly what they all needed to be forced to begin to understand one another, and not just the surface level perception.

Drake's throat bobbed as he reached down to adjust his cock, his grin gone, replaced instead with a look of hunger. Dark eyes bore into mine, and it felt as if Drake wasn't present at all with the primal aura that radiated from him.

Lincoln's lips pulled away before finding my throat and forcing me to arch my back to give him further access. He nipped my skin in spots, making them burn before quickly soothing it with his tongue.

Fuck, Comoară. I...my control is very thin right now.

This was his monster, and he looked hungry...for me.

Lincoln.

He said don't let him interrupt, so I didn't.

I don't think this is having the impact you intended.

As his lips found the sensitive spot of skin beneath my ear, he began to suck on it seconds before I felt the pricks of his fangs scraping against it.

It was a test, actually. This was exactly what I needed to see.

Well unless you're ready to fuck right here, with

Drake as an active participant, we have to put on the brakes.

My mouth popped open in shock as I felt Lincoln's indecision wash over me. It wasn't an immediate no, and that alone had my mind reeling.

He backed away, though, letting me gently drop to my feet and giving me space to breathe. My heart beat wildly and my mind ran amuck with ideas of what this might have led to if left unchecked.

"Shall we?" Drake gritted out, gesturing at the door.

Get your whoremoans under control, Alina.

If Lo wasn't here right now, I'd highly disagree, Comoară.

Tingles spread through my body, but I forced my feet forward one at a time until I crossed the threshold of the room. Looking over my shoulder, my mouth dropped as I watched Lincoln and Drake shake hands.

How was this the same professor who told me he didn't care if I'd fucked someone before him as long as I knew he'd be the only one to do so moving forward?

How was this the same Drake who had been full of absolute rage at seeing me defend Lincoln and feed him my blood in this very room, adamant that I was his mate solely?

The last time the three of us were in this room, they started a pissing match over me like children, and now they were shaking hands and being open to...sharing me?

A shriek was the only notice I got before a hard body slammed into me and arms wrapped around me, engulfing me in a hug. "Alina, my girl!"

With that warm greeting, you'd think that we hadn't just seen each other this morning. Opening up to new friends and accepting their affection was still an adjustment for me. In the back of my mind, there was still a little voice telling me that I didn't deserve new friends after what happened with Skye and Jade.

Shoving that nasty thought out of my mind, I forced my arms to encircle her, squeezing her back. My heart was always warmed by the easy-going presence and kindness she radiated. "Hey, Lo. How are you?"

When we pulled apart, she narrowed her eyes at Drake. "You know, doing whatever my liege asks of me, like I'm suddenly his personal assistant or something."

"You're so dramatic," Drake grumbled in return, rolling his eyes.

She leaned in, her curls tickling my cheek as she whispered into my ear, "I think he's just trying to keep me busy, so I don't have time for a dick appointment."

"You know I can still hear every word you're saying?"

Undeterred, she kept whispering, "Your man's a cockblock. Can you please distract him long enough when we get home for me to take care of business?"

When we get home. The sentiment of her referring to it as home to me was sweet and touched my heart, especially when I was feeling without one right now.

Turning my lips to her ear, I whispered conspiratorially, "Don't worry, girl. If he doesn't let you get some dick, I won't let him get any pussy. Fair is fair."

"What!" Drake roared as he came to my side and tugged me away from Lo, "This is bullshit. Absolutely not."

I kicked my feet out and wiggled, trying to escape his grip. He doubled down, his arms like bands of steel around my body as my laughter rang out.

"Take that, Dracula!" Lo called out, a full smile

consuming her face as her eyes glittered with amusement. Her hip popped out as she pointed a long, manicured nail at him, "Chicks before dicks!"

A playful growl emanated from Drake before he set me on my feet, letting me go.

Remember my warning, Comoară. Whenever I want and no matter who is around. You won't be withholding anything from me. Your pussy is mine.

Yeah, yeah, I think you might be all talk.

I couldn't contain my bratty mouth this time, wanting to see him follow through with his promise one day.

I'll remember that remark.

Bet.

Turning around as I chuckled, I came to a screeching halt when I noticed Lincoln and Andrei side by side, staring at the three of us with slightly parted mouths and wide eyes. The smile on my face fell immediately.

"What?" I asked, my brow scrunching at their shocked expressions.

They glanced at each other before looking back at me, both men shaking their heads. Andrei ran a hand through his shaggy hair, wincing before he said, "It's just that, uh...this isn't what I was expecting from Lo and Dracula, considering their reputations."

Lincoln let out a huff of amusement, "You mentioned enjoying your time with them at the castle, and while I saw a different version of Drake in the hallway, it's something entirely different to actually see the dynamics of two renowned cold, bloodthirsty killers act like playful puppies with you."

"Check yourself before you wreck yourself, boys," Lo murmured in an icy tone that made the hair on my arms stand to attention. "I don't know who you're calling a puppy, but I know it isn't me."

Oh, fuck.

"Lo, he's baiting you," Drake announced in a bored tone as he plopped onto the padded floor and stretched out his long legs in front of him.

Comoară, come sit. We need to get this meeting started. There's a lot of ground to cover.

I blinked at him, shocked at how unbothered he was as Lo and Lincoln remained locked in a stand-off.

Lincoln raised a single brow, offering a lopsided grin at Lo as he added, "I see that take-no shit attitude is still in you. Just wanted to make sure my memory of you as a kid wasn't completely wrong."

"Fuck, that's a weird thought, " Andrei muttered as he lowered himself to the ground as well. Flicking his gaze toward Lo, he asked in a quizzical tone, "Was Lincoln as annoying as a kid as he is now? I picture him stealing his friends' toys and breaking them."

"Fuck you," Lincoln muttered, but there was no real heat in his words as he lowered himself to the ground and reclined back on his hands.

It was the perfect icebreaker, the tension bleeding from the room as Lo let out a sharp laugh. "He was always getting into things and asking questions. I actually don't remember him ever wanting to play with the kids. He was always wanting to learn more about the board and what we did."

For some reason, that thought made the corner of my lips tug upward into a smile. Her description completely matched what I pictured little Lincoln being like. Andrei was right when he said that was a weird thought for Lo and Drake to have known Lincoln as a child. It constantly slipped my mind that vampire's lives were so long, and you really couldn't tell anyone's age just from seeing them.

As I moved to sit where I stood between Lo and Lincoln, Drake shook his head at me and pointed at the spot between his legs.

Here.

It was on the tip of my tongue to tell him that it wasn't fair for me to show any favoritism while I was with them all. But it hit me that while I was trying so hard to make things equal I was denying myself moments with each of them simply to keep the peace.

I'd been afraid to show affection toward one of them at a time out of fear. They'd shown great strides in learning to share, so maybe it was time for me to stop holding myself at arm's length when they were all around.

Striding over to Drake, I plopped down where he indicated and leaned against his chest.

Letting my feelers out, I checked on Lincoln and Andrei's emotions. There seemed to be a small part of each of them that wanted to be the one holding me, but what they were feeling wasn't an unhealthy dose of jealousy.

I was proud of them.

Drake's voice rumbled out from behind me, "Shall we begin?"

And just like that, any lighthearted energy that remained was doused.

CHAPTER 14

ALINA

"Let's start with why we were sent to Jeoffrey's manor to extract Serena," Lo said, taking control of the conversation while she stood in front of us.

I was so relieved that she took control of the conversation and directed it. There was so much to talk about, and I didn't know where the hell to begin.

Pulling my knees up to my chest, I wrapped my arms around them and rested my chin on top as everyone's attention drifted to Andrei. While Lincoln and I knew everything, and Drake probably sensed or heard it in part through the bond now that they were in the same room, it still wasn't our story to tell.

A darkness shadowed Andrei's eyes as the light-hearted energy he'd shown fizzled out. "Long story short," he started, before taking a deep breath and blowing it through pursed lips, "my dad is an abusive, narcissistic, evil asshole. My entire life he's used my mom as leverage to make me fall in line and do what he demands. If I don't, he hurts her."

Lo's pacing halted, offering him all of her attention as unbridled fury flashed in her gaze.

Andrei's eyes fell to the floor. "As of yesterday, he now knows that Alina is my mate and is trying to use her in the same manner as he had my mother. However, he's made it clear that my mother is expendable if I choose Alina."

His sorrow and guilt flowed through the bond freely as our gazes met, making me feel sick at the reminder of what I already knew.

"When I told him about Alina and how I could never hurt her, he slipped up in his rage and said things that led me to believe he's planning to launch a coup to take over the board."

You could have cut the tension in the air with a dull butter knife, it was that bad.

"He said he needed me on the board to have a majority, but now that he likely knows that I've chosen Alina, I don't think he'll wait to make a move. As much as it pains me to say, he's a smart and cunning man. There's no way he hasn't assumed that I would be telling you everything by now."

Drake's body tensed against me, and Lo's fangs snapped out.

"Majority?" she hissed, swinging her face toward Drake and me. "Who the hell would follow that bastard in such a mission? I'll gut them one by one, in front of each other."

Hell hath no fury like a sister scorned, and I was right there with her. A coup meant they would have to kill Drake to take over because there was no outcome in which they could leave him alive and tell him to just ride off into the sunset and never return. Sanguis was his baby. He'd built it from the ground up to provide a sense of community and a way to protect his people.

Drake's voice dropped to a deep timbre that I'd never heard before, sending chills down my spine as he spoke. "I don't care if he has everyone on the board besides myself, Lo, and Alina. We'll destroy them if they even try to step out of line."

"I believe that," Lincoln murmured, glancing between us all until his eyes settled on me. "But I want to make it clear that just because I'm not on the board, doesn't mean I'm going to stand on the sidelines. I will fight."

"As will I," Andrei echoed, lifting his chin and letting his determination bleed through in his gaze and tone.

A sense of approval and pride flowed from Drake at their words, matching my own feelings. This was the team I was hoping to see us become, and I was glad to feel Drake accepting it.

"How do you want to handle the board, Drake?" Lo asked, crossing her arms against her chest as she narrowed her eyes. "We can't leave this to fester."

After silence stretched for a few minutes, I turned to look at him and found him in the depths of what seemed to be deep contemplation. His brow was scrunched with a tightness present through all of his features.

Drake?

One wrong move and everything could fall apart. I have to make the right decision.

You've built Sanguis from the ground up. Trust your instincts. You haven't lived this long based on luck. You're the king for a reason.

I wasn't sure if there was anything out there that could truly take Drake out. I knew from a slayer standpoint that no one had ever been successful in assassination attempts or reconnaissance missions to try to glean insight on the inner workings of the board.

The only thing that could destroy me is if you walked away from us, Comoară.

He pressed a quick kiss to my forehead before his attention bounced to Andrei, giving me little time to dwell on his sweet sentiment. "Do you really think he would kill Serena, or do you believe it's just a calculated ploy?"

Andrei's throat bobbed as he considered the question for a moment. "I've asked myself the same question over and over, and I always come to the same conclusion. Yes, I do think he would. Without hesitation."

"The fact that he hasn't killed her, but left a trail of blood, feels purposeful," Lo murmured, rubbing her chin in thought as she paced,. "I think he's full of shit for saying she was dispensable. He's using her as leverage, like a shield."

Drake grunted, "Agreed, but that's a good thing for us." I could feel my face screwing up in confusion, but he was quick to elaborate. "If he thinks keeping her alive gives him leverage, he won't kill her. I do agree with Andrei that he *would* kill her, but I don't think he will while she's still of value to him.

In his current position, he needs everything he can get to try to survive."

"That gives us time to find them," I murmured, drawing the conclusion between what they were saying. "But how will we do that without tipping off the rest of the board members?"

Lincoln cut in, pulling my gaze to him. "It doesn't matter if they know. We have to assume Jeoffrey already knows that we know everything from Andrei. He would have alerted anyone on his side to this and given instructions on how to proceed if that was the case. Just because he tucked tail and ran doesn't mean he's going to give up. He's going to make bold moves now because what does he have to lose? This is when we need to be on high alert."

"Spoken just like your father," Drake praised, "he was unrivaled in strategy. It's why I've never filled his spot since we lost him. No one has ever come close to comparing."

My breath caught in my throat as I waited for Lincoln's response to that. The mention of his father on the board was undoubtedly a touchy subject, considering the outcome of them leaving. Not to mention Drake's dismissal of him as a kid when he lost his parents.

One day, when we didn't have all of this on our plate, I wanted to know that story from Drake's point of view. Knowing him as I do now, I couldn't picture him turning away a child like that. There had to be more to it.

Grief flashed through Lincoln, cutting into my chest sharply, but quickly fleeting in the bond before he gave Drake a single nod. "Thank you. That's high praise. My father was a brilliant man."

Relief poured through me at the respectful handling of the sensitive topic on each of their parts.

The relief was short lived, though, as a question scratched at my brain, so intensely that I couldn't get rid of it. I fidgeted uncomfortably for a second, almost scared to ask, before deciding to spit it out. "We know that Jeoffrey holds a lot more power than we thought, but does he have enough to have orchestrated the attack on my family? We still need to find the person responsible for that, and I can't shake the thought that someone with enough power on their side to consider staging a coup could be the primary suspect."

Nodding his head, a thoughtful look creasing his brows, Lincoln said, "Don't forget that they would have had enough power and money to get in contact with a witch to help with the ward. Jeoffrey has more than enough of both to achieve that."

Drake directed his next question at Andrei. "Have you ever heard him mention anything about the slaughter of the Van Helsings?"

Slaughter of the Van Helsings.

Despite trying to find my peace in order to continue to live and bring justice to them, hearing those words felt like a bulldozer tossing me on my ass. My chest burned.

In a heartbeat, I was surrounded by Andrei, Lincoln, and Drake.

Concern bled through each of my bonds to them, and I rushed to reassure them, "I'm okay. It's just a fresh and painful topic. Let's continue, okay?"

The truth was that all of us had tough shit to deal with. I wasn't going to make this about me. It wouldn't change what had been done, and it wouldn't get justice for them. Only action would.

With unsure looks on their faces, Lincoln and Andrei finally nodded but didn't move from my side. Thankfully, Lo did as I asked, continuing on seemingly unperturbed.

"I think the best course of action would be for all of you to move into the castle with us until we know that the threat has been taken care of. We don't know who is on Jeoffrey's side. It could even be a kid at the school or a teacher.

While I agreed with her for the sake of our safety, it wasn't my home to agree to take people into. I turned toward Drake, quirking a brow.

What do you think?

I think that my bed is about to be filled with two other men who refuse to be separated from you at night.

His tone was one of humorous annoyance, and I whacked him lightly on the arm.

You didn't seem to have an issue earlier at the thought of sharing me with Lincoln.

Drake cleared his throat before announcing, "We'll move you all in tonight if you agree. There is plenty of room in the castle, and its location offers a much better defense."

I didn't think Andrei would have an issue with it, as long as we were together, but I was worried Lincoln wouldn't be on board. His memories from that place and time in his life weren't ones he wanted to revisit. I found that I couldn't blame him for that.

Lincoln pushed to his feet, running a hand over his dress shirt as if he could get the wrinkles out of it and I wasn't sure if it was from anxiety at the thought of moving into the castle, or him noticing how rough he looked still in his clothes from yesterday. He really needed sleep and a shower. "I just need to inform Estrid of what is going on and my impending departure. I will need to hand over my role as head professor for the interim."

"Understood," Drake acknowledged as the rest of us stood up. "I don't want anyone going anywhere alone. If you must go and gather belongings, do so in pairs. We leave in thirty minutes. Meet at the pavilion near the portal."

Shockingly, no one blinked twice at him taking control.

Lincoln flipped his phone out, quickly dialing a number, and talking to Estrid about the situation as soon as she answered. Lo sidled up to me and linked our arms together, dragging me away from Drake and Andrei.

"Nervous about having them all under one roof?" she inquired, genuine curiosity tinting her tone.

I was so damn grateful that she wasn't judgmental of me having more than one mate, especially considering how protective she was of Drake. It meant the world to me that she was open minded to the unconventional, which further cemented my desire to change the slayers perception of the vampires and mend our rift.

There had to be a world where we coexisted and worked together—I refused to believe otherwise after seeing this side of Lo and Drake.

My brow raised as I considered her words. "It's going to be interesting, to say the least. I can't imagine what we're going to do all day without having classes here to attend or lead. I just hope being forced together like this doesn't put them at each other's throat."

A tinkling laugh fell from her lips as she shook her head at me. "Girl, I can think of many ways for the four of you to pass the time that will leave them too preoccupied to be annoyed with each other, and they all revolve around your p—"

"Lo!" Drake called, his footsteps drawing close to us once more.

My cheeks burned at the very thought of her suggestion.

Even if sharing me sexually was something my men were down for, I was not confident in my abilities to be able to handle them all at once. Hell, I'd never even had two at the same time.

"Yes, my liege," Lo answered, turning on her heel

and bowing dramatically. "How may I live to assist you?"

"You'll take over Alina's combat training, which I want her to keep up with every day at the castle gym. We need everyone at their absolute best, and she needs more training with someone closer to her size and who fights similarly."

My eyes drifted to Lincoln, who was still chatting on the phone. "Does he know that yet? I think he enjoys being my teacher for hand-to-hand combat."

The unexpected change was going to ruffle some feathers for sure.

"As your mates, none of us will be the right teacher for you," Drake said, defending his choice.

While I didn't disagree that they were all tempting and slightly distracting, I was worried how it would impact Lincoln.

"Our body compositions are far too different to be effective. This is for the best."

My eyes widened as I shook my head and laughed. "I'm not going to be the one to break the news to him. Have fun with that."

CHAPTER 15
LINCOLN

Arriving at the castle felt like a punch to the gut. Memories from my childhood washed through me as I trailed behind the group while Drake conducted a tour for Andrei. There had been a few upgrades to some of the rooms since the last time I had been here, like the additions of the theater and the state-of-the-art gym and training room, but it was still very much the castle that I'd grown up in.

My feet stilled as we reached the board meeting room, not needing a refresher of that one at all when Drake swept his hand out, saying, "This is the only room that remains entirely untouched in the past one hundred years."

I knew the long, dark table that sat within. It

was surrounded by sixteen plush, black leather chairs—one for each member. A red velvet rug laid beneath it, giving a stark pop of color to the otherwise cold room. An arched ceiling rose above it all, echoing and amplifying all of the heated discussions that had occurred within over the centuries. I'd sat beneath my father's feet many times on that rug, playing with the laces of his dress shoes while listening to conversations that had gone far beyond my understanding at the time.

My earliest memories were warm ones, and Lo was correct in her memory of my fascination with all things to do with the board. My father had brought me along to some meetings, as did a few other board members with their children, wanting us to have time to play and grow up together. According to the adults, no one else would understand our lives and the power our families held, and the responsibility on our shoulders, besides one another. I'd never wanted to play with them, though. Instead, I begged my father to sit in on board meetings.

For the most part, the other members tolerated my presence, with a few of them even praising my father for raising me to have an interest in such topics so young. But soon enough, those curious glances and approving eyes changed to withering glares as they demanded that their kids be allowed to sit in on meetings as well. They claimed that I had a leg up on their children for a spot on the board when we were of age and if a spot became available.

That was when everything changed.

Alina appeared at the entrance of the room, scanning the area until her eyes landed on me. Her lips did that adorable thing where they pursed before thinning, as determination bled into her steel gaze. It was the look of a woman on a mission, and Alina wore that expression often.

"Lincoln?" she asked as she came to stop in front of me, reaching up to cup my cheek. Her blue eyes were searching me for answers to questions I could easily sense, despite her ability to know my feelings and thoughts through our bond.

It was sweet that she was giving me the chance to feel like I could explain or withhold if I wanted.

I leaned down, pressing a kiss to her forehead as I wrapped my arms around her. Truthfully, I loved the way her presence grounded me in the now instead of letting my mind fester in the memories of the past.

I'm okay, Spitfire. Just having to work through the past.

Her face burrowed into my chest as her fingers trailed along my back, making a shiver run through me at the light touch. Understanding bled through our bond before I felt her concern fast on its heels.

You need to shower and get some sleep. You've been going non-stop the past two days. You'd never let me do that to myself, so it's time I put my foot down in return.

My nose wrinkled slightly as I thought of my current state. It was less than ideal, but she was right, things had been non-stop.

Come, I'll show you to my room, and you can get cleaned up there. I need to check with Drake to see what the sleeping situation is while you do that.

We parted, and she tugged on my hand, pulling me toward the staircase in the foyer.

I was curious about what the sleeping arrangements would be as well. If Drake thought he was going to stick Andrei and I together in a bed while he took Alina in his, there would be a problem. So far, we'd managed to be respectful and understanding with each other, but it was still early, and the thin truce we'd seemed to call could be easily broken.

She quickly led me down the corridor toward a massive room that was definitely fit for a queen. A large sitting space was off to the right, a vanity perched next to the large expanse of windows at the far wall...and the bed, damn. It might be the largest bed I'd ever seen, sitting to my left, a large four post bed littered with cream and white pillows.

"Take your clothes off," she demanded before padding into the adjoining bathroom. "I'm going to get the shower going now."

A knowing smirk worked its way onto my face as I followed her instructions.

She would never have to tell me twice to get naked, and if she thought I was going to let her leave this room without joining me in that shower, she was sorely mistaken. I craved the feeling of her body trembling for me. I needed to hear her moans echo through the room, settling my nerves about what this relationship would look like now that we were all connected by the *Coniuncta* bond. I needed the reassurance that only her body could sing to me.

Maybe that was selfish of me, but I couldn't help it. I'd played as nice as I could for the sake of her happiness, but there were still ways in which I needed the reminder that I wasn't replaceable in her life.

I hated the thought of Alina being caught in the middle of the three of us, but there would undoubtedly be a moment of tension with us all being thrust into this living situation. She'd handled our posturing and inability to initially comprehend the thought of having to share our mate as well as anyone could have expected, but this was still hard to work through.

Moments of doubt, insecurity, and fear had twined through me since I realized that this was the only way I could have her.

Was it even possible for her to not have a favorite or to spend her time between all of us equally? I wanted to think that she could make that happen, knowing how stubborn and headstrong she could be when she felt convicted.

Steam flowed into the bedroom as she stepped through the door from the bathroom and found me stroking my already hard cock, a wolfish grin on my face. She swallowed, her throat bobbing hard as her mouth popped open and her eyes ran over my body. My nostrils flared as I scented her answering arousal.

Fucking game over. There was no way she'd leave this room until she came on my cock at least twice.

The pink of her tongue caught my gaze as it darted out to wet her lips. It was as if she was in a daze before she shook her head and blinked rapidly, holding her hands up. "We cannot do this right now, Linc. They're going to come looking for us any minute!" She hissed, eyes darting behind me as if they would suddenly appear at the mere mention of it.

Crossing the space between us, I grabbed her throat, groaning at the way she let out a breathy sigh of arousal at the move. "Then I guess we'd better be fast, Princess," I murmured, backing her into the bathroom and closing the door behind me with my foot.

She squeaked and ducked under my arm, darting for the door, but I was still quicker than her. With time, she would develop her speed and strength, but as a fledgling, she didn't stand a chance against me. Grabbing the edge of her hood, I halted her long enough to race in front of her and lean against the door, smirking in victory.

"You know I love it when you fight me, Princess," I murmured, voice thick with desire as I thought of forcing her to her knees to choke on my cock.

The way she was so perfectly matched to my own preferences sexually was something I'd never stop being thankful for and wanting to explore. However, there was a very thin line of this primal chase part that bordered on a forceful way that I wasn't cool with. She loved when I took control from her, and I would continue to push her and learn her boundaries, while also learning all of her tells to ensure I never cross the line of her comfort.

The way her eyes heated as she clenched her thighs together confirmed what I felt from her right now.

What she said aloud to me was what she thought she should be saying, but it wasn't what she wanted. She wanted to writhe on my cock as I brought her to the edge. She wanted me to remind her how delicious the feeling of floating on the edge of her consciousness could be with my hand around her neck or my cock shoved down her throat as I pinched her nose.

My cock twitched as I felt her acceptance of the knowledge that only I could give her that.

Fates, I loved this fucking bond. It was exactly what I needed to feel for my insecurity to be soothed and the perfect built-in way to ensure she was always comfortable.

Gripping the front of her hoodie, I yanked her down, demanding in a tone that I knew would get her to *eventually* submit to me, "Get on your fucking knees."

Her eyes narrowed, and I could feel the wheels turning in her head, deciding how much she wanted to fight me today. Lust slammed through our bond at my demand, and the scent of her arousal was heady, even with her leggings covering her from me.

I knew if I tore them off her and slipped my finger between her folds that I'd find her soaked for me.

I jumped at the opportunity in her hesitation, using more strength to force her to her knees. I bent and grabbed her chin, loving her obstinate gaze as she pursed her lips. It only spurred me on. "Be a good girl and suck my cock like you mean it and maybe I'll let you cum quickly enough to return to your other mates before they notice."

We both knew they would notice her disappearance quickly, but I knew I could extend this as long as I wanted because she wouldn't walk away on her own accord now that she was so worked up. My girl was in desperate need of release, and I was more than happy to use her frenzied arousal as leverage. After all, I never promised to play fair.

She tried to rip her chin from my grip, but I didn't allow her any escape, changing my grip to encompass her jaw.

"If you open your mouth to sass me," I warned, barely controlling the urge to flip her over, rip her leggings down her legs, and slide into her in one fell swoop, "I'm going to shove my cock into your mouth, Princess."

The build-up was half the fun, but man, it was so fucking hard to hold myself back when I knew the euphoria that awaited me when her pussy wrapped around my throbbing cock.

She stared back at me as she taunted me. **What if I sass you without opening my mouth, Sir?**

A deep chuckle filled my chest as I shook my head at her workaround.

Then you're still not being my good girl, and you deserve a punishment, Princess.

Her eyes widened before I used my grip on her jaw to force her mouth open, sliding my cock all the way to the back of her throat in one go as I tilted her head back, offering me the perfect angle.

She gagged, and the tears that sprang into her eyes made me groan. Her hands flew to rest on my thighs as she relaxed her throat, taking me deeper as her tongue caressed the bottom of my cock.

I kept myself buried in her throat, pulling out just enough to rock back and forth. I enjoyed the way her thighs shifted together, trying to try and find enough friction for her clit.

Deciding that she deserved a reward for taking

me in so well, I let go of her jaw and pinched her nose.

Relief flowed through our bond, and I smirked as I pulled out completely and commanded, "Take a deep breath through your mouth, Princess."

Without hesitation, she did as I said. When I saw her chest stop rising, signaling her lungs were completely full, I praised, "Good girl. I'm going to fuck your mouth now."

That was the only warning she got before I was back down her throat and bucking my hips in and out at a brutal pace. Tears streamed down her cheeks, and I gathered her hair with my free hand, holding it back and using it as leverage to control her head.

"Fuck," I hissed out between clenched teeth, "tell me who you belong to right now, Princess."

You, Sir.

Good girl.

I felt a sense of bliss from her as I pushed down her throat one final time before pulling out and letting go of her nose. If I kept that pace up, I was going to come in her sinful mouth.

She sagged as she took deep, ragged breaths. Her eyes were wide; the pupils completely dilated.

Whether it was from pleasure, pain, or both, I wasn't sure.

I pulled her to her feet, deftly stripping her clothes from her as she caught her breath.

"Into the shower," I directed, swatting her ass lightly. "It's time for your reward."

As she walked toward the gigantic, glass-encased shower, she tossed over her shoulder, "We have to be quick, Linc. I mean it."

She didn't mean it, but I would let her cling to the idea that she was attempting to get back to them quickly.

Warmth caressed my skin as I stepped into the shower behind her, pulling the door closed. This shower definitely wasn't built with the intention of just one person using it. I smirked at the sight of the huge marble bench that ran the length of the far wall—it could easily accommodate three large men side by side.

So many possibilities.

I stood back for a moment, enjoying the view as Alina submerged herself beneath the hot water pouring from the waterfall head. Water cascaded down her body, soaking through her long hair as she turned to look at me. Her rosy nipples were pert, begging for my tongue and mouth. Her toned legs gleamed under the recessed lighting, somehow making them look even longer.

Fuck, she was a vision.

I needed to bury myself in her, now. In the next breath, I had my hands on her hips, turning her back to my chest and forcing her to hinge slightly at the hips to line her pussy up perfectly with my waiting cock. The water falling down our bodies in caressing rivulets made the moment feel even more sensual.

Pulling her hips back, her pussy enveloped my cock and squeezed, which drew a hiss from my lips as she moaned with our joining. Thank the fates we had eternity because I could spend every day between her legs and never feel like it was enough.

I started off slow, building her orgasm slowly to drive her crazy. If she thought I was going to make this a quick, fast fuck for her to rejoin them, she really didn't know me.

I know exactly what you're doing.

Bending over, I reached between her legs from the front, brushing my fingers over her swollen clit.

I'm not sorry, Princess.

Increasing the pace of my hips and fingers simultaneously, I soaked in her cries and the way she pushed her hips back in time with my own, making me drive that much deeper inside of her.

Having fun?

I would have assumed that hearing another man's voice in my head while fucking my mate would have been a total mood-killer, but for some reason, it only spurred me on. Drake had no idea just how much fun we were having, and that thought made me smirk in satisfaction.

I'd promised to play nice, but Alina had no idea the way we constantly prodded each other internally. I preferred it that way, though. We could figure our shit out this way without bringing her into it.

I'm close to filling her pussy with my cum, so I'd say that's an understatement.

You're welcome for the lubrication that my cum left for you.

I barely contained a laugh at his quip. I didn't give a shit if he'd been in her this morning because all that mattered was right now. My hips smacked against her ass repeatedly, the pace I'd set becoming brutal, spurred on at the idea of claiming her as he spoke to me.

His words wrangled a deep desire from me to finish inside of her. Before, I'd always forced myself to pull out and cum on her beautiful ass, knowing that we hadn't talked about birth control or what that looked like if she wasn't on it. But if she'd given him the green light to cum in her, I was going to take full advantage of the knowledge and enjoy watching my cum drip from her when we were done.

"Fuck, Linc," she moaned. "I'm so fucking close."

I'd never tire of hearing my name pass through her sweet lips.

Listen, Lincoln. For the sake of Alina, how about we learn to share her in every way?

I thought about his question as I drove into her, over and over. If the roles were reversed, I'd definitely want to join in, no matter how awkward it might be at first. It could be a stepping stone to help show her that we wouldn't make her choose between us in any capacity. Fuck, if we could make something like this work, maybe it would be the way that ensured we all got more time with her.

I was willing to extend the offer, and I couldn't wait to see our beauty's expression when she found out.

Bring the kid. I don't know if she's ready to let him back in like that yet, but at the least we can force him to watch so he realizes what he almost lost. But if you touch my dick, I'm knocking you out.

CHAPTER 16
ALINA

My body tingled as Lincoln slowed his pace before finally withdrawing from me completely, causing my desperate pleas for more to echo through the air. "Don't stop, what the hell!"

His deep, throaty laugh sent a shiver down my spine as he swatted my ass and playfully teased me, "Oh, Princess, things are about to get a hell of a lot more interesting, so we're going to slow down even more."

Fuck, I knew I wouldn't walk out of here until I'd had an orgasm—or five—and he damn well knew that too.

My mind raced with thoughts of how annoyed Andrei and Drake were going to be if I stayed in here with him much longer. I was too hazy, too riddled with the edge of pleasure, to have my walls in place, so there was no doubt they could sense what was going on between Lincoln and me.

Shit, should I have put the barriers back up as a courtesy before we started this? I was so helplessly lost on how to navigate this now that they had bonds as well. Would it even matter if I put my barriers up if the guy I was with at that moment didn't?

Fates, you've made this really fucking complicated.

I tried to sense Drake and Andrei's mood but was met with a block. Fuck me, were they pissed enough to close off the bond?

Lincoln's head teased my entrance, and my hips fell back until I was successful in getting him in, though it wasn't even halfway. I really needed him to cut me a break and make me come already.

"My needy little thing," he purred, stroking his hand down my back. "Don't worry, Princess, you're about to have everything you want right now, and then some."

Frustration bubbled within me as I pulled away from him and turned around. I certainly had the intention of taking control of this situation.

"Either fuck me and make me come right now,

or I'm leaving," I bit out, pushing my hand against his chest to stop him from turning me back around.

As much as I loved our dynamic, he was driving me crazy, and I was trying to be conscious of my other mates. While they couldn't expect me to be a saint just because we were all under one roof, it was fair of them to expect us to set expectations and boundaries, which we hadn't done yet.

Water poured down on us as we stood beneath the shower head. I bit my lip as he pulled me close, pressing our chests together. Droplets of water ran down his face, catching on the dark hair above his eyes and sinking deep into the strands.

"Getting a bit demanding there, *Comoară*. Are you truly going to let her sass you like that, Lincoln?"

Drake's voice filled the space, startling me. I blinked repeatedly, attempting to wipe the water from my eyes as I stared through the foggy glass around us.

Shit, this couldn't be good. There's no way Lincoln would continue now. Dammit, all I wanted was at least one orgasm.

I couldn't deny the way my pussy clenched at the idea of Drake watching us, though. If the heated kiss he'd observed outside of the training room was any indication, I was almost positive that he would be down for that.

"Are you going to worry about what I'm doing with my cock or figure out how to use your own right now?" Lincoln retorted, and my body stilled as my mind reeled.

Was he...was he inviting Drake to join us?

A familiar laugh sounded, jolting me out of my shock as I asked, "What the fuck is going on right now?"

Andrei had entered the room as well, and I was so far beyond fucking confused.

Lincoln prowled toward me as the shower door opened, revealing Drake's naked form as he joined us.

My heart hammered in my chest, my eyes slowly meandering between the two exquisite men. I quivered with anticipation, longing for their touch. Was this a dream? Never did I imagine they'd be open to sharing me like this so quickly. I'd hoped that eventually we'd build up to that, but this? They were truly blowing my mind without even having their cocks in me.

I felt the chill of the marble seep through my skin as my back hit the wall, sending a shiver down my spine. I hissed in shock at the frigid temperature.

They each stepped closer, the heat radiating from their bodies and the shower mingling with the cool of the stone that pressed against my back. Our eyes met in a knowing glance as they cornered me.

Drake didn't break eye contact as he called out, his deep voice rumbling, "Are you doing what we said, Andrei?"

Excuse me, what? In my shock of having them both in here, I'd already forgotten Andrei had entered the room as well. What the hell did they tell him to do?

If I was being honest with myself, I wasn't sure if I was ready to invite him back into my body just yet. We'd worked so hard to bridge the gap between us, but in the back of my mind, I was still hesitant when it came to taking the leap sexually. Focusing on rebuilding the trust between us was the ultimate goal.

Relax, Comoară, we figured that would be the case, but we all decided to show you that we're capable of sharing in the pleasures of your body. Andrei is just going to stand out there and watch if you're okay with that.

Relief poured through me, but it was quickly replaced by curiosity. He wanted to watch us?

It felt like the perfect way to ensure he was still

included but respecting my boundaries. Plus, this brought me all the way back to the night he watched me finger my pussy outside of my window without me initially knowing he was there.

After the thought flickered through my mind about not being ready to fuck him, I winced, worried that Andrei heard me through the mental connection.

Understanding and reassurance pulsated through my bond from him, making my shoulders sag with relief.

Baby girl, you never have to worry about rushing things with me. I fucked up, and I'm willing to wait as long as it takes to repair it.

That was exactly what I needed to hear from him in order to relax enough to even consider this.

"Okay," I whispered, glancing between Drake and Lincoln, who towered above me. I had never been shy in sexual situations, priding myself on knowing what I wanted and getting it, but this was uncharted territory. And I wasn't so blinded by lust to realize that it could end up very messy with the level of feelings involved. "How is this supposed to work—"

My question was cut off as Lincoln dipped his head to capture my lips in a hungry kiss that had all thoughts fleeing as I opened up to him. Once more, his hand found its way around my throat, but my focus was ripped away, a gasp falling from my lips at the feeling of a tongue lapping at my clit.

I wanted to look down and see Drake on his knees, eating my pussy, but Lincoln's grip held me in place.

"Trust us, Princess," he murmured against my lips. "Not everything needs to be logical and thought out. Just enjoy."

His kiss became more urgent, and his hands more exploratory. The time for talk was over. My back arched as his fingers tenderly caressed my nipples, grazing them with a feather-light touch before firmly tugging and rolling them in a slow rhythm.

Drake's tongue lavished my clit until my hips bucked him off from the intensity of his attention. A deep growl came from below me before his hands gripped my hips hard, holding me in place as he began to devour me once more. His tongue brought me to pleasure's edge over and over again as I felt my body trembling in anticipation. I was so close already.

Lincoln's hands left my nipples and traveled up to tilt my head to the side, leaving my neck exposed.

Soft kisses were brushed against my neck and across the top of my shoulder before I felt his fangs lightly graze against my skin, scraping and teasing. I gulped in anticipation, expecting the sharp sting of his bite, but he held back.

While I loved his gentle affection, my body yearned to feel the pleasure of his bite. My eyes widened, and a gasp escaped me as two fingers plunged into me. Drake's expert touch stretched me as he curled them up and effortlessly found the sweetest spot deep inside me, sending waves of pleasure throughout my body.

The intensity of the sensation hit me like a wave, and I longed for Lincoln to bite me, to take me to the next level of ecstasy.

"What do you want, Princess?" Lincoln's question sent shivers up my spine as his outstretched tongue brushed against my skin. I could feel my pulse quicken beneath his mouth, now tracing small circles around the quivering vein on the side of my neck. "Tell us and we'll do it."

The words were ripped from me before I could even think them through. "I want to be bitten."

A second later, his fangs were buried in my neck, a deep growl accompanying the motion. The brief sting of pain was quickly replaced with decadent bliss as I felt his tongue lapping at the blood pouring from the wounds and into his mouth.

Pleasure overwhelmed me when I felt Drake's fangs sink into the sensitive skin of my inner thigh just beneath my pussy. His fingers worked me, expertly coaxing me until I trembled. Lincoln's fingers simultaneously teased my nipples, each touch a reminder of the orgasm I'd been denied earlier by him.

I could feel an orgasm rising within me, and my eyes sought out Andrei, finding him naked on the other side of the glass. He stroked his cock, eyes burning a bright crimson as he watched with rapt attention. As our gazes clashed, my orgasm crested over me in an explosion of exquisite pleasure that sang through my veins. My body shuddered around Drake's skilled fingers as I rode out my release, the intensity lingering in the air between us.

Before I knew it, their fangs were gone, and I was scooped into Lincoln's arms. I sank down onto his cock as my legs wrapped around his waist.

Fuck yes.

My mind was a haze of pleasure as he began to fuck me, rutting into me like a deranged man with a tight grip on my ass. My fingers dug into his skin as I held onto his shoulders for dear life. My breasts were smashed between us, and the light dusting of hair on his chest scratched against my nipples deliciously as I bounced up and down on his cock.

I'm going to fill your pussy with my cum, Princess.

I had absolutely no objections. There was something so incredibly hot about being marked by them like that, no matter how primal it was.

I felt the heat of Drake's body at my back as Lincoln roared out his release, pulsing his hips into me a few times before stilling. His eyes were hooded as he pressed a quick kiss to my lips before lowering my feet to the ground.

Taking a step back, he sat down on the marble seat before curling a finger at me. "Come here, Princess. Bend over and put your hands against the wall on either side of my head."

Glancing at Drake over my shoulder as I followed Lincoln's instructions, I found his eyes glued to my ass as I pushed back against him.

Do you trust me, Comoară?

That was a very loaded question—one I didn't take lightly—so I took a moment to think it over before answering.

I do. Don't make me regret that.

Never.

I felt Lincoln's cum leaking out of me, but Drake was quick to use his fingers to prevent it from falling down my leg, instead scooping it up and shoving it back inside of me with a growl. "Can't let any of that go to waste."

I gasped at his words. Feeling him pushing another man's cum back into me was way hotter than it should have been.

"It is vital," Lincoln practically purred, pulling my gaze back around to him.

Vital for what?

You'll find out in a moment, Princess.

Our breaths mingled with how close our faces were, and I couldn't help but lean forward the final inch to nip at his lips playfully. "Tell me," I whispered.

A moment later, Drake had me impaled on his cock, using Lincoln's cum to easily slide all the way into me. "Shit," I breathed out against Lincoln's lips, blinking furiously as Drake stroked in and out of me at a languid pace.

I heard Drake spit right before his finger teased my ass, pushing in easily with how relaxed I was in my state of post-orgasmic bliss. I blinked in surprise at the new feeling as he slowly pressed his finger in further. While not painful, it was still slightly unpleasant.

"You okay, Princess?" Lincoln murmured, eyes searching my face for any sign of discomfort. The corners of his eyes were pinched, showing his worry for me.

Before I could answer, though, I felt his fingers brushing along my clit, making me clench down on Drake's cock.

"Shit, *Comoară*," he hissed. "I'm going to add another finger, so I need you to relax your muscles, not tighten them."

I let out a breath, forcing my body to do as he said while maintaining eye contact with Lincoln as his fingers continued to dance along my clit. When a second finger began to work inside my ass, I winced at the feeling of being almost uncomfortably stretched, but Lincoln was quick to replace any discomfort I felt with pleasure as he increased his pressure on my clit.

"That's good, *Comoară*," Drake praised, rewarding me by quickening the speed of his hips as he fucked me more earnestly now.

Open up for him, baby girl, Andrei whispered to my mind seductively, ***I'm going to enjoy watching***

your tits bounce as you ride me with my cock buried in your ass.

"Mmmm," I murmured, letting my eyes fall shut as so many sensations flowed through me.

The image Andrei was giving me.

The fullness between Drake's cock and fingers in me.

Lincoln's adept knowledge of the exact way to play with my clit.

Drake began to lightly pulse his fingers in and out of my ass, awakening an entirely new feeling with it. Instantly, I clenched as pleasure spiked through me and a moan fell through my half-parted lips.

"I think our girl likes her ass played with," Lincoln murmured, causing my eyes to open.

His gaze was behind me, and something about Drake and him making eye contact while they shared my body had me flying to new heights of desire.

My breath caught in my throat as I felt a third finger pressing into me. "Holy shit," I breathed out, feeling so damn full between his fingers in my ass and his cock in my pussy.

Is this how it would feel if I had each of their cocks in me?

It would feel a hell of a lot better with a cock instead of fingers, Comoară. Double the pleasure. Want to find out?

Hesitation filled me at the thought of their massive sizes in me at the same time.

I don't think I'm quite ready for that.

Understanding radiated from him before I added, *But I want to feel what it's like to have your cock in my ass now.*

He was quick as lightning, pulling his fingers and cock out of me, nudging my entrance with his wet tip that was coated in a mixture of Lincoln's cum and my own arousal.

Fuck, I've dreamed about fucking your tight ass, Comoară.

"Deep breath," Lincoln instructed just as Drake began to press in. My breathing turned ragged at just how different the size was between his fingers and his cock.

Fuck, this was a mistake. How did I think I could do this?

Drake stilled as Lincoln's fingers increased their speed on my clit.

"Look at me," Lincoln demanded gruffly in the authoritative tone that I loved. I hadn't even realized my eyes had fallen shut until he'd shocked them open with his command. "You're going to take his cock in your ass, Princess. Do you want to know why?"

My words were shaky as I asked, "W...Why?"

His fingers pinched my clit, shooting sparks of desire through me and making me forget about Drake's size for a second as he began to push into me further.

Lincoln's eyes narrowed as his lips turned up in a smirk, bringing his lips to brush against mine as he spoke, "Because my cum is wrapped around it, and I want to know that my cum has been in every single part of you."

And I love that my cum will be the first inside your ass, even if it isn't my cock in there first.

Shit, the dirty talk had my eyes rolling in pleasure as his tongue invaded my mouth and they began to work as a team. Each time Drake pushed further and paused, Lincoln pinched my clit, rolling the bundle of nerves between his fingers.

You look fucking beautiful right now, baby girl. You're doing so good. I want you to picture something for me, can you do that?

Andrei's question took my focus just as Drake bottomed out in my ass and groaned.

Yes.

Picture your hair tightly wrapped around Lincoln's hand as he fucks your throat and pinches your nose. He'll be standing while you straddle me. You'll sink down onto my cock at the same time Drake is pressing into your ass from behind.

Drake began to move slowly, making me moan at the feeling accompanied by the image Andrei was painting. He had to have felt or heard my desires that Lincoln satisfied through our bond to know this information.

Lincoln's lips found my ear, running his tongue along the shell, his hot breath making me shiver in delight as fingers pressed into my pussy. "Fuck my hand and Drake's cock, Princess," he murmured before biting down gently on my lobe. "Set the pace."

You'll be taking all of us into you like the perfect little mate you are because you're meant for us, baby girl.

I felt like I was going to cry at the level of pleasure coursing through me. It was so fucking intense I wasn't sure I could handle it as I began to push my hips back at the rhythm I wanted.

"Shit," I moaned as my body trembled, a pleasure so deep building within my core that I felt like I was going to be knocked on my ass when it crashed through me. "You all feel so fucking good."

While Andrei wasn't even touching me, his thoughts had me feeling so much desire that he might as well have been caressing me with how intimate it felt.

Drake grunted as his hips smacked against my ass over and over. "Fuck, your ass is milking my cock, *Comoară*. I need you to be a good girl and come for us."

One day we'll all come inside of you at the same time, baby girl. We're going to stuff you so full of our cum that no one will ever doubt who you belong to.

I flew over the edge. My entire body tightened as my orgasm rolled through me in unrelenting waves.

Andrei's and Drake's groans filled the air alongside my own moans. My mind and body felt fuzzy as the pleasure seeped into every molecule of my being.

This was bliss.

They were bliss.

And they were *mine*.

CHAPTER 17

ALINA

I breathed in the scent of all the new equipment in the training room as I glanced around to take it all in. It was beyond spacious, with towering, vaulted ceilings and floor to ceiling mirrors that made it seem even bigger. The floor was adorned with colorful mats, stretching equipment, and fitness machines on the other half of the room.

As Lincoln and I stretched on the open mats of the sparring section that had a wall of weapons nearby, a knowing smirk filled my face. Lo sauntered in, dressed in a white leopard print legging and sports bra set that made my plain black set look dull in comparison.

She seriously had the best taste in clothes. While she had been the one to stock my closet, she'd expressed her fear of giving me anything too bold or unique when she'd had to shop for me without knowing me. I was thankful for everything she'd gotten me, but I wanted a shopping trip together as soon as our lives were no longer hanging in the balance. While I'd grown up partial to the black leathers of slayers, the more time I spent around her, the more I felt myself wanting to try out new things.

Her brow scrunched in confusion as she glanced at Lincoln before giving me a pointed look that screamed, *Did Drake not tell him?*

I shook my head and shrugged at her.

To my knowledge, no one had told Lincoln that he'd been fired as my teacher, and I had been extremely careful to protect those thoughts in my head from him. I meant it when I said I wouldn't be the one to break his little heart with the topic, so when he'd asked me as we finished breakfast if I wanted to head down to train, my answer had been a squeaky and pinched yes.

Drake had had all the time in the world to update Lincoln on the decision he'd made, seeing as the four of us had all piled into my bed after washing up and drinking our dinner. I'd fallen asleep to the three of them having casual conversation and a smile on my face.

"Morning, lovebirds!" Lo called out in a tight tone, a cute bounce in her step as she crossed to drop down next to us.

Rolling my hips forward, I reached out on the mat with my legs spread, folding myself over. I couldn't hold back my slight wince as I straightened back up, resting on top of my sit bones. My ass was sore as hell from the way Drake fucked it last night, despite all of the pleasure it'd given me.

Despite the aches, I couldn't help but nibble on my bottom lip as I thought of what tonight would bring now that we'd opened the door to having joint sessions.

Heat blossomed on my cheeks as Lincoln taunted me.

Wanting a round two, Princess?

Before I could respond, Lo focused her attention on him as she stretched to touch her toes over her straight legs. "Hey, Lincoln, did Drake happen to talk to you about the change in Alina's training?"

He paused mid-stretch, an arm across his chest with his hand on the elbow, forcing it further. His eyes narrowed, voice dropping as he answered, "No? What did his *highness* decide?"

While all three of my mates had been getting along surprisingly well, considering Lincoln and Drake's staunch opposition to sharing me at all initially, the condescension dripping from Lincoln's tone made me wince.

Trying to lighten the blow, I murmured, "Lo calls him *liege* in that same tone. You guys should be friends."

When silence stretched between us, showing that my joke had clearly flopped without the intended effect, I sighed heavily.

Fuck you for leaving this to us to tell Lincoln.

Comoară, talk to me in that tone of voice one more time and I'll bend you over my knee and smack your ass cherry red.

The threat should not have had me snapping my legs together and my core aching, but here we were.

You owe me for this, Drake.

It really shouldn't be that big of a deal. The decision was based purely on logic, not emotion. Lo makes more sense to be your trainer in all aspects.

He still wasn't getting it.

Deciding it would be best to just rip off the bandage and not shove this onto poor Lo, I announced, "Drake thinks it would be beneficial to have Lo take over my training completely. He's ordered her to work with me every day now."

To my shock, Lincoln showed no external outburst, but if he was a dragon shifter, there would be smoke billowing from his mouth and ears right now with the way he was vibrating with rage.

His jaw was so tightly clenched I wasn't even sure how he got his next words out while staring a hole into the mat beneath him. "Am I not good enough after proving myself as a capable trainer for Dark Imaginarium Academy, churning out countless skilled fighters that are employed all over Praeditus?"

I knew his ego would take a huge blow from this, seeing as he'd literally dedicated his life to training the best of the best.

Crawling over to him on my hands and knees, I sat back on my thighs and grabbed his hand. "Hey, you are amazing at your job, but Drake has a point about Lo being closer to my size and similar in fighting techniques because of that. Maybe you can still join us for her to demonstrate things for someone our size fighting you?"

I swung my head to Lo, eyes pleading for her to give me this to soften the blow on him.

She was immediately nodding way too enthusiastically as she pushed to her feet. "Yes! Of course, what a great idea, Alina."

A growl came from Lincoln as he dropped my hand and ambled to his feet, muttering, "I don't need the pity. What I need is to show Drake just how capable I am."

He flashed out of the room, leaving me to straighten to my feet and face Lo. Tossing my hands in the air, I groaned.

Seeing as he was without a doubt on his way to try to get a few hits in on Drake, I tried to quickly explain to him what was coming his way.

After finishing school in Sanguis, he had nothing, Drake. He was offered the position by Estrid and has built his entire life around his job. He has a lot of pride in it, so to be brushed to the side is going to hurt not only his ego but will make him feel worthless if he feels like he isn't good enough for the one thing he has to his name.

Guilt flowed from him through our bond.

That wasn't my intention.

Just because it wasn't your intention doesn't mean it won't still hurt someone. Telling someone you didn't mean it that way doesn't take the sting away. I understand why you made the decision, but you need to own up to your decision to him yourself and understand why he feels the way he does because of it.

He's here. I'll apologize.

Good boy.

Watch yourself, Comoară.

"Done talking to them?" Lo questioned as she pulled a short broadsword from the weapons rack along the far wall. "You had that concentrated look."

"Yeah," I muttered, dragging my hand over my face before dropping it to my side. "I think there's hope for them yet."

She nodded in agreement, her curls bouncing with the move as she offered me a gentle smile. "Your situation is a lot to take in as a whole. It's going to take time to work out the *kinks*."

My mouth dropped open at her implied inflection. Cheeky girl.

It was a reminder for me to get the down low of her fuck buddy situation soon. I needed all the details. It was only fair since she knew everything about mine.

We shared a laugh before she quickly switched over to the side of her I'd only seen flashes of before. She went full-instructor mode, all mirth fading away as she pointed the sword at me. "Call forth your soul sword, now. Drake told me about it, and we're going to work on your ability to wield it today."

I hesitated a fraction of a second too long before letting my fangs lengthen to knick my lip enough to bleed. As Devorare materialized in my hand, I found myself flat on my back with the tip of Lo's knife pressed into the hollow of my neck above my collarbone.

"Fucking hell," I breathed out with wide eyes. "I'll never be able to fight you."

"You will," she corrected in a sharp tone while flashing to her feet and holding a hand out to help me up. "With training and age, you absolutely will be able to. If you can actually connect to your sword, you'll have a leg up on most, if not all, vampires."

A single eyebrow raised at her as I took her outstretched hand and pulled myself up, letting Devorare's flaming length lay flat at my side. "How do you know we aren't connected?"

I tried to not get defensive, but the reminder of my inability to find my connection to my sword, past the surface level one we innately shared, hurt. Every time I thought of the lack of connection, it served as a painful reminder that I had failed during my time as a slayer. I was unable to do the one thing everyone around me with a soul weapon had on the very first day of being gifted one.

A huff of laughter came from her, but it was tinged with an iciness I'd never heard from her. She looked me in the eyes as she responded, "I've fought many slayers in my time, Alina. Anyone with a soul weapon was always ten times the fighter than a slayer without. It allows you to move faster, to react without thinking, to trust in your instincts on a whole new level."

I let my head hang, glancing down at Devorare.

Please, let me in.

"You're still moving like a slayer without a weapon," Lo observed. "But if we can get you to tap into that connection, I'd feel a hell of a lot better about your odds of fighting any vampire besides Drake. You'd definitely be able to hold your own, and with the threat hanging around you and your men, we need you to have that edge."

Letting my insecurities out, knowing it did me no good to keep them inside, I glanced back to her and confessed, "There's never been a soul weapon by her name, to our knowledge. Every other weapon has a book kept, detailing their powers, how each wants to be connected to their slayer, and their achievements together. I'm in the dark with Devorare."

Although, those achievements that were often boastful of how many vampires they'd slain seemed like less of an accomplishment. Especially now that I knew some incredible vampires that would have been on the receiving end of the blade.

"Lincoln thinks she was destined for me, seeing as she's the first of her kind and I'm the first Van Helsing vampire," I mused, wondering if there really was any merit to it.

"Devorare," Lo mumbled, brow furrowed in deep thought as she stared at my sword. "To devour." Her lips thinned as her eyes blew open. She blinked repeatedly before looking at me. "I think Lincoln was onto something with that, but you're going to think I'm crazy for what I'm about to suggest."

"What are you thinking?" I hedged, curious as hell.

I was willing to try anything—do anything—to finally connect to my soul sword. There was nothing Lo could say that would make me blink twice in regard to my weapon.

She shook her head, taking a deep breath before blowing it out. "Put up your mental walls to all three of your mates," she instructed, making my curiosity fucking palpable now. "If they get even a *whiff* of what I'm about to tell you to try, they will be down here in an instant, stopping you and probably beheading me for even suggesting it."

I gently coaxed my walls into place with each of them, not wanting to alert them to it because it would only make them come check on me anyway. As it was, I still didn't think we had much time until they noticed.

"Okay, I put the blocks up, but they will notice pretty quickly," I said, encouraging her to spit out whatever the hell she'd concocted in that beautiful head of hers.

"What if she quite literally needs to devour you to connect?" Lo murmured. "I noticed how you called her to you after spilling your blood. What if you couldn't connect to her until you were a vampire because you wouldn't survive what she needs when you were a slayer?"

A shiver ran down my spine. Maybe I spoke too soon in saying there was nothing I wouldn't do to spark our connection.

I ruminated on her words, pacing around as I kept my gaze on Devorare.

You crazy bitch, is there truth to her words?

Coming to a halt, I cocked my head and sighed, knowing it was time to try something drastic with the threat hanging over my head. "What do you have in mind?"

Lo's throat bobbed as she looked me in the eyes and whispered, "Drive her through your heart."

I choked on my spit, completely caught off guard by her idea and spluttered, "Are...are you fucking serious?"

While I knew driving a sword through my heart wouldn't kill me now that I'd changed, it would still be a pain I never wanted to experience in my life. Healing from that would be an immense process that would probably knock me on my ass the rest of the day.

Tossing her sword to the ground, she came to stop in front of me, holding my shoulders tightly as she reassured me, "If you don't want to do this, I understand. It's insane, but I think we're running out of time to find the connection when you really need it."

I swallowed, the motion feeling like I was forcing cement down my throat as I contemplated her idea. My eyes danced around her face as I shook my head.

Was I seriously about to run my sword through my heart?

Her warning to keep my mates from hearing this plan made so much fucking sense now. There's no way they'd ever let me do it.

It was a gamble. Either way, I'd be susceptible as I focused on healing afterward. If anything happened during that time, I'd be shit out of luck without someone to protect me. But what's the point in having three big, strong mates if I couldn't get them to dote on me when I was down and out?

Fuck, I was going to do this.

"Have blood ready for me to drink in surplus at the end of this," I finally relented as I took a few steps back from her to give myself enough room.

"Girl, I'll force feed you the blood myself if you don't have the energy," she answered, placing a hand over her chest as if in sympathy of what a sword through the heart was going to feel like. "I won't let anything bad happen to you while you heal. You have my word."

She reached out with her pinky, and I smiled at the simple gesture, glad to see the tradition transcended species. Reaching out with my own, we linked them together and shook.

With a deep breath, I dropped her pinky and

took Devorare's hilt into both hands, guiding the tip of her flaming blade over my heart to the best of my ability with her size.

If this worked, Devorare and I were going to have a stern talk about how fucking insane she was for choosing this as our bonding method.

CHAPTER 18
ALINA

I stood there for what felt like an eternity, trying to hype myself into actually plunging my sword through my heart, but each time I began to press in, I chickened out. Blood dripped down my chest, soaking my sports bra at the small cut I'd continued to reopen from my attempts.

Panic gripped me, and I turned my attention to Lo. "Fuck, I don't think I can do it. My brain keeps convincing me that I'm a human and that this is going to kill me."

She blinked once before grabbing her sword from the ground and sighing heavily. "Fine, fine. We'll stab ourselves at the same time, so you aren't in it alone, alright?"

My head reeled back, shocked by her suggestion.

"Lo, no," I argued, shaking my head emphatically. "You don't need to stab yourself too."

This whole situation was already crazy enough.

Waving her hand as if she was just going to join me in a dance, or something equally insignificant, she moved her own sword over her heart. "It won't be the first time I've been stabbed in the heart, but it will be the first time it's happened on purpose."

I stared at her with my mouth open as she tipped her head back and let out a cackle, eyes dancing with mirth as she collected herself and cocked an eyebrow at me. "How much do you think Drake is going to regret introducing us when he inevitably ends up down here the second your pain breaks through the bond, and he finds us with swords in our hearts?"

The image actually got a smile out of me.

"Oh, he's going to be cursing us out and regretting letting you take over Lincoln's position as my trainer," I agreed, chuckling for a moment before I pinned her with a look. "Seriously, though, put the sword down, Lo. I appreciate the sentiment, but it's not needed."

A grin I could only describe as insane took over her face as she mused, "What's that saying, friends who stab themselves together stay together?"

I blinked twice. "That is absolutely not a saying."

With a shrug of her shoulders, she retorted, "Well, it is now, bestie."

Clearly, there was no talking her out of it. With an exasperated and dramatic sigh, I caved. "Fine. Let's do this, but Lo?"

She tilted her head to the side, smiling still, "Yes, Al?"

"Al?" I echoed in question, completely side-tracked.

"Well if I'm just Lo, that means you have to be Al to match. It'll be the story of Lo and Al, the dumb bitches who stabbed themselves in the hearts for shits and giggles."

What was initially an overwhelmingly fearful thing was turning into a moment we'd look back on in a hundred years and laugh at. All because of Lo. She was exactly what I needed in a friend at this point in my life, and I could only imagine the shenanigans we'd get into in the years to come.

"Fates," I breathed out, shaking my head toward the ceiling, "I know I don't give you credit, often choosing to curse you instead, but thank you for bringing Lo into my life."

"Aww, bitch," she cooed, wrapping both hands around the hilt of her sword. "Don't make me cry, I have on my good mascara today. On the count of three, we stab, okay? Also, don't forget to pull the sword back out so your body can begin to heal immediately."

I gave her a nod as fear spiked through me.

"Three."

I wanted to tell her this was crazy and that we weren't going to do this, but she was counting down already.

"Two."

There was no damn way I was going to let her stab herself for nothing. I was following through with this. I kept my eyes on hers instead of down at my chest that was about to be a bloody mess.

"One."

I didn't allow myself to pussy out despite the way my hands shook with fear.

Steel met flesh and both of us grunted in pain, and I watched, fascinated as crimson spilled out of her chest around the wound. I dared not look down, knowing I'd look exactly the same, and I feared that I'd stop if I looked. A burning wildfire engulfed my entire body as the blade drove deeper into my chest, until slowly, I felt the tip piercing through my heart.

Apparently Lo was right about the pain ripping

through the measly walls I'd put up to block my mates from hearing or feeling me.

Their voices flooded in like a tsunami, one after another.

Comoară! Stop whatever you're doing right now.

Princess, talk to me. What is happening?

I'll be right there, baby girl. Hang in there.

I had to finish this before they got here and intervened.

With one final shove, I felt Devorare slide entirely through my heart. I choked, trying to take a breath but finding that I couldn't. Blood spilled from my mouth, and Lo's voice echoed around me, as if there were multiples of her surrounding me.

"Alina! Pull her out!"

I attempted to do what she said, but it felt as if my body was completely frozen. Finally braving it, I looked down in an attempt to see why I couldn't pull her out of my chest. Panic seized me as the sword disintegrated in my hands.

I gasped, realizing I could breathe all of a sudden. *What the hell was going on?*

The pain subsided completely, replaced by a feeling of emptiness as I saw the hole left in my chest, gaping and the size of a fist.

How...how was that even possible?

I fell to my knees, legs quivering like jelly. My head tilted downward to stare at my heart beating and pumping blood all over the ground beneath me. A scream tore from my throat at the sight, and I whipped my head up to get help from Lo. The scream quickly died in my throat as I saw that I was in a black void of some sort. With another version of me staring back at me.

The training room was gone.

Lo was gone.

And I couldn't feel or hear my mates anymore.

Did I...die?

The reflection of me was lounged on the ground, laying on her back as she blew a bubble with gum, popping it loudly.

"About time you showed up," she mumbled, pushing up to sit cross-legged as her gaze ran the length of me.

Staring back at a perfect replica of myself was eerie as hell. The only difference between us were our eyes. While I knew mine were blue under normal circumstances, and red while under the influence of a bloodhaze or bloodlust, hers were completely black like Drake's were at times.

"Where are we?" I demanded, voice trembling as

I glanced around for anything distinguishable, but it was like we were in a black hole.

Nothingness wrapped around us from every angle, making me feel like I was suffocating.

"What, you didn't like the gushing, bloody heart on the ground when you got here? I worked hard on that," she pouted, shoving her bottom lip out. "This is the only time we'll ever be able to meet like this, face-to-face so to speak. I wanted to make it a flashy entrance."

She was fucking crazy.

"What are you talking about?" I demanded, needing answers from whoever this was, but finding myself more confused with each passing second. "Am I dead?"

Holy shit. I was dead and this was the nothingness that awaited me in the afterlife, not being allowed to be at peace with my ancestors for dying as a vampire.

Tears sprang to my eyes as the realization hit me squarely in the chest. The knowledge somehow hurt more than running the blade through my heart. I would be alone for eternity.

I let my head drop, eyes on the black ground as tears began to roll down my cheeks to drop off my jaw and into the void around us. They never landed anywhere, making this place feel even more disorienting.

"Stop that," she hissed, suddenly in my face as she gripped my chin and forced my eyes up to meet hers. They blazed with a strength I wasn't sure I ever possessed. It poured out of her in what felt like waves, slamming into me as she said, "You will never, ever be alone, Alina. We are bound now. Your heart for my soul. We've devoured each other's essence finally."

I blinked away the tears obscuring my vision as her words sank in. "Devorare?" I questioned.

Hope broke through my sorrow.

"Yes," she answered. "I've been waiting for you for a very long time, Alina. I watched my brethren come and go, over and over as I waited for your soul to be available to bond to."

Plunking down onto my ass as she let go of my chin, I tried to wrap my brain around the information she was so casually dropping on me. We'd actually done it. We'd connected, and I wasn't dead.

She moved to sit as well, tilting her head as she gazed at me intently. "I just have to say this, Alina...I don't know how I feel about being used as your safe word during sex. It feels a little too intimate, even for us."

I blanched at her words, my eyes widening to the size of saucers.

"And also, I think you should run me through Andrei for good measure to make sure he learned his lesson with betraying you. You let him off way too easily."

My mouth flopped open. "Wait, you've been able to watch and hear everything around me?" I questioned, reeling over how that was possible when I couldn't sense her until now. "For how long?"

"Ever since the coming-of-age ceremony when I materialized in your hand for the first time. My bond to you was open and complete with your acceptance and vow to me as your soul weapon, but I've been waiting for you to complete your end of the joining ever since. That was complicated, as I came to you before you were turned."

My mind whirled with what felt like thousands of questions, but somehow I landed on one that knocked the breath from me as I voiced it.

"So, you were there with me...that night?"

We both knew what night I meant.

She reached out, grabbing my hand and squeezing it as she nodded. "I was with you and saw it all as you did. I felt what you felt. I wished with everything in me to have our bond complete then so that you could know then that you weren't alone, but it wasn't possible yet."

My throat tightened with emotion as I murmured, "I wish I would have been able to hear you then too."

For some reason, it brought me an odd sense of comfort that she had experienced that night from the same viewpoint I had. I didn't have to explain any part of it to her. She knew my pain and anguish...the horrible images that plagued my mind from that night...the memory of Skye's fearful eyes on an endless loop.

There was so much I wanted to say, but it was as if someone punched the box we were being held in as the world around us rattled and cracked like a black mirror, crevices and refractions of light shining through. Some shards held images of the training room and others the concerned looks of my mates and Lo.

"Our joining is complete, Alina," she rushed to say, grabbing both of my hands once more and pulling me to my feet. "I'm not an affectionate soul, but seeing as this will be the only time we can do this..." She trailed off, looking slightly uncomfortable before flinging her arms around my neck and squeezing.

The second I wrapped my arms around her... Well, the only way to describe it would be like the sigh of relief you let out when you came home after an eternity away.

I tried to open my eyes to look at her one more time, but the nothingness consumed me, the darkness of unconsciousness threatening to drag me under.

Her voice whispered to me.

Just because you won't be able to see me now doesn't mean I'm not there with you every moment. Just think of me as your built-in pain in the ass.

The last thought I had before being swept away was my gratitude for finding her finally. She was everything I could have ever asked for. Despite not knowing her for long, the way our souls became one and everything clicked into place made it feel like an eternity.

Finally, I felt complete.

CHAPTER 19
ALINA

M y breath caught in my throat as I jerked awake, the fluorescent lights of the training room searing through my eyelids like a hot knife. I squinted against the oppressive brightness, gritting my teeth together as I groaned in discomfort.

Was all of that a dream?

If you wanted it to be a dream, I have bad news, Devorare murmured in a sassy tone that made me picture her with her hand on her hip. **But if you don't want it to be a dream, here I am. You're welcome.**

Thank fuck I didn't go through all of that for nothing.

I tried to push myself up from the cushiony mat,

but I felt like an invisible force was pressing me down, making even the slightest movement impossible. I let my head collapse back against the mat, feeling the immense weight of gravity bearing down on me. Sweat beaded on my forehead as I fought to maintain any semblance of control over my body.

Yeah, you're down for the count, girlfriend. Chill out for a bit and let your mates pamper you.

Why the hell did you choose this as our bonding method? Are you a masochist, Dev?

The voices around me seemed to come from a great distance, distorted and muffled like I was submerged in a deep pool. I tried to take slow, even breaths to calm my racing heart and steady my attention on my surroundings, but anxiousness crawled beneath my skin, making it difficult to focus.

I hated feeling weak and defenseless.

It's not my fault other soul weapons just go around willy-nilly letting anyone wield them if they so much as sneeze the correct way. I wanted my wielder to prove their dedication to me. What better way to do that than to stab yourself?

You're fucking crazy.

And you were destined for me, so what does that say about you?

I attempted to open my eyes as I felt a hard object pushing against my lips, causing them to part slightly and inviting a trickle of hot, salty blood to enter and fill my mouth. A low, guttural sound escaped me as the sharp points of my fangs slowly descended from their hidden place inside my gums.

The first bag of blood was replaced by a second, then a third, and then more. I felt my eyes roll back into my head as the dark liquid filled my veins. An overwhelming rush of pleasure coursed through my body, like an orgasm, but somehow more intense and consuming. Every inch of my body seemed to tingle with anticipation as the nourishment filled me.

I could feel the damage to my heart, bone, and muscle being repaired piece by piece.

Then suddenly it came to a halt. Glaring at whoever was helping me, I let out a grumble of discontent.

"Shhh, it's okay, baby girl," Andrei soothed as he gathered me in his arms, letting me slump against him, incapable of doing anything else. "We'll get you more blood, but we're going to get you cleaned up. Lincoln and Drake are edging closer and closer to killing someone just to get their fury out the longer they see you covered in your own blood like this."

Guilt slammed into me at the thought of what I'd put them through, but it was something I had to do. I wouldn't change what I'd done or take it back, ever. Though, it didn't escape me that not only was Andrei able to see through his fear or anger at what happened to me and take care of me, but he was also making decisions to help lessen the blow to Lincoln and Drake.

These were the moments that proved I was right in forgiving him and holding onto the truth of what I knew about him from almost the very beginning. He was a good soul.

It's hard to stay mad at him, but he's still not my favorite.

A huff came from me as I burrowed into Andrei's warmth. You'd think since she was bound to me that she wouldn't be able to have a favorite.

Oh, yeah? Who is your favorite?

The way Drake does that thing with his tong—

Dev! Have you been watching like a total creep?

I mean, yes? But in my defense, it's not like I can just close my eyes.

We're going to need to learn boundaries, Dev. And if

you're such a little peeping tom and like Drake the most, why aren't you okay with me using you as my safe word with him, huh?

Before she could answer, my attention moved to Andrei as he asked, "Hey, baby girl?" I hummed in answer, prompting him to continue, "Did it work? Are you connected to Devorare now?"

Tell him I'm here and stuck to you like herpes. There is no cure.

If I'd had control over my body right now, I'd be bent over on the floor, tears streaming down my face with laughter. How did I end up with the sassiest and nastiest soul weapon? *How do you even know what herpes is?*

In our shared, conscious state I know what you know.

My throat felt like it was slick with sludge, but I managed to nod and croak out, "Yes, she says hello."

No I fucking didn't. Tell him what I actually said.

No.

"Wow," he breathed out as we made our way into my room. The light was dim, allowing me to fully open my eyes. "So she's like her own entity inside you?"

He makes it sound so dirty. What a weirdo.

I really don't think you have room to talk, perv.

"Yes," I murmured. "She's definitely her own person."

Understatement of the century.

"That's pretty neat, baby girl," he answered as he gently deposited me onto the bed. "I'm going to fill up the bathtub really quickly. I'll be right back."

As I watched him go, I took the moment alone to ask Dev one of the questions that had been burning in my mind.

Dev, you mentioned watching your brethren come and go as you waited for me.

Yeah, talk about boring.

How did you not have any other matches before me?

Fate is a funny thing, Alina. We are each created when destiny is set, and the person who needs us is set to become a part of the world. I was created specifically for you. Who knows what Fate has in store for me after our story. Perhaps I will have another user after you.

It warmed my heart, hearing that she was specifically created for me. It made sense, with how well we were meshing already. But she'd made it seem like she'd been waiting around forever for me. There's no way that destiny was set that long ago.

Wait, but how long ago were you created?

Mmm, time is irrelevant for us as we wait, but if I had to guess and put a number to it, I'd say three hundred years ago.

I choked on the spit I was trying hard to swallow, sending me into a coughing fit that had Andrei back at my side in an instant. He helped pull me into a sitting position and patted me on the back to try to help clear it. "Easy there, baby girl."

How was I destined to be born and have you as my weapon three hundred years ago? That's insanity. There had to have been so many little choices my ancestors had to make for me to even be here. You'd basically be declaring that none of us actually have a choice in the paths we take.

Not at all. Fate just knows what path you are going to choose—always.

I wasn't ready to accept that at all.

My breaths slowed and deepened as I began to relax. Andrei gently tugged my tattered clothing from my body and discarded the pieces carelessly on the floor. His arms enveloped me as he carried me to the steam-filled tub and slowly lowered me into its depths. The hot water soothed my skin, and I moaned in pleasure as the bubbles caressed me.

"Can you straighten your legs to touch the end of the tub, baby girl?" he murmured, helping position my back to lean at the perfect angle to allow my head to rest on the cushion on the rim. My arms shook, the muscles burning as I tried to put them on the edge as well. He quickly moved to help me, settling my arms and hands down softly as I did as he asked with my legs. My feet touched the edge, anchoring me in place.

"Done," I answered, giving him as much of a smile as I could manage right now. "I won't fall under."

He grabbed a loofah before dragging a stool over to sit next to me. Dipping it into the water, he began to wash each part of me, starting with my feet and calves despite there being no blood there. "Even if you did, I'd follow you under," he murmured softly, not meeting my eyes as he kept his attention intently on his current task.

Be still my heart.

You don't have a heart.

Semantics—I have yours.

Each stroke of the loofah against my skin sent tingles through me, the tender and light touches matching exactly who Andrei was. Life had forced him to create a tough exterior, but there was no doubt in my mind that he was the most gentle and kind mate I had.

He smiled to himself as he washed me, as if the mundane task brought him genuine happiness.

It does, baby girl. I'm so thankful to be here with you after what I did. I'm honored that you're allowing me to take care of you while you're hurt. I don't take your forgiveness for granted.

My heart was bursting with affection for him, and once more, words fell from my mouth without thought. "I love you."

Fear snaked up my throat after I'd uttered the words, the reminder of how he'd reacted last time still so prevalent in my mind.

He froze, and time seemed to stand still for a moment until he slowly turned his head in my direction. His Adam's apple bobbed as his bright green eyes glistened with unshed tears.

His voice cracked as he admitted, "I didn't think I'd ever hear those words again from you, baby girl."

And then he was at my side, leaning over the tub and gripping my face between his hands, consuming me in a kiss that I wished I could return with the same vigor. He pulled back far enough to be able to murmur, "I love you too."

This. This was the response I'd wanted from him the first time. This was the memory I needed to replace the old one with, bringing my soul peace.

I half expected Dev to have a snarky comment about letting him back in so easily, but she remained quiet.

We fell into an easy silence as he finished washing my body before making quick progress rinsing my hair out. Thankfully, only the ends of my hair had blood in them since we couldn't wash my entire head of hair in this position.

Before long, he had me tucked into bed—after ripping the bloodied comforter I'd laid on earlier off and replacing it with a soft, beige blanket. Leaning down to kiss my forehead, he sighed, "As much as I've loved this time with you to myself, the others want to check in on you now."

I was shocked I hadn't felt or heard them through our bonds already, but maybe they needed the space to process their emotions.

I nodded in understanding as the door opened to reveal Lincoln, worry lines etched between his eyebrows and on his forehead. His arms were full of blood bags, and after giving Andrei a nod as he left, he crossed to sit on the edge of the bed, dropping them onto the empty space next to me.

I waited for him to say something—anything—but his lips were pinched in a thin line as he began to feed me the bags. After I'd downed six bags, I'd had enough of the silent treatment.

"Are you mad at me?" I whispered as my eyes searched his face for any tell of how he was feeling past the silence. I was pleased to find it easier to speak now, my strength beginning to return.

His head snapped to me as his nostrils flared. "No, I'm not, Spitfire."

My brow furrowed. "Then why haven't you spoken at all yet?"

"I'm angry with myself," he admitted, dropping his eyes to prepare another bag for me to drink from.

As he lifted it to my lips, his eyes finally settled on mine as he continued, "I lost myself in a bloodhaze when I saw you on the ground with a sword through your heart and a pool of blood surrounding you. Andrei was the first to react, and Drake shortly after, but it was like I lost myself in the fear of potentially losing the woman I love. All I saw was an image of what you would have looked like dead if you were a human still. I didn't understand what had happened —didn't want to hear it when Lo explained it."

Not falling in love with, but the woman he loves.

Happiness exploded in my chest.

Oh, Lincoln. The broody professor who stole my

heart the second he walked into Estrid's office. The man who drove me fucking crazy but also pushed me to be better as I did the same for him. The man who patiently waited for me to tell him about my past, never pushing when I made my boundaries clear. The man who'd held me in the shower while I sobbed over feeling like I'd never be able to complete my blood oath with Dracula as my mate.

The man I loved.

Inching my hand toward him, I brushed my fingers on top of his hand. "I'm sorry I scared you like that, but it was something I had to do."

"I know, Spitfire," he murmured and smiled softly, reaching out to cup my face tenderly. "Never the easy way, huh?"

"Never the easy way," I breathed out, feeling like the first time he'd said those words to me on the stairs in the dorm building was an eon ago.

My how things had changed.

My voice caught as I took the leap of faith and stared into his eyes. "I love you too, Lincoln."

His thumb brushing my cheek halted as he quickly demanded, "Say it again."

My smile grew bigger. "I love you, Lincoln."

"One more time," he murmured as he leaned in close, touching our noses together.

"I—"

He pressed a kiss against my lips.

"Love—"

Another kiss and a groan.

"You."

His tongue tangled with mine at the end, devouring me like he was afraid I'd disappear any moment. He pulled back quickly, though, resting his forehead against mine as he looked into my eyes.

"I love you, Alina Van Helsing, with everything inside of me."

A vampire who used to burn with hatred for slayers, and a slayer who used to burn with hatred for vampires.

When it came to my mates, I was willing to admit Fate got some things right for my life.

After he fed me a few more bags, I felt sleep trying to claim me. I blinked, eyelids heavy as I asked the one question I needed an answer to before I gave in to the sweet reprieve of rest. "How's Lo doing?"

"Drake's taking care of her now, but she's doing much better than you. Human blood has more of the nutrients that we need, so her feedings have sped up her healing process comparatively."

As much as I wanted to be back to normal, I

wasn't going to compromise on my morals and the decision I'd made to not drink human blood ever again. I was relieved to hear Lo was doing well, though.

Knowing the consumption of human blood was a moot point, Lincoln easily moved on. "He wanted to be here with you, but we're taking turns watching over you both until you're back to normal. He'll be next to see you."

"Okay," I murmured, as my head fell to the side, eyes gently closing, "I think I just need to sleep for now."

His voice was soothing as I let myself be dragged under, burrowing into his warmth as he laid down next to me and pulled me against his chest. "I'll be here, Spitfire, always. Sleep now."

Throughout the night, I woke up each time they took turns watching over me. Each time I came to consciousness, I felt closer to my normal health, and knew that by morning I would be back to normal.

Everything had worked out.

CHAPTER 20
ALINA

My eyes slowly opened, and I took in the warm, fragrant aroma of coffee wafting up from the mug on my nightstand. Blurry images of my mates surrounding me and treasuring me in my dreams trickled into consciousness with me. I savored the feeling of being wanted, cherished, and loved no matter if I was awake or asleep.

"Ugh," I groaned groggily as I found Lincoln perched on the edge of the bed with another cup of coffee in one hand and a phone in the other.

"Morning," he murmured, lifting the mug in his hand. "Lo said this is how you take your coffee, but if you want blood instead, I can run and grab you some."

"No," I quickly snapped, pushing to sit up. I was pleasantly surprised to feel completely back in working order. "Gimme," I muttered, grabbing the cup before he could threaten to take it away from me again.

He chuckled and lifted his phone, shaking it lightly. "I hate to do this to you, but if you want to stay enrolled at DIA, you have to give Victoria a phone call to make up for the therapy session you were supposed to have last night."

I glared daggers at him over the rim of the mug as I took a tentative sip of the scalding coffee.

Drake's head poked into the room, blue eyes crinkling at the corner as he smiled, before adding, "Morning, *Comoară*. When you're done with that, we've started conducting one-on-one meetings with each board member today, and if you're feeling up to it, I'd love for you to take part."

Yes. Fuck yes I wanted to be a part of that. It was time to get answers and find Serena and Jeoffrey. I hated that it sounded like I'd already missed out on some of the meetings.

I blew him a kiss before he retreated, leaving me to glare at the phone in Lincoln's outstretched hand. "Can't I get a pass on this week's session after stabbing myself last night? I feel like that's a pretty good exemption excuse."

He shook his head, attempting to look stern but failing as a knowing smirk turned his lips up. "Estrid and Victoria were firm in their decision when I spoke to them last night about it. Andrei and you will continue to collect points for classes as long as you keep up training here and do your sessions. They've reinstated classes as usual in our sector, so it's this or fall behind."

Well, fuck. It looked like I was going to have a chat with my pal Vic. Maybe I could try to get an update on how Alexandra was doing from her, though, seeing as we both saw Vic. It would be the one silver lining of having this conversation.

"Fine," I rumbled before taking a big gulp of coffee and setting it on the nightstand in place of the one he'd just picked up from there.

Snatching the phone and navigating to Vic's name in his contacts, I paused as I scrolled through the short list, smirking at one in particular. Peering up at him as he stood to leave, I quirked an eyebrow before asking, "Pain in my ass? That better be me, or else I'm going to be jealous."

His lips turned up in a devilish smirk. "The one

and only," he answered, turning on his heel to head out the door. "Have fun with Vic!"

Note to self: change Lincoln's name in my phone to something in retribution.

As I pressed the call button, I leaned my head back against the headboard and sighed. She only made me wait three rings before answering, surprise tinging her tone. "Hello, Alina. I'm shocked to have the pleasure of hearing from you."

"Well," I drawled, looking at my nails, "it doesn't really seem like I have a choice in the matter if I want to stay at the academy, and I've come to grow quite fond of it."

"I'm happy to hear that," she answered, seeming genuine. "How have you been since our last session?"

I hummed in contemplation. Where to begin? There was just so damn much going on.

I began to list everything in a nonchalant tone, ticking them off on my fingers as I went, "Well, let's see. I found out I have three mates. I became queen of Sanguis. I made some new friends. I'm in the middle of tracking down a corrupt board member who may or may not have a hand in the slaughter of my family, oh, and I stabbed myself through the heart yesterday in hopes that I could connect to my soul weapon because I'm that desperate, but thankfully it worked out."

I had to take a deep breath at the end of that word vomit.

"I heard about that last one," she mused.

There was a hint of disapproval in her tone, and I changed direction with our conversation. After all, I was supposed to be showing progress in some manner in order to not look like a basket case and a danger to the students at DIA.

"Oh!" I exclaimed, continuing on, "I got Maya reinstated at the academy, despite my personal feelings for her. So do I get like a smiley face sticker on my report card for that, Vic?"

She scoffed at my question, her tone only mildly bemused. "Do you really think I have smiley face stickers, Alina?"

"Probably not, but I think you should get some because I deserve them," I argued half-heartedly.

"Mmm," she hummed. "I'll think about it if you can drop your humor and talk to me about how you're really doing.

Damn, she went for your throat.

She's one of the only people that continuously calls me the fuck out. I hated her at first for it, but now I tolerate her and understand why they assigned me to her. I admire her take-no-shit attitude.

I could just picture her sitting in her chair, tapping the end of her pen against her clipboard with her mouth pulled into a tight look of disapproval. "You're a peach, Vic, don't let anyone tell you otherwise."

"I'm going to sleep so well tonight having that approval from you," she muttered, throwing it right back at me in the way I expected from her. "Really, Alina, how are you handling all of that? It's a lot, and yes, I am proud of you for standing up for Maya when she's caused you a huge headache, for the record."

Reaching for my coffee, I took another sip, thinking over how much I wanted to admit to her. This is where things got tricky with Vic. I liked her well enough and thought she was great at her job. Honestly, I felt like I *could* really unload onto her and not be judged, but when I spoke things out loud, it uprooted all of the neatly planted problems sitting in my mental cemetery of shit I hadn't handled yet.

Deciding to start small, I sighed and set my coffee back down before staring out the window across from me. I was offered a stunning view of the mountain wrapped around us and overlooking Sanguis.

"It's been hard," I admitted, already feeling the emotion I'd kept at bay coming up to rest in my throat. I swallowed thickly before clearing my throat and continuing, "I've learned a lot about myself and my mates, though, and it's made everything a little more bearable."

She was quiet for a moment, but I could hear the strokes of her pen against paper through the phone, before she asked, "What have you learned about yourself that has made it easier?"

My chest heaved with a big breath before I ripped the bandage off. "That I'm not defined by my mistakes. That I can learn from them and be better. That I can have grace for not only others, but for myself as well, because no one is perfect."

Sure, that was the type of thing I knew Vic wanted to hear, but I wasn't feeding her bullshit lines. I meant it. The chaos of forming these connections to my mates was the best lesson in learning grace all around.

"That's immense progress," she praised. "I'll go get you a smiley face sticker for that if you promise to call me any time if it feels like too much. I know you have your mates and your friends, but I want you to feel like I'm a safe space for you in case you ever need it, Alina."

Which reminded me...

"I know that, Vic," I agreed. "But hey, can you tell me if Alexandra is doing okay in the demon sector? The last time I saw her was the night the student was found dead, and I'm worried about her."

A heavy sigh came from her, before she admitted, "I was actually hoping that you would have information for us on where she went. She's not at the Academy, and we haven't had any success in locating her, even with the help of tracker witches."

My heart dropped, and my gut churned with all the possibilities of what could be going on with her.

Was she hiding from someone or something?

Was she okay?

Had the attacker gotten to her?

I needed to get back to the academy as soon as possible when the issues with Jeoffrey and the board were all wrapped up here. I wasn't going to leave this in their hands and hope for the best. As the Queen of Sanguis, I had resources, and I wasn't going to rest until I knew Alexandra was safe.

I blinked repeatedly, trying to force myself to focus as Vic spoke, "I'll keep you updated if we hear anything, okay? I know she was your first friend here, but please don't do anything rash in the meantime. You already have too much on your plate."

I agreed easily, knowing Vic would call me on my shit no matter what I said. "Sure. Sounds good, thanks."

"Alina," she hedged, a warning in her tone.

"Can't wait to have a session again next week, bye!" I chirped, hanging up before she could continue.

Dropping the phone onto the bed, I pinched the bridge of my nose, letting my eyes fall closed as I shook my head. "Fates, look after Alexandra wherever she is, please."

Her destiny is already determined, remember?

Yeah, well, fuck Fate if she gets hurt or killed. I'm going to continue to fight against it. I won't lose anyone else just because Fate said so.

Throwing the blanket and sheets off me, I made quick work of getting ready for the day while finishing my coffee. Throwing my hair into a high ponytail, I nodded at my reflection in the mirror. I'd chosen a pair of ripped, black skinny jeans and an oversized white t-shirt, topped off with black slip-on Vans. A swipe of red lipstick really elevated the look in a chic, casual way.

"Let's do this."

The faster I tied up the loose-ends here in Sanguis, the quicker I could handle finding Alexandra as well as beginning to try to repair my connection to the slayers. I knew it would take time to try to win them over, but I hoped that with Jade's family in charge, they would at least listen to what I had to propose.

Speeding to where I heard Lincoln and Andrei talking in the kitchen, I handed Lincoln his phone back with an apology, "Sorry. Vic might call you later to discuss the end of our conversation, but don't worry, okay?"

His eyes narrowed, but I rushed to press a kiss to his forehead before doing the same to Andrei, giggling at the red lip marks left behind on each and their half-hearted protests.

Breezing out of the room, I headed to the meeting room, not wanting to miss out on anything anymore. Cracking the door open and peering in, I didn't see anyone, but the sounds of grunting pulled me into the room regardless. Closing the door behind me, I neared a section of the far wall where the sounds were loudest.

A faint outline surrounded a massive mural of Dracula, so I pushed on it. A secret room? Cliche, but cool, nonetheless. Immediately, I was rewarded with the sound of it clicking. Success. Pulling the door open, I hurried into a tunnel that was dark save the spots lit by the torches lining the walls. I quickly rounded a corner and stopped in shock at the sight of the dungeon that lay before me.

Cells lined either side of the large room as far back as I could see, with the only light coming from the torch Lo was holding. It smelled of mold, piss, and blood the further I went, approaching Lo and Drake. My mate towered over someone that was begging for mercy.

"Please, I know nothing!" a feminine voice cried out. "How could you do this to me? I've been nothing but loyal. Have mercy, I'm begging."

A chill crept through me, though I wasn't sure if it was from the torture I'd stumbled upon or the room itself. The walls felt cold and damp, and the floors were slick with a thin layer of water that ran along the walls and pooled at the entrance.

"What did I miss?" I asked, knowing damn well that Lo and Drake would have heard my approach long before now.

As I came to a stop at Drake's side, it took everything in me to not show a reaction to the sight that met my eyes.

The woman's bloody hands were tied in front of her, and she wore no shoes. Three fingers with perfectly manicured nails lay on the ground directly in front of her feet. Her clothes were ripped and torn in some places, and it looked as if her body had been cut open from the way blood soaked into each spot. There were no open wounds, but that meant nothing considering how quickly we healed from flesh wounds.

She was bent at the waist with her head hung low, long dark hair covering half her face. As it was, I wasn't sure who exactly this was yet. Piss pooled beneath her, and I had no doubt that she was sitting in whatever didn't make it to the ground.

I'd heard of Drake's and Lo's vicious natures, but to see it was something else entirely. I wasn't afraid of them, or even disgusted by their ways, I just hadn't been expecting it this morning. When they'd told me we were conducting meetings today, I hadn't thought that it meant torture sessions.

The sound of a low chuckle drew my attention to the side where Drake and Lo watched with amusement. Lo held an empty glass of what looked like whiskey in her free hand.

"What's so funny?" I asked, waiting for someone to catch me the hell up.

"She wasn't begging like this until you walked in," Lo answered, a smirk on her lips before downing the rest of the liquid. "She thinks she can use you as a weak link to free herself."

I was actually fucking offended that whoever this was thought so little of me.

"Prior to your arrival, *Comoară*, she was telling us, in graphic detail, how Jeoffrey planned to kill each of us," Drake rasped, voice dark and void of emotion, gaze entirely focused on his victim.

And with that, the woman leaned back in her chair and lifted her head up to gaze at me. The manic look to her eyes instantly put me on edge. She watched me with something akin to rabid hunger as she licked her cracked lip.

"Do you want to know the plan for your death, hmm? It's the most delicious of them all."

CHAPTER 21
ALINA

My upper lip curled as I shook my head. "Nah, I'm good. It's probably as basic and dull as Jeoffrey himself."

Her face contorted with rage, and she inhaled sharply through clenched teeth. Her eyes dilated, swallowing the unique purplish hue of her irises that struck me as familiar as she leaned forward with a sneer. "Don't you dare insult him like that! He will bring us into the future instead of keeping us oppressed and in the Dark Ages like Dracula!"

The Dark Ages? Oppressed? Yeah, I'd say the life she seemed quite comfortable living with the wealth and power of a board member was far from that.

Despite my nonchalant attitude toward her, I couldn't help the tightness in my chest at the thought of Jeoffrey's plans. There probably *was* a special place on his hit list for me, considering my bond to his son seemed to be the catalyst that exposed his plans. I wasn't sure how long he'd been on his quest to gather forces to take over the board, but I had to imagine it had been a while. All it took was a week with his son for me to blow it straight to hell.

That probably destroyed him on the inside. How many times had he cursed my name in a scream of rage by now?

The thought gave me a sick thrill and quickly blotted out any fear that began to creep in. Fuck Jeoffrey. He'd used fear to manipulate people for too long. I was only sorry that no one had exposed him earlier.

Dismissing her rant, I turned to look at Lo and Drake. "Is that Silvyn?" I asked, trying my damnedest to remember the names and faces from the party where I'd met everyone. Silvyn was a Rook, if my recollection was correct, but I wasn't willing to bet on it.

Lo nodded in confirmation. "Yes. She was assigned upon hire to protect both Jeoffrey's and Lincoln's fathers. Ever since we lost Allan, she's served Jeoffrey directly. The other Rook, Tania, tipped us off this morning, after our actual meeting, of her suspicions." She lowered the torch to hover dangerously close to Silvyn's head, showcasing the green and yellow bruises that littered her face. "Apparently, Silvyn here has been doing Jeoffrey's dirty work since he went into hiding, pushing those not loyal to him into supporting him with scare tactics."

A cackle rang through the air from Silvyn as she tipped her head back and let it all out. She rocked back and forth on her chair, threatening to tip or break the chair if the groan of the wood was any indication.

"Is she on drugs or something?" I murmured as we stood and watched, her laughter quickly increasing into hysteria.

I knew you had to be fucked in the head to support Jeoffrey, but this was some next level shit. With the way vampires metabolized everything so quickly, whatever she was on had to be some strong stuff.

"It would appear so," Drake muttered before flashing to grab her face and force her to stop rocking around. He was eye to eye with her, and his voice was glacial as he seethed, "After everything I've done for you and your family Silvyn...You fucking disgust me. But I'm willing to forgive you if you give up Jeoffrey's location and the names of the rest of the traitors on the board."

She let out an amused huff, eyes darting between Lo and I before turning her attention back to Drake. "These bitches might believe the shit you serve to them on a silver platter, but I learned not to give any merit to your words after you fucked me a year ago and told me to leave my husband for you."

My stomach dropped. He said he hadn't been with anyone in so long.

She's lying to rile you.

I believed him instantly with the anger and disbelief flowing through him and chided myself for entertaining her words for even a split second.

Drake's grip on her jaw tightened as she tried to continue, cutting off her words as I saw the bone giving way beneath his hand. She cried out, and I heard the crunching continue slowly as he hissed, "You've now lost the privilege of any chance of redemption, Silvyn. Say one more thing to try to rile my mate, and I'll cut your tongue out."

Her eyes once again found mine over his shoulder, and if looks could kill, I'd be dead. Visceral hate shone in her eyes as she attempted to speak around his hand and her pain, "B...B...Bi...tch."

She really was out here tempting fate after Drake's ultimatum. He moved to make good on his promise, a knife suddenly appearing in his hand, gleaming from the light in Lo's torch.

"Stop!" I ordered, knowing in my gut that this wasn't the right move.

I could almost feel an invisible hand shoving me forward, pushing me toward my revenge. I had to do this—to make sure nobody else suffered under Jeoffrey's cruelty and deceit.

Cutting her tongue out would ensure she couldn't speak her secrets, no matter what we did, but I wasn't ready to give up yet. Not when I had deaths to avenge, mates to protect, and a blood oath to fulfill.

He immediately halted at my order, straightening and turning to look at me. I held out my hand for the knife, my movements sharp and sure. His grip on the hilt loosened until he relinquished it to me. I stood tall in front of Silvyn, menace radiating from every movement, and narrowed my eyes as I gazed upon her mangled face.

I leaned in, pressing my face near hers, and spoke in a low and deadly tone that promised retribution. "You see, your first mistake was thinking that I would be the one you could play, due to weak, soft emotions."

Twirling the knife through my hand for a second, I saw her nostrils flare as her eyes glanced at the weapon. I wrapped my fingers around the hilt tightly a second before sending it through her left eye, but not far enough to hit her brain. She screamed as eye matter and blood dripped onto her cheek, but her wails didn't stop me from twisting the knife as I spoke over her piercing screams. "You *wanted* your tongue removed to prevent yourself from talking, but I figured I'd take your eyes instead. You don't need those anymore."

For the first time, I understood what Drake truly meant when he said heavy is the head that wears the crown. Having to question and hurt those that were supposed to be loyal was a horrible situation to be in, and I didn't enjoy hurting someone, but he was right—someone had to do it. I wouldn't allow Drake to take this on alone anymore, not when it was so obvious how much it pained him to be in this situation with his board members.

He tried his best to hide it, but I knew his soul.

I had no allegiance or fondness for her, and this wouldn't even come close to being on the list of shit that kept me up at night.

I felt stone cold at the thought of hurting her more to get what we needed—like nothing could tether me back to reality as I gave into the festering rage I'd tucked away since arriving at DIA.

"Stop screaming or I'll give your right eye the same attention," I snapped, grabbing a fist full of her hair and yanking her head back, leaving the knife in her eye. "Give me names."

She attempted to clamp her mouth shut but didn't get very far with her fucked up jaw.

I yanked the knife out of her eye, ready to cut into her more to see just how far she needed to be pushed until she broke. A hand caught my wrist, stopping me from stabbing her right eye as she screamed in pain from the removal of the knife.

"She's too high to even think rationally," Drake muttered. "We won't get anything out of her right now. Leave her to sober up, and we'll come back and try again."

My jaw clenched as I tried to let go of the aggression that had snaked its way up my spine. Soft fingers trailed down my back, but they did nothing to calm me.

Come back to me, Comoară. This isn't the end. We will get our answers, just not right now.

Feeling the bloodhaze was like I'd tapped back

into the burning thirst for retribution that I'd had the night my family was murdered.

Dev broke her silence then, trying to coax me back down alongside him. **I swear to you, Alina, we will get vengeance. I don't care if it takes us years to hunt down each fucker that had a hand in that night—we will make sure each one of them pays.**

Slowly, my grip on the knife loosened and my shoulders sagged. Standing up straight, I blew out a breath, letting my rage leave with it to the best of my ability. Turning around, I felt the shift in air as Silvyn moved.

She didn't get far, though. Drake's hand shot out to grab her throat, squeezing and twisting until a loud crunch echoed through the room. Letting go, she slumped to the ground, her neck broken and twisted as she stared up at us.

"Piece of shit," Drake spat down at her, disgust filling his tone as he clenched his hands tightly at his sides.

I felt hurt flowing through our bond, like a small trickle he was trying to hold back from me. He didn't want to hurt anyone. The pain of all those he'd hurt in his past followed him daily, like shackles he'd never escape.

It's okay to feel hurt by her betrayal, Drake. You thought you could trust the vampires around you. It would shake anyone's foundation to learn those you gave everything to were actually plotting to stab you in the back. While you say Lo is your only family, I feel in your soul that you considered each board member an extension of that.

"Put her in one of the cells and chain her to the wall," he instructed Lo before turning to face me. My eyes dropped to Silvyn's battered and broken body as Lo dragged her into the nearest cell and did as instructed.

What did I do wrong for them to feel like they had to dispose of me?

The pain in his tone crushed me. I hated that he was putting the actions of a mad man on his own conscience.

I've prided myself upon being a just ruler. One who cares about all of my people. I might appear cold and calculating to them, but it's just because to show weakness would be to invite even more people like this to think they could usurp me.

Tossing the knife to the ground, I pulled him to me, placing my hands flat against his chest and peering up at him. "You are an amazing king. You've done what's needed to protect your people and ensure prosperity in Sanguis. There will always be assholes who want power that was never meant for them. That doesn't mean you did anything wrong— it just means they are pieces of shit."

Lo's voice echoed my sentiments as she walked back to us. "Amen, sister."

It seemed he wasn't ready to accept my words, though, opting to switch the topic of conversation, but I wasn't going to give up on making him see the truth of them eventually. "We've put out the call for a shadow witch to come and pull the location that's Jeoffrey's hidden from her mind if we can't get it from her ourselves, but they won't be here until tomorrow morning."

Anxiety poured through me, hating to leave Serena with him any longer than necessary. Taking a deep breath, I reminded myself that I had to have faith that she would be okay until we could get to her.

"We have three more meetings," Lo announced, glancing down at her watch. "Let's get those done and see if we can pull anything else out of them. After that, you and I *are* actually going to train now that you have Devorare."

While I knew I should be focused on training and honing my skills, there was a nervous energy pouring through me, putting me on edge. I was distracted, and I wasn't sure I'd be able to concentrate at all on lessons today.

"Okay," I murmured as chills broke out over my skin.

With a last glance over my shoulder to make sure Silvyn was definitely contained, I focused my attention back on the path ahead of us. Something didn't feel right, and I had a burning urge to take everyone far, far away from here.

Stop stressing, Alina. You're being paranoid.

CHAPTER 22

ALINA

"I've never had a good feeling about Jeoffrey," Heather murmured, eyes narrowed and lips pinched tightly. "We all play nice to not rock the boat. Plus, he's above me in his station, so I never felt like I could say anything since I'm just a Pawn."

Lo moved to sit on the edge of the table near her, placing a reassuring hand on Heather's shoulder. "Every member on the board is equal in importance, hon. A game of chess can't be won without every single piece on the board doing their job perfectly." She stopped and threw her hand in the air, scoffing. "Hell, if Pawns play the game perfectly, those on the back line don't even need to do anything. So I'd go as far as to say Pawns and Rooks are the most important pieces as the first line of defense."

Heather glanced up, admiration and respect bleeding through her blue eyes. A smile tugged at her lips for the first time since she'd been in the room with us. "Thank you, Lo. Jeoffrey and Silvyn have often put many of us down in private."

"You know the best part about being underestimated?" Lo retorted with a laugh that had her head shaking. "They never see you coming when you shove a blade into their neck. They're idiots for dismissing anyone."

As Lo stood and returned to her seat next to us, Heather's gaze slid to Drake and me, bouncing back and forth as she asked, "Is there anything I can do to help? You have my sword, always."

Drake had remained quiet during the meetings with Rin and Elaine, allowing Lo to take the lead. She was intense, but also delicate as she tried to play to their emotions. I'd followed Drake's lead and stayed silent, opting to watch for body language and facial cues to try to glean their tells.

Although, as we watched earlier, I noticed that there seemed to be something weird that passed between Rin and Lo. Their gazes lingered longer and in a different manner. Almost like...past lovers? Current lovers?

What do you think of Heather, Rin, and Elaine?

I've had a good feeling about Heather ever since the night of my introduction party. My gut says she's to be trusted. I can't say the same about Rin or Elaine. They were both tense and struggled to meet your eyes for longer than a few seconds.

Do you think it's just their nerves of being suspect, or do you think they're guilty?

I think they're guilty. What about your meetings with Joely, Tania, and Kiyomi this morning? Obviously, Tania ratted out Silvyn, but was it to save her own ass and draw suspicion off of her? Andrei said his father needed him on the board to have a majority, so that means if Rin, Elaine, Silvyn, and Jeoffrey are all on one side, there should be one more to give them a majority.

Having Andrei on their side would put them only at six to our six, with not all the board positions filled. That's not a majority.

Wrong. It puts them six to your five. Jeoffrey was concocting this plan before I became Queen, remember?

I shifted in my chair, hips aching from sitting so damn straight for hours despite the plush leather chairs being comfortable enough.

Lo let out a heavy sigh, "Sorry, Heather. They do this thing where they have private, mental conversations and make everyone else around them wait awkwardly."

Drake rolled his eyes, and I couldn't hold back the single, short laugh that bubbled out of me.

Lo's words confirmed that she believed Heather was on our side, though. She wasn't this relaxed around Rin or Elaine.

"Heather," Drake started, leaning forward to rest his hands on the table as he stared her down, almost daring her to squirm. She didn't, though, maintaining unwavering eye contact as he asked, "Who else do you think might be on Jeoffrey's side? It seems like there is a lot being hidden from the three of us since many fear Lo and I, and Alina is just joining us."

I was shocked by his straightforward question to her, but quickly rationalized that it made sense to ask her if she truly was on our side. If she wasn't, she could cast suspicion onto those who were loyal to us, to make us waste time chasing the wrong people.

I was intrigued to see if her suspicions were the same as ours.

Creasing her forehead in concentration, she squinted and bit her lower lip. Drake stood tall, attempting to intimidate her, but she didn't flinch. Her gaze was steel, her face a mask of calm determination.

"I don't like to speak badly of others without them here to defend themselves," she started, making me nod in respect of her words. "But given the sensitivity of this situation and the lives on the line, I will confess that there are a few who have let their guard down around me because like Lo said, they've never viewed me as a threat."

With a deep inhale, she lifted her chin and rolled her shoulders back, voice ringing out confidently as she admitted, "Silvyn, Rin, Elaine, and Joely would be on the list of people of interest if I were in your shoes.

I saw Lo tense as Rin's name was mentioned, and I couldn't help but wonder if I was putting pieces together where they didn't belong.

Did you notice Lo's reaction to Rin during the meeting and when Heather just said his name?

I did, and every name she's saying is in line with who I've begun to distrust. Tania and Kiyomi were similar in their meetings to the way Heather is acting now. Forthcoming, open, and asking what they could do to assist us. Elaine, Joely, and

Rin all simply answered the questions asked of them—nothing more and nothing less.

"Are we done here?" Lo asked, voice tight and lips pulling into a flat line, clearly trying to not show her feelings on the matter. Her eyes were guarded and cold, so unlike her usually expressive warmth that emanated from them.

Shit, this wouldn't be good.

"Yes," Drake answered, pushing up from his chair and buttoning his navy suit jacket as he did. "Thank you for your time, Heather. As always, I appreciate your loyalty and dedication to the board."

I'm going to promote her when all of this is done.

From what little I've seen, she's a good one. I approve of it.

She stood and offered us a small bow before turning to leave. As the door clicked shut behind her, Lo sprang up and moved quickly to exit. I felt dread drop in my stomach like a lead weight, knowing that whatever came next would likely be unpleasant.

"Stop, Lo," Drake commanded, letting every ounce of his power seep into his words. "We need to discuss our findings from these meetings. The three of us."

Her slender shoulders were stiff, her back was pulled into a tight arch, as she paused before turning to face us. When she did, a flush of embarrassment and shame flooded her face, accompanied by a tell-tale puffiness around her eyes. Her lips trembled, and she drew in a shaky breath speaking. "Can I please have a moment to myself?"

Oh, she is definitely fucking Rin.

Thanks, captain obvious. That's all you had to add for your observations of the meetings?

I'm a soul weapon, not a detective. What do you want from me?

It was hard to not let the sass from Dev make me laugh out loud. She was funny as hell and had great little quips, but there was no way I was going to let it show right now. I'd hate for Lo or Drake to think I was chuckling at the situation we found ourselves in, because it was so far from amusing.

I'd never seen such vulnerability in Lo before. She was always a fountain of positive energy and enthusiasm, but now she seemed deflated, her eyes carrying the weight of pain. In the past, she shared enough to help me understand the difficulty of her life, so I knew that whatever was happening right now was likely very hard for her to process. It was heartbreaking to see this woman, who had been an unstoppable force since I'd met her, seem so drained and defeated. But then again, it reminded me that even the strongest people have their limits.

Her petite frame stiffened, but her eyes stayed fixed on Drake's chest. Her jaw clenched so tightly the muscle spasmed. She spoke in a shaky whisper, her voice quavering with emotion, "Rin can't be on Jeoffrey's side."

"And why is that?" Drake rumbled out in a deep, suspicious tone.

Don't make her admit it unless she's ready to, Drake. This is personal.

We don't have the luxury of time right now. If there is something we need to know about Rin, now's the time.

Slamming my hands into the table, I raised my voice to Drake. "She cares about him, you idiot! Stop pressuring her into talking about it. She knows the severity of this situation, and that's probably why she's crying. Leave her alone."

I didn't like having to speak to Drake like that, but he wasn't listening to me. He didn't see the pain his sister was in in the light he needed to. All that mattered to him was how this situation impacted us. But there were other people and other emotions involved in this, clearly, and he couldn't just brush that off.

We couldn't just say fuck everyone else around us as long as we were good.

A tear slipped down Lo's face as Drake vibrated beside me with anger.

"Please, give us a moment alone, Drake," I pleaded as he turned to look at me, hoping he would see that he was only making this harder on her.

The seconds stretched into minutes as Drake held my gaze, neither of us giving in. Then, in an instant, he flashed out of the room, the heavy wooden doors slamming shut with a thud behind him. Lo sank to the floor, and her chest heaved as she began to sob. I rushed to her side, pulling her close and reclining against the wall as she wept, my free hand caressing her back.

"You don't have to explain anything to me," I reassured her, leaning my cheek against the top of her head as her tears soaked through my shirt. "But I'm here if you just need someone to listen without judgment. Remember, we're Al and Lo. We handle shit together."

Her cries grew louder, and her breaths came in thick and fast. Tears burned the rims of my eyes as I felt the raw emotion radiating off of her.

"I love him, Alina," she muttered, her voice trembling and barely audible through the emotion that wracked her body. Tears streamed down her face as she pulled back to look at me. "But I never told Drake because he's never approved of anyone I've been with before. He always finds some fault with them and tries to drive them away until I eventually give up on them."

Having family members who loved you deeply was a different kind of burden that no one really spoke of. Those who loved you the most always thought they knew exactly what was best for you. Sometimes their expectations for you were unattainable and suffocating, though, and you have to make the choice to break away from them.

It felt like a full circle moment for me, having a similar experience with my own family. The expectations of me to be the perfect heir, the best slayer in my class, and to have a forced marriage. I wanted to say that I would have broken free of it, but if they were still here with me, I don't think I ever would have. Even now, I still wanted to make them proud. It's why I was pushing myself so damn hard to fulfill my blood oath.

With a last, shuddering breath, Lo's sobs subsided to quiet tears. My heart ached for her as she continued, "I didn't want that to happen with Rin. I wanted to be selfish for once and do what felt right, without anyone else's opinion muddying my feelings."

Reaching out to brush the tears off her cheeks, I said, "You have to be true to your heart, Lo. No one else has to live your life besides you. You can't live it for other people, no matter how much you love and respect their opinions."

I knew Drake only acted out of love for her, but he was to the point of smothering her now. She was a strong woman now and didn't need him to protect her or fight her battles anymore. Evidently, convincing him of that was going to prove to be difficult.

"I know," she choked out, her lips pinching. She heaved a heavy sigh before she asked, "But what if he played me and is using me? Everyone else seems to see something that I don't. I saw the way you and Drake looked at each other during our meeting with him and when Heather said he was a person of interest. What if this is just another moment for Drake to say, 'I told you so' about my bad taste in partners?"

A crease of worry spread across her forehead as she searched my gaze for answers to the doubt that I heard creeping in her voice. My gut was telling me that her emotional reaction to this situation meant this was the first time she was even thinking through her own suspicions—suspicions that the man she had grown to love had been playing with her emotions all along.

I swallowed hard, unsure of how to answer her question delicately. My lips parted as I took a deep breath before finally responding, "I think that love can be blinding. It's overwhelming and beautiful. We want to see the good in those we love, always, because to think of them any other way is heartbreaking. In your heart and soul, do you think Rin could be on Jeoffrey's side?"

Her lower lip wobbled as she nodded, tears renewed as she whispered, "Yes."

I didn't expect that level of transparency, but damn was I proud of her. How did we move on from here in regard to him, though? Her love for him wouldn't just disappear overnight, and I didn't want to put her through more pain.

"What do you want to do about this?" I asked, voicing my inner conflict. "I'll support you in whatever you decide, babe."

She'd stood by my side, loyal and steadfast since the first time we'd met in the kitchen. I'd repay that in whatever way I could right now. If it meant going toe to toe with Drake over what we were going to do, I'd do it. She needed my support and love more than ever.

Lowering her head to my shoulder, we sat in silence for a long moment before she quietly admitted, "I don't know, Al."

"We'll figure it out, I promise."

CHAPTER 23
ALINA

I felt my eyelids growing heavy with fatigue as I stumbled to my bed, legs trembling like jelly. The day had been a whirlwind, both mentally and physically draining. From the business meetings to the emotional rollercoaster with Lo and Rin, to training with Lincoln in the evening after Lo needed some time to process it all…I felt like I was close to breaking point. As I slid beneath the satin sheets of my bed, I felt the softness envelop me in a comforting hug, finally allowing me to relax.

"Fucking hell," I muttered into my pillow as I stretched out on my stomach, allowing Andrei to climb onto the bed and throw his leg over me before sitting back on my ass to get the vantage point he needed. "Today sucked."

"You know it won't always be like this," Andrei reassured me as I felt his large hands come down to massage my shoulders through the long t-shirt I'd donned for bed. "Emotions are running high, but we're getting closer to the answers we need."

I felt his near-constant anxiety and fear for his mom bleeding through the bond but appreciated that he was doing his best to try to stay outwardly positive for us all in this shit situation.

A moment later, Lincoln settled on the mattress at my right side, his weight causing a slight dip in the bed. "And Drake will come around. I know he's been sulking somewhere all day, but he's not a complete idiot, unlike I previously thought."

Normally his attempt at a joke would have brought a laugh out of me, no matter how obvious it was that he was just saying it to make me smile. I knew he didn't ever think Drake was an idiot. A calculating, cold bastard? Yes. But an idiot? No.

My eyes fell shut at the mention of my third mate. I hadn't seen him since he'd left Lo and I in the meeting room. Thankfully, he'd left the bond open between us, so I didn't feel completely shut out. While we didn't talk directly, I could sense his confusion and the pressure he felt to make decisions that were for the good of the group while not hurting any of us in the process. The worst part for him, though, was how awful he felt for not providing Lo the space to feel like she could share personal details with him anymore. I hadn't actively told him what happened during our conversation, but he seemed to be able to pick up on my thoughts and infer for himself what his sister was feeling.

Please come to bed, Drake.

I'll be there soon, Comoară.

Relief flooded me, and I relaxed under Andrei's touch. I wasn't sure how long he would need space to work through it all, but I wanted them with me—I needed a moment to have them all with me and relax. Tomorrow would bring a lot to our plates, of that I was sure. There was still so much to unravel and so many decisions to be made. We still hadn't managed to pull anything from Silvyn, whatever drug she was on had a serious extended effect, and I wasn't sure what Drake wanted to do about the other board members we were suspicious of. Everything was bound to come to a head tomorrow when the witch came to pull Jeoffrey's location from Silvyn's head.

"You did great during training today, Spitfire," Lincoln praised in an effort to change to a light topic of conversation. "We just need to work on you not fighting the instructions Devorare gives you, but overall your speed and agility have already improved drastically with the connection."

Yeah, listen to me. He's growing on me for that spot of favorite mate.

You told me to knee him in the balls, Dev.

And? I don't see the dilemma. You have to use every resource available to win! There might not always be an opening to use a weapon unless you create one.

"In my defense," I muttered loudly, hoping he could understand me despite the pillow covering my mouth, "she told me to knee you in the balls on five separate occasions. Are you sure you want me to listen to her?"

Andrei's deep, guttural laugh filled the space, the sound of it warm and inviting. I couldn't help but smile in response until Lincoln's grumble pierced through the pleasant moment. "Well that's fucking rude. Thanks for not listening to those specific instructions, Spitfire."

See, this is why Drake is my favorite and no one else comes anywhere close.

Your loyalty leaves much to be desired, Dev. Your opinion changes direction like a leaf in the wind.

The only loyalty that won't change is mine to you.

My lips tugged into a smile. Dev's serious moments really caught me off guard whenever they were interspersed between the humorous ones, but I cherished them nonetheless.

Thanks, Dev.

By the time Drake joined us, my eyelids had fallen shut and I was spooned between Lincoln and Andrei. Each of them was asleep, the sounds of their steady, deep breaths soothing my anxious nerves. The bed dipped at our feet before Drake draped his large frame across my lower legs and feet, kissing me through the sheets.

I'm sorry I disappeared for a bit, Comoară.

How'd you know I wasn't asleep?

I can sense the restlessness in your brain. It matches my own right now.

I let out a sigh, opening my eyes to gaze at Andrei's back. I nibbled my lower lip, anxiety pooling in my stomach over what I was about to ask him.

What are you going to do about Rin and the others?

Nothing, for now. My focus is completely on saving Serena and taking Jeoffrey prisoner. We'll figure out what to do with the rest after. Maybe

they'll do me a favor and disappear before I have to treat them like I did Silvyn. Honestly, I think I'd prefer that. I don't want any more blood or deaths on my hands, Comoară.

We'll figure it out, I promise. You don't have to make these decisions alone anymore. Allow me to be the queen of the board, not just in title, but in actions as well. You've carried on alone for so long, but I'm here to share the weight of that crown now, okay?

He peppered more kisses on my legs, working his way up to my knee and back down.

You always know the right thing to say. Do you have a handbook on how to handle Dracula or something?

His words, echoing my own to him not that long ago, brought a smile to my lips. I decided to use his back to them because they were still the truth.

That's why the Fates put us together as mates, Drake. We complement each other's souls and give the other what they need as naturally as we breathe air.

I'm fucking crazy about you, Comoară. Promise me you'll never give up on us?

Never.

They were mine and I was theirs—it was as simple as that.

And just like that, my anxiety melted away, and I

finally drifted off to sleep with that damn smile still on my face.

***

Wake up, now! Take a deep breath and hold it, immediately.

Drake's bellowed order jolted me from my fitful sleep, but I instantly did as he said, filling my lungs as much as I could. I froze as three figures burst through my door and into my bedroom. I couldn't make out their faces in the eerie darkness of their hoods, but I could see their long, black robes sweeping their feet as they advanced. One of them carried a device that emanated a strange, acrid smoke that hung thickly in the air, quickly spreading out and engulfing the room.

Lincoln must not have gotten the memo from Drake quickly enough, collapsing two steps into trying to attack them. My stomach coiled with fear for him, but I found our bond alive and well, so I didn't immediately think he was dead. Fuck, please let him be okay.

Drake, Andrei and I moved at the same time as our intruders, each of us running to take on one. I was overwhelmed by the flurry of movement, and I struggled to track my men and their opponents in the darkness.

Focus on you, Alina. Trust them.

Dev's command was an eerie similarity to that of my instructor growing up, and it hit home, stealing my breath away. However, there was no way I could put myself first anymore. I wasn't capable of forgetting about my friends and family around me in the midst of battle like a robotic soldier. I don't know if I ever was truly capable of that, but was that a bad thing really? I'd give up my life to save those I loved a hundred times over.

Drake! I shouted through our bond, seeing a fourth figure come through the doorway, raising a gun in his direction.

At this point, I didn't know what the hell our enemies had up their sleeves, but anxiety churned in my gut with the thought that whatever was in the gun might be a hell of a lot more damaging than a regular bullet.

Suddenly, there was a shout, and I felt a hard blow to my head, but I fought through the daze of it, running on autopilot. Slamming my shoulder into my attacker's stomach, I took advantage of them doubling over and slammed my knee up into their crotch, hoping they had a set of balls to crush.

A grunt came from the person, and I called Devorare to me as they slumped, feeling the trickle of blood on my forehead from the blow they'd delivered. She appeared in my hand, glowing brightly in the dark room and illuminating the scene enough for me to see clearly.

Don't hesitate—these people aren't here to befriend you.

Swiping her through the neck of the attacker who was slumped in front of me, I whipped my head around to search out the fourth intruder with the gun.

Get down! I yelled once more through the bond as I saw Drake running toward the figure who now pointed toward Lincoln's unconscious body. Was he going to get in front of that fucking bullet for Lincoln?

Time slowed around me.

No. I would not let any of them be injured.

Devorare's thoughts became mine at that moment, and I gave in, pointing the burning sword toward the man at what felt like triple the speed he was moving as Drake tucked and rolled to the ground. I didn't know what I was doing, but I knew to trust my connection to Dev. With a roar, I pushed the energy glowing around the blade toward him. Red flames shot out, faster than lightning, and engulfed him in an inferno, the smell of charred skin and hair filling the room. Within seconds, his screams tapered as he fell to the floor.

Move to the next. He's going to die.

Flicking my attention to Andrei, I found him pinned to the ground, and the figure restraining him was pulling a gun from beneath their robe. I couldn't shoot flames at them, knowing Andrei was in the direct path. *Fuck.* Charging toward them, my hand shot forward to grab the person's wrist, sending the aim of the barrel toward the ceiling as I sliced through his neck with Dev.

Andrei bucked the last intruder off of him, before moving to pin him. The sound of the intruder's neck filled the room in the second before the sound of tearing tendons and crunching bone met my ears. Andrei screamed as he ripped the intruder's head clean from their body.

I glanced around as Drake flipped the light to the room on. Thankfully the smoke had dissipated, because my lungs were burning despite our enhanced ability to not need as much oxygen.

Is the air safe?

Yes, it should be clear now, Comoară.

A deep, gasping breath fell from my lips before I inhaled big breaths of fresh air.

Doing a quick scan of Andrei and Drake, I

breathed in a sigh of relief to see them injury free, save a few cuts on their faces that were already healing. Letting Dev disappear, I ran to Lincoln and fell to my knees, pulling his face into my lap.

"Lincoln," I murmured softly, tapping his cheek gently to try to pull him back from unconsciousness.

Andrei came to my side, dropping to his knees and resting a hand on my shoulder. His silent presence provided me a grounding strength, allowing me to not immediately spiral into the worst-case scenario. I needed to feel like he was never going to leave again when things got hard, and this was a step towards repairing that broken faith.

"Lincoln!" I yelled this time, as he laid prone and unchanging. "Wake up, you bastard!"

Drake's voice cut through the panic that began to grip me. "He'll be okay. I recognized the scent instantly. It's a harmless gas only meant to knock people out, and it should wear off soon. I'd like to go check on Lo, *Comoară,* but I'll be right back. Andrei, do not leave her side."

My gaze snapped to Drake, panic jolting through me in an electric current, just as he disappeared out of the door.

Holy shit—Lo. In the frenzy, I completely forgot that Lo was in the castle with us. With her being in a separate wing, it was easy to sometimes think we lived in different homes entirely.

Brushing Lincoln's hair away from his forehead, I leaned into Andrei's side, needing his strength. My body was shaking now that the adrenaline had worn off.

How the hell did your flames kill that vampire? I thought beheading was the only method.

This is why I had to ensure I ended up in the right hands, Alina. My power is beyond that of a normal soul weapon. I needed to be wielded by someone who wouldn't abuse the power and think of themselves as judge, jury, and executioner. It's why you had to become a vampire first, to see the other side.

Her words were heavy, but they made sense. This was a huge responsibility to carry, holding the only other method of killing a vampire that was known.

"Who were they?" I muttered as I chewed my lip.

"Did you not see the faces after the lights came on?"

Confusion pinched my brow, but as I moved to glance around him, he caught my chin in his hand and shook his head. "You don't need to see the aftermath, baby girl. It's Elaine, Joely, Elaine's husband,

and someone I don't recognize because they're charred from your attack."

Oh my fucking hell. Was it Rin?

A wave of nausea rolled through me, and I almost vomited at the thought. Lo would never forgive me. Suddenly, Lincoln's eyes flew open, and he leapt to his feet, shocking me into silence as he poised in a fighting stance with a fist raised and ready to swing. His pupils were dilated, and I could see the pulse in his neck racing as his eyes darted left and right, searching for an invisible foe.

"Linc," I whispered when I finally found my voice again. "It's over."

It took a moment for his adrenaline to wear off as his breathing evened out and his tense shoulders relaxed. He eventually really took in the room before his gaze landed on Andrei and me. "What the fuck happened?"

Andrei took over the explanation as I leaned against the side of the bed, letting my head fall back as he caught him up. A smirk tugged my lips up when he ended with, "Drake was diving in front of a bullet for you until Alina saved both of your asses and fried the fucker."

Lincoln's head reared back in shock. "Are you serious, he did that?"

Drake appeared in the doorway, looking just as manic with disheveled hair, and deep, ragged breaths as Lincoln had when he woke up.

"Lo," he whispered, voice cracking as his lip trembled, eyes pooling with devastation. "She's gone."

The pain bleeding through our bond would have brought me to my knees if I wasn't already on them.

CHAPTER 24
ALINA

The first morning rays broke through the window, painting stripes of orange and yellow across Drake's room. All of us were gathered here since my room was off-limits– since, you know, it was acting as a temporary mortuary.

Drake paced as the rest of us remained still, trying to keep a brave face for each other in the face of so much uncertainty. It wasn't safe to leave the castle, so we paced and agonized in silence, waiting to hear from Lo. Drake sent out the board members we trusted to look for Lo, while we waited for the witch to get here.

Even after a thorough sweep of the castle, none of us were ready to face the darkness of sleep. Our anxieties about what was happening, and if further attacks were in store, were too heavy to be ignored.

A mixture of grief, anger, and relief flooded Drake when he saw who our attackers were. Grief over their deaths, anger at them choosing this path, and relief that he no longer had to worry about what to do with them and their betrayal.

Down in the dungeon, Silvyn was still talking about how Jeoffrey would save her. I was too emotionally exhausted to tell her that his minions had come to attack us, not free her. She was nothing more than a disposable Pawn on his own board. Everyone on his side was. I just wasn't sure how they didn't see it.

This was my worst nightmare all over again: all of the friends I'd managed to make since leaving my home were gone, and I had no idea if they were okay.

Drake's arms wrapped around me, pulling me to his chest as his hand ran through my hair as he murmured, "She's strong, she'll be okay."

I knew he was saying it for me as much as he was himself, to remind us of her strength.

We dialed Lo's number relentlessly, desperately hoping that she'd pick up and tell us where she was and if she was alright. The unanswered calls left us feeling like an eternity had passed in a void of despair, spiraling Drake and I further and further into the depths of darkness with each passing second.

We took turns trying to be the outwardly strong one for each other, but in my soul, I knew it wouldn't be okay until we had her back with us, unharmed.

Andrei and Lincoln came back to the room and tossed bags of blood onto the bed, the latter demanding, "You guys have to eat. We have to be at our best in order to take on anything that comes our way next."

When they'd offered me blood earlier, I'd quickly declined, feeling like my stomach was so unsettled that I wouldn't be able to keep it down. I knew he was right, though, and I pushed off of Drake and begrudgingly sat on the bed, grabbing a bag marked animal blood.

Andrei took a few bags and crossed to Drake, clapping him on the back when he came to a stop next to him. "Come on, man. Drink them for Lo."

With a heavy sigh, Drake took the bags and quickly sucked them down before dropping them onto the floor.

It took me what felt like an hour to get three

bags down, and as I was finishing my last, my phone rang, making me choke on the crimson liquid pouring down my throat. Everyone's attention snapped toward me, their bodies tensing as they waited for me to answer.

My hand trembled as I pulled my phone from my pocket, dread pooling in my stomach as my chest tightened with fear. "It's Lo," I mumbled, staring at the name flashing across the screen.

"Answer it!" Andrei demanded through clenched teeth, forcing me out of my daze.

This was too good to be true. I knew before I even heard the voice that Lo wouldn't be on the other end of the line.

Pressing the button for the speakerphone, I answered, "Hello?"

"Have an eventful night?" Rin's voice practically purred through the phone, making my hackles rise as fury welled within me.

"Where the fuck is she, Rin?" I demanded, voice hitching with anger as I forced myself to take deep breaths.

He laughed before muttering, "She's where she's supposed to be—at my side."

I looked up at Drake as I took in Rin's words. His eyes were black, and his chest heaved with barely restrained anger. His fingers lengthened into gleaming black points, black veins traveling up his hands that matched the ones slowly beginning to show beneath his eyes.

His monster was out to play.

There's no way she's willingly there with him and against us now. Absolutely no fucking way.

I know. I'm going to fucking gut him and string him up from his intestines.

"Well, anyway," Rin drawled, as if this was a relaxed, normal conversation. "That wasn't what I called to talk about."

"So then spit it out, you piece of shit," I seethed as I stared daggers into the phone, wishing I could somehow kill him through the tiny piece of technology.

"Your behavior is unbecoming of someone who is supposed to be Queen of Sanguis, Alina," he chided, voice taunting. There was a note of laughter in his tone as he continued, "Unless you trade yourself to us, Serena will be killed tonight."

Andrei's emotions slammed into me as he let out a hiss of anger, punching the wall he was next to immediately.

My mind raced on what to do.

"We have Silvyn," I countered. "We'll trade you for Serena."

Seeing as they didn't bother with having anyone free her when they broke into the castle, I wasn't holding my breath over my barter being accepted. I was willing to try anything, though.

Another laugh boomed through the phone, so long and obnoxious that I scoffed at the phone as I rolled my eyes. "You think we care that much about Silvyn? You can kill her if you want. She's become weak and dependent on drugs. She is a liability."

Despite my disgust over Silvyn turning on us, a part of me felt bad for her, hearing their thoughts of her so clearly laid out. When I met her at the party, she was stunning. Regal as could be and quiet as a mouse. Nothing like what I'd seen from her earlier. Drugs were a terrible path to go down, and part of me wondered if she had anyone around her to support her and try to get her help.

"If that's the way you all treat your comrades, you were destined to fail," I hissed out, shaking my head to clear it of thoughts of their treatment of someone who helped them.

I already thought they were the scum of Praeditus, but somehow they continued to set the bar even lower than I thought possible.

"Yeah, whatever," he rebutted quickly, completely unfazed by my judgment. "Text Lo's phone with your decision within the next two hours, and I'll give you a meeting location."

Two fucking hours? Fuck, I didn't know when the witch was supposed to be here.

"Four hours," I snapped.

"No. Two hours." A growl ripped from my chest as he tossed out, "Oh, and Alina? If it's even a minute past, Serena's head rolls."

Fucking hell.

The line went dead, and I dropped the phone onto the bed before I could throw it at the wall. Jumping to my feet, I dug my fingers in my hair, pulling tightly at the roots as I paced.

Andrei sank down the wall to his ass, letting his head fall into his hands.

"What the fuck are we going to do?" I asked, desperation breaking my voice. "I don't know where to start."

As if on fucking cue, a heavy pounding sounded through the castle. Drake rushed out of the room with all of us quick on his heels, Andrei scrambling up from his position against the wall to bring up the rear. Glancing at his phone for the cameras he had in place around the perimeter, he nodded once. "It's the witch."

Unbolting the heavy locks, he pulled the door open to reveal our guest.

A figure draped in flowing black fabric stood on the doorstep, face hidden by a large hood and a pool of dark, swirling shadows at their feet.

Their eyes appeared to glow silver beneath the shadows of their hood, and the air surrounding them crackled with energy and an otherworldly presence that made my spine tingle with caution.

"Please, come in," Drake offered, sweeping his hand toward the foyer as their shadows disappeared and they pulled the hood back to reveal their face.

Holy, Goddess.

White hair that shone as if imbued with moonlight was revealed first, followed by stunning, rich brown skin that was highlighted by beautiful silver eyes. Her smile was soft and kind as she nodded her head in greeting at each of us. "It's a pleasure to meet you—I'm Nimia. I'm sorry I couldn't make it any earlier, I was wrapped up with another assignment."

Honestly, I felt momentarily too stunned by her beauty to speak, but I quickly snapped myself out of my trance as she reached a hand toward me. As our hands met, I felt a jolt run through me with the contact. I hadn't met many witches other than in passing at DIA, but I could innately tell that this woman was a force to be reckoned with.

"Hi, I'm Alina," I murmured before dropping her hand to introduce my mates. I indicated to each of them in turn, naming them for her where they stood. "That is Dracula, Andrei, and Lincoln."

They each nodded their greeting to her before Drake took over the conversation, leading us to the meeting room as he spoke. "Thank you for coming, Nimia. This situation has escalated since I last talked to your point of contact. The person we're trying to find has two hostages and has threatened to kill one of them in two hours unless we trade Alina in for them, which we will not be doing."

"Oh my," she murmured as we swept into the room and took seats around one corner of the long table, save for Drake who went toward the hidden dungeon to grab Silvyn. "It seems that evil lurks in every corner of reality, no matter the species."

"Very, very true," I agreed, feeling more ashamed than ever to have once thought the world was as black and white as the defining species between slayers and vampires. I'd thought it enough reason to judge and condemn.

How fucking naive I'd been, raised in a community of people that didn't wish to see outside of the bubble of life we'd been conditioned to accept.

"How long will it take to locate our target in her mind?" I asked as Drake dragged Silvyn out of the dark hall leading to the dungeon.

Nimia's eyes narrowed on Silvyn as she was shoved into a chair across the table from her. "It depends on the level of resistance in the target. There can be few or many layers to pull back to find our answer, but sometimes a person is so damaged inside that it can be near impossible to sift through their thoughts."

Shit, was she already sensing Silvyn's brokenness?

"What's the name of the target you're looking for?" she asked, reaching out to grab Silvyn's hand that Drake pinned atop the wooden table.

"Jeoffrey DeLuca," Andrei answered.

Nimia nodded at him and grabbed Silvyn's hand firmly. In an instant, the room grew as cold as ice and the space around Nimia filled with shadows. Her silver eyes clouded with shadows as the wafts began to slowly slink toward Silvyn.

Silvyn tried to fight off Drake, shoving back

against her chair and attempting to pull her hand back as she let out a scream. "Stop this! Stop!"

Her screams grew louder until the shadows filled her mouth, and then eerie silence filled the room as Silvyn's purple eyes clouded over.

The room vibrated with power as Nimia worked, and I fought the urge to rub my arms as a shiver ran through me. More and more shadows were pumped into the room, clouding the floor and curling up to tease our skin.

Fear spiked through me until Nimia whispered, "They won't hurt you, Alina. They are merely saying hello. I've entered this woman's mind, and as I suspected, it's a bit of a mess. I need at least an hour, I'm sorry."

The shadows were saying hello? What the fuck, were they alive?

Beside me Andrei let out a heavy sigh, and I grabbed his hand, squeezing it, trying to give him the same strength and reassurance he'd provided me. *We'll find them.*

His emerald eyes turned to gaze at me as he took a deep breath and nodded.

We waited with bated breath for Nimia to say anything. As the minutes dragged on, my anxiety built and my faith in us getting to Serena and Lo in time waned.

The shadows were suddenly sucked out of the room as Silvyn sucked in a deep, gasping breath. She slumped forward onto, passing out, as Nimia exclaimed, "Got it!"

We all breathed simultaneous sighs of relief.

My relief was short-lived when I glanced down at my phone, seeing that we had forty-seven minutes left to get to the location before I was expected to give them an answer. I could only hope that the location Nimia pulled was where they actually were.

"They are at Jeoffrey's childhood home," she announced, pushing to her feet. "If you get a map of Sanguis, I can pinpoint it for you. From what I could tell in her mind, it's abandoned and hasn't seen use in many years."

"No need," Andrei answered, pushing to his feet as well. "I know where that is."

After saying our goodbyes to Nimia, and Drake writing a check to her for her services, we locked Silvyn back in her cell until we could find a better solution for the problem she raised. After securing her, we headed to the armory in the castle, wordlessly loading ourselves up with weapons and ammo. I strapped on a bulletproof vest and forced them all to do the same, just in case. I wasn't taking any chances.

"Follow Andrei to the house," Drake instructed, filling his ammunition belt to the brim with loaded clips. "Once we get there, hang back until I give you the signal to advance. We take our time to get a proper understanding of the situation and try to locate Lo and Serena to ensure they aren't hurt in any crossfire that may ensue."

After we all nodded our understanding, he tapped his fingers against his temple. "No speaking out loud. Communicate anything and everything through our bonds."

I rushed to give them each a kiss before we made our way out of the castle. Never did I think I would see us all working so cohesively as a unit. I was so damn proud of how far we'd come in such a short time, and despite the uncertainties and fears I had of how this situation was going to go down.

It's time for you to pay for your sins, Jeoffrey.

CHAPTER 25
ALINA

I pushed my body to move as fast as I could, my feet flying over the ground. The wind grabbed at me like an icy claw as I ran, and chills covered my body despite the blood pumping through me at the exertion. The longer we ran, the harder I could feel my pulse racing. My breathing grew ragged and desperate until we finally stopped in the shadow of a small forest. As Andrei slowed and held up a hand, I drew to a stop near him and caught my breath. Crouching low, I scanned the perimeter of the house, searching for signs of life or movement.

The home was a two story, standard brick structure, with a few of the upper shutters hanging at a slant. The white paint on the shutters had long since faded to a dingy brown color with paint peeling off the edges. Several windows had been shattered, and debris and garbage littered the property. From what I could see the roof had large gaping holes in it, and overall, the house looked like it might collapse at any moment. The property was overgrown with hedges and tall grass, but despite all of this, it was easy to picture how charming it was once upon a time.

So *this* was the home that produced a monster. I wasn't sure what I expected to see when I'd found out we were going to Jeoffrey's childhood home, but it wasn't a house that spoke of warmth.

The front door creaked as the wind pushed it on its hinges and I tensed, waiting for someone to appear.

"Close the fucking door!" Jeoffrey screamed from inside, his voice carrying easily out to us from the many holes in the structure. "Get ready to move out. There's no way that bitch doesn't take the bait and come, but I know she's going to bring muscle with her. She's not brave enough to face us alone."

I found it hilarious, honestly, hearing him act like bringing back up made me weak. It made me smart, but whatever helped him sleep better at night, I guess.

A low growl rumbled from Lincoln on my right.

Don't let his words bother you. They're spoken by a man who hides and lets others do his bidding. He's the one who isn't brave enough to face us alone. I could very well run in there with Devorare and fuck shit up, but why would I when I have a team around me? What Jeoffrey thinks of me does not matter.

At my words, Lincoln's bunched up shoulders fell before shaking his head as if to clear away the anger.

"Let go of me, you fucking bastard!" Lo roared, a split second before glass shattered, echoing out to us.

Lo. She was alive.

My heart leapt into my throat at the sound of her voice, and Drake moved like he was acting on instinct to rush in and save his sister. Andrei's hand snapped out to grab his arm. They shared a look, and I knew Andrei was reminding him of the plan that Drake set himself.

It was damn hard to not let emotions control you in these moments, and I was reminded so much of my inability to let go of my overpowering emotions when I stumbled into my family home and found my mother. I'd been instantly overwhelmed by sorrow and let go of all the training and knowledge I had in that moment, giving the vampires the perfect opportunity to turn me without a real fight from me.

Who knows what might have happened differently if I'd only stuck to protocol.

Fate and destiny, remember?

Incapable of using that concept as a way to ease the pain of my family and friend's deaths, remember?

One day you'll understand.

My eyebrows hitched as I let out a huff of air. I wasn't sure I ever would accept or understand the concept, but now wasn't the time to argue it with her.

"Baby, don't talk to me like that," Rin said, actually sounding offended by her tone. My stomach turned. "I love you."

"You don't know what love is," she spat back, right before the cracking sound of skin on skin rang out.

Fury rolled through me like a vat of acid being poured out.

Jeoffrey's snarling voice met my ears. "If you don't keep your pet in check, I will."

Oh, fuck no. I was going to bitch slap the fuck out of him while calling him my pet when we had him in custody.

Glancing at Drake, I spoke to him as I chewed my lip. *It doesn't seem like anyone else is in there besides Rin and Jeoffrey. Should we get closer to attempt a look inside? I don't see anyone watching the perimeter. Plus, we haven't heard Serena yet, and we need to make sure she's in there.*

He gave a nod. **Go closer and take Lincoln with you. Andrei and I will move around to the back of the house and let you know if we see anyone else.**

I quickly relayed the message to Linc before we split off into our teams. Speeding to the side of the house, we dropped to our asses with our backs to the wall just below a broken window. My heart rate increased, pounding lightly in my ears at the thought of being seen or heard.

"I'm going to grab Serena from upstairs," Jeoffrey announced, voice growing more distant as I heard the pounding of feet on what I assumed were stairs. "Our underlings are already in place at the designated spot. We'll kill Dracula and his little bitch today and live like the kings we are by the time the sun sets, Rin."

He promised to rule alongside him, and Rin actually fucking believed him. Jeoffrey would decapitate him the moment he got what he wanted.

No doubt, I easily agreed with Lincoln's assessment.

"Baby, I—" Rin started, before Lo quickly cut him off.

"I don't care what you have to say to me. I came to you last night to try to help you. To save you from this path you are so hellbent on going down. Now you have me tied up as a hostage and are allowing him to hurt me, Rin. I showed you mercy and compassion, and you spat in my fucking face by doing this. You're dead to me."

A mixture of pride and sorrow flashed through me at Lo's words. So she was never in the castle to begin with during the attack. She'd sought out Rin to try to work things out and probably try to sway him back to our side because of her love for him. She had such a big heart, but she was finding out the truth behind what I'd said to her before. We wanted so badly to see the good in those we love that we often gave them more credit than they deserved.

Rin's voice softened to a hushed whisper, barely carrying out to us. "Baby, this is all part of the plan. Once we get rid of Dracula and Alina, we'll kill Jeoffrey and rule together."

I had to shove down the groan that threatened to burst out of me. Jeoffrey and Rin each planned on double-crossing the other. Truly, they were wonderful partners.

"Did you ever stop to think that maybe that isn't what I want!" She hissed, venom dripping from her tone. "Dracula and Alina are my family. Why would I ever, *ever* betray them?"

Pride rolled through me at her standing her ground. That's my girl.

I'm going to look in while they're preoccupied.

I offered Lincoln a nod, and he quickly flipped to his knees and eased his head closer and closer to the edge of the window.

"I'm all the family you need, Lo!" Rin argued, sounding a bit unhinged. "You'll see that when this is all done. I promise."

It's just them as far as I can see.

Relaying the info to Drake, I waited to hear their report.

We have eyes on Jeoffrey coming back down the stairs with Serena. She's thrown over his shoulder and looks to be unconscious. She doesn't look well. We need to move, now. Go through the front door with Lincoln and distract them. We're going to come through the back door and try to catch them off guard to prevent any weapons from going off.

On it.

Be careful, Comoară.

I could feel his indecision over sending me to be a decoy, but we both knew this was our best course of action with needing to choose immediately. Time was not on our side.

Lincoln and I sidled around toward the front and shared a nod and a deep breath.

If anything goes sideways, get out of here. Don't look back or wait for any of us.

I could lie to you and say okay, but I will never, ever abandon any of you. If we go down, we go down together.

The muscles in his jaw clenched, and his nostrils flared as if he was planning his rebuttal. I knew we didn't have time for an argument, though, so I quickly hopped onto the porch, spinning around to face him with my chin held high. My heart raced as I waltzed through the entrance, praying my confident façade was convincing.

"Hello, friends," I called out, leaning in the doorway as Jeoffrey and Rin whirled around with wide eyes.

A smile tugged my lips up at the corners when I spotted a genuine flicker of fear in their eyes. Were they afraid of this little bitch? The one who needed muscle? Funny how that worked.

Jeoffrey grabbed the limp body of Serena, haphazardly flinging her over his shoulder before carelessly dumping her onto the ancient and stained couch.

"Alina, get out of here, they—" Lo tried to call out before Jeoffrey rushed to her, striking her in the temple, making her drop unconscious before he deposited her onto the couch next to Serena.

My hands clenched at my side, anger coursing through my body in waves at the sight of him laying his hands on either of the women. I wanted to call Devorare and burn him to a crisp right here and now, but I knew we needed to take him alive to get answers to the questions I so desperately needed.

It was damn hard not to let my eyes go over their shoulders as I watched the sliding glass door open.

What was Lo trying to warn us about, Drake?
Fuck.

I don't know, but all we can do is proceed with the plan. Stay on high alert.

They were outnumbered by us—Lo had to know that Andrei and Drake came with us. So what scenario could we possibly be in that would make her want us to get out of here rather than rescuing her?

"I suppose you want to take our offer," Jeoffrey

began, putting on a sense of bravado as he clasped his hands in front of him, a smirk growing on his face. "How kind of you to come all the way to us."

"Eat shit, motherfucker," Lincoln responded, stepping past me. "We're giving you one chance to hand Serena and Lo over without us killing you in retribution. This doesn't need to get bloody."

His voice was strong, steady, and confident. None of what he said was true, of course, but he acted his part perfectly. We would kill them a hundred times over if that's what it took...Once I had my information, though.

"You know," Jeoffrey murmured as he dipped his hands into his pocket, unaware that Andrei and Drake had made it into the house behind him. "You really shouldn't underestimate me. I thought Andrei would have told you that by now, right son?"

My eyes bulged in shock as the weight of our plan's failure sunk in. My heart squeezed in terror as I watched Jeoffrey pull out two syringes and turn for Serena and Lo.

Get him, now.

We all moved at once, Lincoln homing in on Rin as the rest of us descended on Jeoffrey. He was old and fast, managing to inject Serena and Lo before we could reach him. In a blur of movement, he flashed to intercept Andrei when he was done. Jeoffrey grabbed him by the throat as Andrei landed a right hook on him—Jeoffrey grunted but refused to let go.

Drake pulled Lo to him, shaking her lightly to try to wake her up. "What the fuck did you inject them with!" he screamed, spittle flying from his mouth.

Lincoln pinned a thrashing Rin on the floor, pressing the man's arms into the small of his back as he screamed at Andrei's father. "That was not a part of the plan! What the fuck is wrong with you, Jeoffrey? I'm going to fucking kill you!"

Rin's fury was palpable, and his unrelenting fury only made my fear of whatever had been injected into Serena and Lo increase tenfold.

I moved to help Andrei, but Jeoffrey snapped his gaze to me as he let go of him. "Leave with me, and I'll tell you the location of a single vial of the antidote. Kill me, and you won't save either of them."

There was only one vial of the cure? He injected them both, knowing one would die anyway.

My heart clenched at the choice that would put on us. Andrei's mom or Lo. It was an impossible one to make, and Jeoffrey fucking knew it.

Indecision plagued my heart as blood pounded in my ears, loud and fast.

"No, Alina," Andrei murmured, shaking his head as our eyes met.

"Don't you fucking dare, *Comoară*," Drake growled.

You said we were a team, Spitfire. Don't give up on that now.

I glared at him, fury rolling off of me in waves as a sneer took over his face. "The antidote needs to be injected soon or they'll both be dead. So, what'll it be, Ms. Van Helsing?"

CHAPTER 26

ALINA

Take the emotion out of it, Alina.

Breathe.

Focus.

I closed my eyes for a brief moment, knowing everyone was waiting on my move.

One thing at a time. I needed to find the vial first. I'd face the hard decision of what to do with it after that.

I wasn't walking out of here with Jeoffrey, so how else could I get the vial?

A lightbulb went off. *Rin.*

"Are you going to sit there and meditate over what to do?" Jeoffrey taunted just before my eyes snapped open. "You're out of options, bitch. Admit it."

Maybe I would have felt like I was out of options if I was still the same girl I was the night of the attack on my family. But now? I was a woman who knew she wasn't going to roll over and take whatever Fate sent her way, crying over how unfair life was after the fact. I was going to grab my own destiny in my hands and mold it into what I wanted it to be.

I kept my face void of emotion with my lips in a tight line as I nodded at him. "Not quite."

I tuned into my bond with Lincoln. *I'm going to threaten to kill Rin if Jeoffrey doesn't give us the vial, which I know he won't do. He doesn't care about Rin— but that gives us an excuse to remove Rin from the room under the guise. Rin has to know where the vial is. He's been against Jeoffrey this entire time and clearly knew about the poison to begin with. There's no way he didn't track where the poison and antidote went. Assure him that the dose will go to Lo, so he gives up the location. I think he's holding back his knowledge because he doesn't want Jeoffrey to kill him, and he doesn't trust us to not use it on Serena.*

I'll take him to the backyard, so Jeoffrey can't see me talking. I'll squeeze the answer from Rin and let you know when I have the location.

Jeoffrey crossed his hands across his chest, puffing it out with self-importance as he scoffed at me. "Enlighten me."

As quickly as I could, I conveyed the plan to Andrei and Drake before I cocked my hip out and tapped my finger against my lip as if in deep thought. Neither objected, so I continued on.

"I'm going to kill your partner here if you don't tell us. Then who will you have left to do your bidding for you?" I asked, letting my voice drip with condescension as I crossed my arms to mimic him. "It's clear that you don't have the strength or numbers to carry out your coup, so what now Jeoffrey?"

I stepped closer to him, seething as I shot him a look of pity. "Run away with your tail tucked between your legs? We all know you can't finish this on your own. You're *weak*," I bit out. "A pathetic excuse for a man who used fear to control those around them."

His features contorted, fury painting his face as his lip curled up in a snarl and blood rushed to his face. "I don't need Rin to finish what I started," he barked, flinging his hand at him. "Kill him. I don't hide behind *anyone.*"

I held out a hand and snapped for Lincoln to move, swallowing the urge to laugh at how easy it was to manipulate the manipulator. Everything was going according to plan so far. Rin thrashed in Lincoln's grip as he forced him past Jeoffrey toward the back.

A hocking sound came from Rin seconds before he let a glob of spit fly and land of Jeoffrey's cheek. "I hope they give you a long, painful death, you piece of shit."

I couldn't agree with his sentiments more, but I kept my face neutral despite loving the disgust lingering on Jeoffrey's face as he wiped the offending spit away. Swiping his hand on the front of his shirt before crossing his arms again, he made one last attempt—a desperate sort of one that I saw coming from a mile away. He was so fucking predictable, using anyone's life to save his own.

Get out of the way, Andrei.

Jeoffrey whirled on his foot to use his son as leverage, but I was already at his back, biting into my lip on instinct and calling Devorare forth. My hand wrapped around her hilt as Andrei darted to the left at the last possible second, sending Jeoffrey crashing into the wall with the burst of speed and momentum he had going.

My blade dug into the back of his neck before he could react. "Make one move and I won't hesitate to cut your head from your body," I hissed, letting my words come out with a strength that dared him to test me. "I'd love to do the realm a favor and rid it of one less monster."

His cheek flattened against the wall when he craned his face to look at me out of his peripheral line of vision. His bravado echoed around us once more as he laughed and spluttered, "As if you would risk the lives of both of those women."

I have the location. It's here in the house, upstairs in his old bedroom. Third door on the left and tucked into a small hole in the beige teddy bear on the bed.

Drake darted up the stairs when I relayed the message, and the sound of my mate taking the stairs two at a time made Jeoffrey's teeth gnash together as a guttural growl vibrated through him.

"Turn around and face me," I ordered, voice tight through my clenched teeth. "I want to see the look in your eyes when you see that you've failed."

To my surprise, he did turn, holding his hands up in surrender. But instead of the scathing anger I expected to see in his eyes, a look of victory gleamed in the dark depths instead. "You won't kill me, Alina, because I know everyone who was involved in the slaughter of your family."

A cold wave of anger burst through me, threatening the loosening grip I had on my control. I felt the pulsing, primal energy of a bloodhaze threatening to pull me under.

I had to play the best bluffing game of my life.

Forcing a smile to my face, I cocked my head and blinked at him, pushing the tip of Devorare into his throat just enough to draw rivulets of blood from the wound. "It's cute that you think I don't already have answers about that night. I already know the witch that helped you get into our territory. You really underestimated me, Jeoffrey."

My thirst for vengeance filled me, and I gave into the bloodhaze, baring my fangs at him as I hissed, "The only reason I kept you alive was to get the antidote. Now that we have the location from dear old Rin, who you let us walk out the door with without second thought, give me a reason why I should let you live. I want to hear you *beg*."

He blanched, the color draining from his face as his mouth popped open in shock. His eyes bugged, and he worked his jaw for a moment as his breaths puffed through his lips faster and faster. "Please, no," he begged, fear finally beginning to shine in his seedy eyes. "You can't possibly have all the answers. Even if you knew Astaroth helped, that doesn't mean you know everything."

Astaroth, huh? Must be the witch. Thanks for that, Jeoffrey.

Neither Rin nor Jeoffrey knows what the poison is. A witch delivered it to him, and because of the price tag, Jeoffrey only paid for one vial of the antidote. All the witch said was that the poison would cause the most excruciating and slow death a vampire could have.

Lincoln was still pulling valuable information from Rin. Knowing that it was supposed to be a slow death, at least, brought me a small bit of room to breathe for the moment. Of course Jeoffrey tried to make the situation sound like it was life or death, in that very second, to try to force my hand.

I graced Jeoffrey with a menacing smile.

It was funny, the way weak men like him trembled and begged—just like their victims did for them—when their own mortality stared them in the face. These were the same men who thought they'd never be in positions like this, who looked down on their victims as weak for begging for mercy.

It brought me so much fucking satisfaction to stare the devil in the face and smile, unflinching and in control. Beyond doubt, I knew I would have a lot of fun with Jeoffrey when we brought him back to our dungeon at the castle. I'd inflict on him every single injury he'd ever doled out to Andrei, Serena, or Lo. I'd make him scream until I remembered the sound by heart.

He must have seen that I was the devil then, the distinct scent of piss rolling from him as he shouted, "The slayers that came to us with the plan—I'll give you their name!"

My body tensed as my hand tightened around Dev's hilt, betrayal flowing through each crevice of my body like a slick sludge. It felt like all of the air in the room was sucked away, and I was left gasping for breath and reeling.

The slayers? He had to be talking out of his ass to try to save his life now. There was no way any slayer would turn on their own to orchestrate a massacre like that. We were family.

I heard the pounding of Drake's footsteps on the stairs as he reentered the room, pulling me out of my spiral.

I have the antidote.

My eyes narrowed as I increased the pressure on

Jeoffrey's neck with Devorare. "Speak now or forever hold your peace."

His eyes widened and he choked, no doubt my blade beginning to cut into his trachea, before spewing out, "They requested that you specifically be turned and left to make a mess, to show how far the Van Helsing name had fallen! I merely requested my team pin the blame on Dracula for my own plans, and it worked out for everyone involved. We all got what we wanted."

"A name," I hissed, baring my fangs and curling my lip back to display them. My mind was spiraling with all of the names he might say, and the anxiety churning through my gut left me wanting to heave. I needed answers now, before I lost the thread of control I had over myself. "A name for your life, Jeoffrey."

There was nothing this pathetic excuse of a man wanted more than his life, and I wasn't above bartering for it. Though I had no intention of keeping my word.

"How do I know you'll let me go?" He argued, a small glint of his usual bravado peeking through. I bared my teeth at him as he damn-near smirked at me despite his current situation. "I need some kind of guarantee."

What would he believe from me?

"I'll make a blood oath to you," I answered with a shrug. "You know slayers don't break their blood oaths."

It was true, but I had no intention of holding onto those traditions or giving a fuck about the consequences on my soul if what he had to tell me was true. There were also three other vampires in this house who would gladly kill him for me, absolving me of any oath I made.

"Do it," he hissed, eyes darting downward as I lifted my finger to my fangs.

Pricking the pad of my finger, I brought it down to draw the Van Helsing emblem—a V trapped within the H—on the inside of the arm that held my sword to his throat.

"I swear that I will let you go if you give me the names of the slayers who assisted with the plan to slaughter my family."

A sigh of relief fell from him, and I barely restrained myself from laughing at how far he'd fallen to actually believe this. He was a man staring death in the eyes, and he was a fool if he believed, even for a second, that he had a chance of living.

I don't want him kept alive if you get all the

answers you need here, Alina. I don't want him living a moment longer than absolutely necessary.

Andrei's request shocked me, but I agreed, knowing that if anyone deserved the ultimate say in what happened to Jeoffrey, it was him. While I'd dreamed about the way I would extract justice against this pathetic excuse of a man, husband, father, and friend, I still wanted Andrei to have the closure he deserved.

Do you want to do the honors, or would you rather that I do it?

Could...could you do it? I know it probably sounds weak, but I don't think I could manage it. There's still a part of me that hasn't grieved the death of the father I never had, and if I have to look him in the eyes, I'm going to keep searching for that part of him that never existed.

Of course, my love.

His relief was palpable through our bond, and not a single part of me thought him weak for it. I thought he was incredibly brave to admit that to me. In stories, it was always the man who had the strength to save the woman from her demons. I loved that he was willing to flip the switch and allow me to help give him this closure.

Showing my fake, good faith, I retracted the

blade from Jeoffrey's throat, though I enjoyed the spray of blood that sprang from his wound.

His shaking hands came up to staunch the blood flow, and he gurgled around the blood pouring into his throat as he said, "Devaroux."

Jade's family.

No. No, that couldn't be the truth. They were our closest allies. They were the only family to ever invite us over for dinners and treat us like normal people. Other slayers were always so guarded, acting on their best behavior because my family was in charge.

Agony tore through me as I considered his words. The Devarouxs were in charge now. Had they smiled to our faces, acting like we had their undying support, when behind closed doors they wanted us sated and unsuspecting?

Did Jade know? *Fuck.* How did I miss the signs of their hatred for us?

Jeoffrey tried to push against the tip of Devorare, and I glared at him, eyes narrowed to slits as I tried to intimidate him into admitting he was a fucking liar. Fuck, all I wanted was for him to fall apart when he saw that I didn't immediately believe him. I desperately wanted him to tell me he was making this shit up to save his ass.

"You made an oath!" he hissed, making me cock my head as I ruminated over his bombshell.

Time for one last attempt to make him squeal.

"You're lying to me," I deadpanned, trying to keep the thick emotion I was feeling from reflecting in my words. "Why would I make good on a blood oath when you didn't uphold your end of it, Jeoffrey?"

If this was the truth, Jade had acted the part perfectly when I'd stared at her, begging her to end my life because of the agony of guilt that was consuming me for killing Skye. She said I deserved to live with that guilt, but was the truth actually that her family demanded that I live because of the deal they made?

His eyes bulged as he blubbered, devolving into hysterics. "Why would I lie to you? Why would I protect a slayer instead of choosing my own life? That's the fucking truth, you've got to believe me!"

The truth was that he was so much of a fucking narcissist that he wouldn't ever choose anyone over himself. He'd never sacrifice himself to save another.

The fact that the Devarouxs betrayed my family *was* the truth.

In an instant, I thought of the way I'd snubbed Drake for not recognizing the corrupt members of his board at first. Yet here I was, oblivious to the betrayal my family faced by one of my best friend's families. I bit down on my lip, trying to use the pain to ground me as tears threatened to spill over. Love really was blinding.

Forcing down the bile that rose in my throat as the truth sank, I took a deep breath and spoke to Devorare.

Incinerate him.

She didn't respond verbally, instead the flames burst from my sword instantly and consumed him, sending him to his knees as he howled in pain. "You made an oath!" He screamed, clawing desperately at every part of his body, trying and failing to douse the flames consuming him.

"Oaths clearly mean nothing to slayers," I spat, fighting the spiral that was threatening to take me over.

Don't lump in all with the actions of some, Alina. You've learned that with the vampires, and it applies to the slayers as well.

How do I know they weren't all in on it? I seethed. *How do I know they weren't all plotting to take my family from me?*

You don't, but what I can promise you is that we will get to the bottom of it, together. Don't

pass judgment until we have the answers. It will only torture your mind and heart that much more.

Andrei's relief flowed through me, staunching my own burning rage in conjunction with Dev's promise to me. The weight I felt removed from Andrei's soul as Jeoffrey expired beneath the flames before us was enough to make me focus on the present moment. This was a huge victory, and though I didn't feel settled yet, for now, I'd take solace in Jeoffrey's death and the knowledge that he'd never be able to hurt anyone again.

Lincoln came back into the room with Rin, forcing him to his knees with a grunt as he wept. "Please, please save Lo. You promised."

Lo.

Serena.

Tucking away the problem about the slayers into my shit-to-deal-with-later pile, I turned to find both women in the arms of men I loved. They sat on the couch next to one another, cradling Serena and Lo to them.

Drake tenderly stroked Lo's cheek as black tears dripped from his eyes. Her eyes were open, but she didn't seem to be fully cognizant.

Andrei pressed a kiss to his mom's forehead,

murmuring, "It's over mom. He's gone. He won't hurt us ever again."

My eyes burned as I swallowed the emotion threatening to engulf me. The pain and grieving that both of them were going through right now, in anticipation of the decision we had to make...it made me feel like I was being crushed by the weight of it.

We killed Jeoffrey.

We found the antidote.

But what the hell were we supposed to do now?

I couldn't force the emotions away to make a logical choice because there wasn't one in this fucked up moment.

I fell to my knees as I let Devorare go, staring at them and shaking my head as the tears began to fall.

What decision am I supposed to make, if Fate already has it figured out, Dev? Tell me.

That's not for us to know ahead of time, Alina. I'm sorry. I'm so sorry.

Andrei lifted his tear-stained face to look at me. "My mom is so fucking broken inside from what Jeoffrey did to her," he gritted out over a sob. "She is a shell of who she was, and I don't think there's any coming back from that. She'll finally be at peace."

Fuck, why did his offer to choose Lo make me

feel even guiltier? How was I supposed to just accept that and let him lose both of his parents tonight? I knew how holding my mother as she died felt, and that gut-wrenching, heartbreaking feeling wasn't something I wished on my greatest enemy, let alone one of the men I was in love with.

"Are you sure?" Drake croaked, eyes still streaming with black blood as his eyes widened in shock, lifting his gaze to meet Andrei's own tearful one.

Andrei dropped his head to Serena's, the tears flowing endlessly as he rocked back and forth with her held tightly in his grip. A sob wrenched its way free from my own throat.

Spitfire, I know it doesn't feel like this is going to be okay. I know this is shit and it's suffocating, but I need you to breathe and know that we are all in this together. We will bear the weight of the choice together and learn how to move forward together.

How are we supposed to move on from this, Lincoln? This isn't okay. It was never supposed to end like this.

We will find a way, I promise you.

"No," Andrei whimpered, pressing a kiss to his mom's head. "But Lo has a better quality of life ahead of her if she gets the antidote." His hand came up to wipe away tears that had fallen from Serena's eyes as well. "I'm so sorry."

She had to be able to hear us right now. Fuck. My heart hammered in my chest, and bile churned in my stomach.

My vision blurred as Drake lifted the vial to Lo's lips before stilling and looking at Andrei one more time. "Andrei, I—"

Lo burst to life, cutting him off as she grabbed the potion from Drake and moved to stand in front of Andrei and Serena. The bottle was at Serena's lips and falling in before any of us could even comprehend what just happened.

I couldn't react, couldn't speak, couldn't even think as she crossed to the floor where Rin was crying uncontrollably. She wobbled heavily before falling to her knees and whispering, "I forgive you."

Her head swung around to glance between us all, eyes pleading with us to understand. "I couldn't live with the guilt," she croaked out, eyes brimming with tears. "I couldn't leave that choice to the people I love."

"Fuck!" Drake screamed, speeding to grab her and hold her as she began to fall toward the floor. I crawled over to them, throwing myself around them both as the implications of her choice hit me. Sobs wracked my body as I held onto them tightly, as if I could hold us all together for the rest of time. As if I could give Lo my own life's essence to cure her.

Lo sacrificed herself to take the damnable choice away from us all.

Taking advantage of the moment of shock, Rin broke free of Lincoln's grasp, and without looking back, ran out of the house and left us all behind. Left Lo behind, like she was nothing at all to him.

"We still have time," Lincoln whispered, voice thick with his own emotion.

I sat up, shaking my head at him as I muttered, "What do you mean?"

"We don't know how long the potion takes, but he said it's the slowest death," he reminded us, voice cracking as he stared down at us huddled together on the floor. "So let's do something about this."

His words hit me square in the chest, and it was like the force of an army thrummed in my heart and soul as I realized he was right. She wasn't actually dead.

Fate hadn't made her final move yet.

"Looks like we're going to Carmina to hunt down a witch," I breathed out shakily, trying to find the strength needed to follow through with this plan. Everything in me screamed that we wouldn't get there in time, but I had to say the words out loud to try and believe them anyway. I had to for Lo. "Get up. We leave now."

I angrily brushed the tears from my face as I pushed to my feet, trying to staunch the flow and focus on the small kernel of hope Lincoln had given to me instead.

I wouldn't give up on her.

I wouldn't accept this.

I wouldn't lose another person I loved

"I know the name of the witch who brewed it," Lincoln murmured softly, trepidation filling his tone and confusing me. Shouldn't that be great news? "Rin told me earlier before Jeoffrey even said it. He's the same witch that helped kill your family, Alina."

Just as I was trying to focus on the microscopic amount of strength I could muster within me, it felt like it was blown to pieces with that admission before he even said the name.

He ran a hand through his hair, sighing heavily as he said, "Astaroth."

I bit down on my tongue to keep from screaming. I'd have to make a deal with the man who helped slaughter my blood family to save my found family.

I turned away from them all to stare out the

window and forced myself to take a breath, one so deep it filled my lungs to the point that my chest ached with the pressure. I clenched my eyes shut, trying to work through the mess of rage, grief, and despair rolling into me in unrelenting waves.

I held the breath until I heard my heart pounding in my ears, the blood whooshing quick and hard when I slowly let it out through pursed lips.

There was only one choice to make here.

"You know what they say," I whispered, accepting the path before me as I opened my eyes and stared at the dark storm brewing in the sky. It matched perfectly how I felt inside. "Keep your friends close and your enemies closer. I'll do it for Lo."

ORDER THE FINAL BOOK, Bite of Justice, here: mybook. to/bite4

TURN **the page for chapter one of Monsters Within, which is Alexandra's story at DIA!**

. . .

Curious about Alora's parents who run Hell in this world? Read their series here:

Monarchs of Hell (Completed Series)

Co-write with M Sinclair

Insurrection: mybook.to/Monarchs1

Imbalance: mybook.to/Monarchs2

Inheritance: mybook.to/Monarchs3

OTHER BOOKS BY R.L. CAULDER

The Creatures We Crave

Monsters Within: mybook.to/MonstersWithin

Monsters Below: mybook.to/MonstersBelow

Monsters Above: mybook.to/MonstersAboveNEW

Monarchs of Hell (Completed Series)

Co-write with M Sinclair

Insurrection: mybook.to/Monarchs1

Imbalance: mybook.to/Monarchs2

Inheritance: mybook.to/Monarchs3

The Vampyres' Source (Completed Series)

Co-write with M. Sinclair

Ruthless Blood: mybook.to/Ruthless1

Ruthless War: mybook.to/Ruthless2

Ruthless Love: mybook.to/Ruthless3

The Pack Prophecy (Completed Series)

Outcast: mybook.to/Outcast

Outlaw: mybook.to/OutlawPP

Oracle: mybook.to/OraclePP

Darkness Rising (Completed Series)

Desolation: mybook.to/Desolation

Detonation: mybook.to/Detonation

Devastation: mybook.to/DevastationDR

Monster's Naughty List (Standalone novella)

mybook.to/Naughtylist

Inferno (Standalone book)

Co-write with M. Sinclair

mybook.to/InfernoMC

Captured by the Monsters (Standalone book)

Co-write with M.J. Marstens

mybook.to/CapturedMonsters

ABOUT R.L. CAULDER

R.L. Caulder is a USA Today bestselling author who lives in her writing cave away from the intense heat of the Florida sun with her husband and furry writing assistants, MeowMeow and Winrey. Life is never boring for R.L., who has hundreds of imaginary friends constantly vying for her attention and begging for their stories to be told.

If you're looking for ways to interact with R.L., you can find her on Facebook in her group:

The Cauldron: R.L. Caulder Reader Group

ALEXANDRA
THE CREATURES WE CRAVE: BOOK ONE

I knew life wasn't sunshine and rainbows for everyone, but eventually the clouds always broke, revealing the sunlight once more for them. But in my case, the darkness that seemed to follow me never cleared.

I had learned a long time ago, life wasn't fair, and at some point, I just accepted it.

The only bright spot was when I was able to climb into my bed, crack open a spiral notebook, and forget reality even existed while being transported into the world I created when I put my pen to paper.

I poured all of my despair and desire onto those sheets. The ink was my pain, and the pages were my savior.

It's where I found myself now, contemplating

the events of the day and how I would cope with them. I was lounging on my bed in an oversized Aerosmith t-shirt I'd found at the thrift shop and some black sleep shorts.

Shoving the rest of my chocolate chip cookie into my mouth, I grabbed the plastic cup filled with the delicious delicacy known as RumChata. Taking a gulp of the cinnamon alcohol, I swallowed down the lump of cookie that lodged itself in my throat before setting the cup back down on my nightstand.

The alcohol had been given to me as a bribe to not tell on the girl across the hall for smoking a joint. I honestly didn't care what she did—I wouldn't have turned her in anyway, but I wouldn't turn my nose up at alcohol.

Despite not having any friends here, I kept to myself...it was just easier. My life had enough chaos without me creating enemies. I had my own shit to worry about. If the girl wanted to smoke pot to get through her days, who was I to judge? We all had our own ways of coping.

The RumChata left a trail of light heat in its wake as I reached for my black spiral notebook that had seen better days. The edges of the pages curled slightly from being bent a bit when I wrote at odd angles. Flipping to the next blank page near the back of the book, I realized that I would need to grab another one soon and add this full one to the plastic bin beneath my bed. That bin held the only things in the world I cared about, the only things that held any value for me.

As a ward of the state, I hadn't enjoyed many luxuries in life growing up. Even now, being on an academic scholarship for my junior year at a small private college, I wasn't afforded much. *The single dorm room was definitely a plus, though.*

I couldn't dwell on the fact that all the possessions I cared about could fit into one measly bin beneath my bed. One day, things would be different —that day just wasn't today. I was what you could call a "pessimistic optimist."

My scholarship covered my classes, school materials, boarding, and a small stipend for food. I'd be the first to admit I had a pretty shit diet. I wouldn't eat all day, then I'd use my budgeted allowance for the day to order a large pizza and cookies and binge eat as I wrote through the night.

Another terrible habit was my almost non-existent sleep schedule, and I often found myself cursing the first rays of morning light as they streamed in through my small window. They took me away from my fantasy world filled with delicious men I was unhealthily obsessed with, signaling that I'd once again be heading to classes running on fumes.

Often I dreamt of being one of the supernatural creatures of the world instead of an isolated, forgotten human stuck in an endless loop that kept reminding me of my place in life.

But unfortunately, this seemed to be the hand I'd been dealt. I just needed to find a way to make the most of it.

That didn't stop me, though, from checking my teeth to see if they'd elongated to sharp points like a vampire's, trying to conjure fire into existence in my hand like a witch, or wishing I'd grown a pair of demon horns overnight.

Maybe I was just a late bloomer in the supernatural community? At least, that's what I liked to tell myself when I found myself sinking in the bleakness of my life.

Grabbing a pen with a slightly gnawed black cap from my nightstand, I backed into the corner of my bed against the wall, a cozy space where I had my pillows arranged and smashed in a nest of sorts to engulf me. Drawing my knees up, I rested my notebook against them, closed my eyes, and tipped my head back to rest against the wall, thinking of where I would be transported to this time.

It was time to cut myself loose from reality and escape to the world between my pages. A world that inspired awe and forged hope within my soul. Hope that one day the world I lived in would be a better place.

My fantasy world was one in which I righted the wrongs of the world. Where the monsters most people were afraid of helped me hunt down the true bad guys—the humans.

Because I can assure you, my monsters were angels in comparison to the true evil that lurked in my reality. Humans just happened to wear skin suits that were more pleasing to the eye.

Closing my eyes, I allowed my mind to drift to the image of my monsters, sinking into the alternate life I'd created for myself.

At first, when I'd created them, there had been nothing beautiful about my monsters, but they had morphed in my mind over the years. Before I learned how to write, I drew them as faceless shadow creatures draped in the fabric of black cloaks with ripped edges at the bottom. They moved in the darkness, shifting with the shadows, undeniably hidden from the human eye.

Then, as I wrote them in stories instead of drawings, when they weren't traveling in the darkness, the lower halves of their bodies were still mostly swirling shadows, but there was a section in the middle of their chests that thrummed with a steady glow, like a human had their heart.

Each of my three monsters had a different color that emanated from the piece of them I liked to think of as their soul, spreading into their necks and up into their faces like veins beneath the surface.

Lucien was red.

Elwin was green.

Kylo was blue.

Then, to top it all off, they had four arms, two on each side, with razor sharp claws at the tips of their fingers. Some might find them disconcerting, being so devoid of humanoid features, but it's what I loved about them. What you saw was what you got, unlike humans.

I had met too many dark, ugly, twisted humans for me to trust them.

They'd smile to your face to placate you, whispering the words you wanted to hear, all while taking what they wanted before leaving behind a husk of a person.

The ones who stole.

The ones who raped.

The ones who thought they deserved everything simply because they breathed.

In my fantasy world, my monsters and I snuffed the arrogance and entitlement out of every single one of those fuckers. Sometimes discretion was needed, so, in addition to their monster forms, they had a human form so they could blend in with society and be at my side.

Which brought me to the task at hand. Opening my eyes, I thought of where I wanted to begin with this one. Today's chapter was about the Dean of Students who had lifted my skirt this afternoon and told me he'd forget the claims of me cheating on my essay if I *helped* him.

I hadn't cheated.

There was no need to when academics were a natural gift of my mind. The only way I was even able to attend this college was due to the academic scholarship I'd been awarded. Without it, I'd be on the streets without a penny to my name, like most kids after they aged out of the system.

There was definitely no way I'd risk any of that by cheating on a dumb creative writing essay that I could ace without struggling.

The problem was that Chloe Blufount didn't like that I continuously ranked above her for the top spot in the undergraduate class for English majors. Our creative writing professor instituted a public ranking board to encourage excellence, and with my talent for writing, I edged Chloe out every year. But Chloe was a girl who was used to getting her way, especially since her father's money usually got her everything else she wanted. He could buy her lip injections, lash extensions, a constant fake spray tan, and her continuously revolving hair colors, but he'd never be able to buy her top rank in our class.

I was proud of that.

So this was how she got me out of the way instead. Feeding the skeevy dean lies, knowing full well what his reputation was. Chloe was one of the monsters beneath a pretty human skin suit, offering me on a silver platter to a man who took what wasn't freely given, knowing I had no one to help me fight my battles other than myself.

In reality, I had smacked his hand away lightly, told him I'd take the zero on the assignment, and quietly left his office, not wanting to ignite the temper I'd heard about many times.

It finally came to me, how I wanted this scene to go. The specific way I wanted the dean to suffer. I let the ink glide on the page, closing my eyes and summoning my bloodthirsty monster to reenact the scene in the manner I truly wanted.

Lucien.

He'd slaughter for those he loved without blinking. Touch what was his and die a painful death as a result. It was that simple to him.

The scene was finally set. There I was, sitting with my legs crossed in the chair in front of the dean's oak desk, with the dean standing and leaning against the corner of it, eyeing me like a pig.

As Lucien stepped from the shadows in the corner of the office, his fingertips gleamed like freshly sharpened obsidian daggers. His form shifted as he approached slowly and intentionally, like a predator stalking his prey, confidence and danger radiating off of him in waves. His blood-red eyes with black slits were pinned on his target with unwavering intensity.

Truly, he embodied the creature of nightmares kids would fear coming from the shadowed corners of their rooms.

Just as the perv put his hand on my exposed leg and drew it up toward my skirt, as he had in reality, Lucien tutted at him. "That simply won't do. The only person allowed to touch my angel is me."

The dean stood, frozen in fear of my monster,

and I smiled wickedly when his beige dress pants darkened and the scent of urine permeated the air. All it took was Lucien's talons touching his skin in the faintest whisper of a touch.

The dean knew he had just become the prey.

The shadows on Lucien's face parted to reveal his lips as he smiled at the dean, putting his rows of sharp teeth on display. The dean screamed, begging for mercy, in the seconds before his hands were swiftly cleaved from his wrists.

Maybe that act should have scared me—it was what I truly wanted, and craving that type of violence wasn't normal. But instead, it unfurled a sense of justice and satisfaction within me, perhaps even a hint of desire toward Lucien for the vicious move.

Alright, it was more than a hint of desire.

It wouldn't be the first time their possessive and sometimes barbaric actions had turned me on. But it wasn't a surprise because I had written them to be exactly like that.

The thing was—my creations weren't just monsters. They were my soul mates, and I had created them to be extremely protective and territorial over me. Something I'd lacked in my life growing up. They all had distinctively different personalities, but their underlying love and need to keep me safe shone brightly through their shadowy depths.

The dean's screams echoed through the expanse of his office, but no one came to his rescue. No one could save him—he was damned from the start of my story.

He fell to his knees as blood poured in rivulets from his severed wrists, pooling beneath him in an ever-expanding crimson lake. Snot poured from his nose as he sobbed and begged, "Please, spare me. I'm sorry. I'm so sorry."

Narrowing my eyes as I stood from my chair, I planted the bottom of my boot on his chest before kicking him backward. "Too bad you won't be able to say sorry to all of your other victims," I sneered. Then, huffing out a dry laugh, I added, "Though, your death will be enough of an apology."

As the words left my lips, Lucien towered over the dean before ramming the tips of his pointer fingers into his eye sockets. The dean only screamed for a few seconds before the bliss of silence descended through the small office with his death.

I soaked the moment in, smiling smugly at his fate. He wouldn't be able to abuse his position of power again.

Meanwhile, Lucien retracted his talons from the

dean and grabbed a handkerchief from the desk, wiping off his top hands' talons with his lower two before tossing the rag onto the dean's body. Dramatically, he rolled his eyes and murmured, "I hate when they make me get my hands so dirty."

A true laugh burst from me as I called him on his bullshit. "You're such a liar. You get upset when you *don't* get to handle our situations this way," I reminded him as I leaned back onto the desk with my hands on the edge. "Though I'm sure Kylo and Elwin would love to hear if you're changing your ways," I added teasingly. "You'd make their lives so much easier."

It was his turn to laugh, and the sound truly made my heart skip a beat. I lived for their love and joy—it fed my own.

"Don't let Kylo lie to you either, angel," he rebutted. "He'd be bored if he wasn't constantly trying to contain my urges under the blood haze."

As Lucien came to float in front of me, leaning in close, I widened my eyes and fake pouted. "But what about poor Elwin who has to deal with calming Kylo down when you inevitably go against his commands?"

He paused as if truly giving it a thought before chuckling. "Yeah, I feel bad for the bastard, but we all know I'm not going to stop. No one fucks with you or my brothers and gets away with only a slap on the wrist."

The reminder of his wrath had my eyes falling down to the dean, and my body shivered at the memory of his touch on my leg.

Lucien sensed my distress, his voice dropping low as he whispered, "You're okay now, angel. He'll never touch you again. You are ours."

The possessiveness of his words, combined with the deep tones of his voice, made heat pool between my legs. An ache began to build, demanding I find a way to satisfy it.

I had yet to bring myself to cross the line of being intimate with my creatures as I wrote my stories, but today felt like the day that was going to change. I needed a little something extra to cheer me up after having to swallow my outrage at the dean's actions. I'd wanted to punch him in the mouth and tell him where he could shove it with his suggestions, but seeing as I couldn't give in to that desire...I'd give in to this one instead.

Keeping reading here: mybook.to/MonstersWithin